OUT OF A FOREST CLEARING

Out of a
Forest Clearing

An Environmental Fable

RANDALL BETH PLATT

John Daniel & Company, Publishers
SANTA BARBARA · 1991

Design and typography by Jim Cook

Published by John Daniel & Company, a division of Daniel &
Daniel, Inc., Post Office Box 21922, Santa Barbara, California
93121. Distributed by National Book Network, 4720 Boston
Way, Lanham, Maryland 20706

LIBRARY OF CONGRESS CATALOGING-IN-PUBLICATION DATA
Platt, Randall Beth, 1948–
    Out of a forest clearing: an environmental fable / Randall Beth
Platt.
        p. cm.
    ISBN 0-936784-89-X
    1. Animals—Fiction. I. Title.
PS3566.L29309 1991   91.8637
813'.54—dc20   CIP

For Charles and Alta Lechner
Never for a moment did they think I couldn't.

"What is man without the beasts? If all the beasts were gone, men would die from great loneliness of spirit, for whatever happens to the beasts also happens to the man."

—CHIEF SEATTLE
upon relinquishing his
lands to the white man

PROLOGUE

I T WAS DURING the spring, when all wild creatures are delivered out of their wintering-thoughts to consider their future seasons and to do whatever they must to survive. It was during this recuperative season when the Great Blue Heron heard the Voice. His initial reaction was to shudder in terror. He had suspicions of having heard the Voice before, but it was only a faint whisper then. This time, the Voice nearly bellowed and it was, above all, terrifying . . . and not to be ignored.

It was a Voice summoned forth by the Will of the Great Council of Beasts and it implored him to forsake his favorite fishing stream, to go forth and tell certain chosen animals to appear before the Council. Being a solitary bird, he was, at first, hesitant to leave his autonomous haven. But he realized that, ultimately, the Council Voice must be obeyed, even though it had rudely invaded the sacred privacy of his sanctuary.

According to his instructions, he was first to find a wolf by the name of Neera and inform the creature of the Council's request. Next, he was to locate a certain buffalo, a raccoon, and so on until the chosen ones were summoned.

"And just where, in all this land, does a Heron find the wolf you request?" he asked aloud, questioning the Council's choice of him as Its messenger. "What makes You think I know any of your Council animals? Don't they have pigeons for these purposes?" he

9

asked. He waited and looked around, half expecting a bounding, angry reply from the Council. But only the breakfast sounds of the other early animals could be heard.

"So why me?" he ventured, daring his resentment further.

And again, no reply.

"What makes you think I don't have better things to do with my time and life?" he boldly demanded.

His voice grew in intensity as he spit out each question. "What you ask is impossible! Even if I were to find all these animals, what makes you think they'll listen to me?"

His boldness and anger multiplied. But still there was no answer. Then, the Heron wondered if perhaps he had only dreamt the entire thing. Maybe the Voice, the Council and Its demands were merely dream-players.

"Is that it? Was I only dreaming? Am I showing my age by creating reality from fantasy?" the bird asked aloud, hoping that there would be no reply.

And there wasn't.

"Well, then if that is the case, I'll just get on with my life . . . senile or not."

The Heron, then convinced it was all a mere self-imposed fancy, prepared to leave for bluer waters. But the Voice this time was more frightening and powerful than ever before. There was no more doubt in the Heron's mind as he listened to the crashing Voice of the Council's Will. It was not a dream, nor was it a matter to be treated lightly from that day forward. Any feelings of self-doubt had vanished with the Voice's words, and after listening in fright, the Heron was left trembling with the fear and trepidation that the future of many great animals was helplessly interwoven into the fabric of his own life.

CHAPTER ONE

N EERA. WAKE," the Great Blue Heron whispered. "I regret having to disturb your slumber, but I bring you word from the Council."

The wolf opened a lazy golden eye and looked up as if still dreaming and thought briefly about the voice. "What?" she asked softly. Her den was dark and the Heron's silhouette near the entrance made him a difficult focal point.

"It is I, the Blue Heron. The Great Council of Beasts sends Its summons to you, requesting your attendance."

The wolf then opened the other eye and examined the large winged creature gracing her doorway. She tilted up her regal head and yawned, displaying a massive set of fangs.

"Please forgive me," she said politely. "I was sleeping and momentarily mistook you for a dream-player." She rose and stretched. The early rays of sun streamed past the Heron and made the wolf's coat shine with a silvery gleam. Her size was immense, yet the Heron stood his official ground, without fear of a natural predator. And after all, Neera was well known as a wise and just being, whose own gentleness had never intervened with her inherent qualities of courage.

"It is I who must be forgiven, for I seem to have arrived too early." The Heron's fair head nodded lightly and his long dark bill carved the air gracefully as he talked.

Neera stretched forward, unfolding her body full length, and approached the cave opening. "Come into the daylight and let me see what a heron looks like close up. My youngest still sleeps and I don't want to wake her."

The bird and the wolf walked a short way down the path together. Neera stopped and faced the Heron. Their eyes met respectfully and the bird was stunned at the depth in Neera's soul-eyes.

"Now, did you say the Council, or was that my dream?" she asked gently.

"No, you heard right. The Council has sent me to inform you. You must leave immediately in order to arrive on time."

"This makes me very happy, Heron," she said, smiling. "All my life I've waited to be summoned. I'll prepare to leave this moment." Neera's tail wagged as she spoke, yet her voice still remained quite low. The Heron never realized how magnificent a wolf's smile could be until that moment. "What is the reason for the Council?" she asked.

"I cannot say, for I do not know. All I can tell you is how to find the Council Ground. You realize, I'm sure, that the Great Council of Beasts is a private matter and requires a certain sense of discretion. So, go silently, Neera."

And so the Heron explained where the Council was to be held as the wolf listened and nodded her head attentively. When he had finished, she smiled again and asked, "Have you been in this business very long?"

"What business?"

"The notification business, of course. You seem to have a very professional delivery system worked out. So unlike most birds I have known," she added with a chuckle.

"I shall take that as a specific compliment rather than an overall insult to my race. But, to answer your question: No, you are my first summons, in fact. I am educated, well-versed, and have traveled extensively throughout the land, making me, I suppose, a likely candidate for the vocation of convocations. But believe me, Neera, the choice was not mine by any means." He walked about as he spoke and then flew to a nearby rock down the path in a restless urge to be on his way.

"Then you too were summoned?" she asked, sitting down.

"To an extent." He spoke from the rock, looking skyward. "Suffice to say that I do this as an involuntary compulsion. The Great Council of Beasts seems to be as unavoidable as tomorrow's sunrise. I shall, therefore, do my best and fly swiftly. I'm anxious to get on with my own life."

As he spoke, a breeze rolled up from the lush valley below and the Heron knew the Council had heard his words. Neera herself was enjoying the breeze and she listened with hospitable interest.

"I should think you would feel honored the Council spoke to you," Neera said, her sly smile shining upon the Heron.

"Well, I am, I guess. But, I would have been just as happy having never heard the Voice at all. I am a monad, singular unto myself."

"Well," she said brightly, changing the subject, "none the less, you are a likable, crusty sort, even for all your haughty reserve. I, for one, am delighted to have been chosen. I know you're anxious to be on your way, so I'll say goodbye and thank you." Neera rose and shook the dust from her coat. And as the Heron took wing, she added, "I'll look forward to seeing you and knowing you better. I am an animal with a social nature and sometimes, in the intimacy of my pack, I wish I were more like you."

Circling low over the wolf's head, the Heron said, "Take care on your journey, Neera. Maybe we will get to know each other better. Maybe we won't. Who knows?" He smiled and vanished on a swift draft, carrying him skyward.

Neera laughed at the Heron's curious and most conflicting nature and dismissed it as the beguilement the Council held over him. And, she reminded herself, he *was* a bird.

She trotted up the path to wake her daughter and inform her of the news.

She entered the cool, dark cave and gently walked toward the back where Bright One slept. "Wake up, Bright One," she whispered. "It's time for me to go."

The young wolf stirred and yawned. "Go? Go where? Must we hunt so early, Mother?"

"Now you hunt alone. I am going where I am needed."

Bright One stood up on awkwardly long legs and faced her

mother. "But you are needed here," she said, blinking away the rising pup-tears. "I need you."

"Please understand. I'll be back."

"But by then I'll have forgotten you, and when you return, I'll fight you for this den. I'll kill you."

"That's foolish. You have your own den to find and your own cubs to raise. Besides, the pack will look after you. Someday, I'll pass your home and you'll invite me in to show off your babies."

"But where?" the young wolf protested. "Where do you go? Where would you rather be than here with me?"

"I have just received notice to attend a gathering of great importance. You know I would not leave if it weren't essential. Don't ask me more, for I cannot tell you."

"But Mother, it may be a trap. A clever man will be there waiting to take your beautiful coat. You are the foolish one."

"Enough! I will go and you will stay, Bright One."

"But why can't I go too?" she insisted.

"Because you have not been chosen. But if you are ever called, as I have been, then you too will be honored and leave your family and den as I am doing now." Neera began to stalk her den, seeing if everything was in order.

"I'm too young. I won't survive alone. How shall I hunt?" Bright One whined, following her mother about the den.

Neera turned and looked her daughter in the eye and said solemnly, "With the knowledge I have given you and your wits and your courage and the love of the pack."

"I have none of those things! None at all!" she cried, sitting down impudently.

"Then, to live, you must quickly find them, for I am all but gone."

"Mother!"

"Don't cry. Go back to sleep now and when you wake again, I'll only be a fading dream. It was difficult when my mother left too," she whispered. Neera felt an identical hurt inside her at that moment and her confidence was slightly shaken.

"Will you send word when you get there? So I'll know you arrived safely?"

"Ha! Who is the mother now, Bright One?" Neera laughed.

"No, I won't send word. You can assume I'll arrive safely. Don't forget. I am Neera. And remember my song." She lovingly touched her daughter's nose with her own and kissed her good-bye.

And so Neera, the great she-wolf, was gone . . . gone from the warmth of her den, the fruit of her hunting grounds, and gone too from the memory of the secure, serene peace of her valley home.

She stopped high on a hill, turned and listened to the small, shrill young voice of Bright One as she echoed her mother's song:

> My heart once sang in the rhapsody
> Of my birth.
> And my song worshipped the Father
> King of all packs.
> But now my cry is for my children,
> And the children of my children.
> For my hunting fields grow smaller,
> And my Man-brothers hunt me.
> And I weep. I weep.
> I am the wolf.
> And now my song is seldom heard.
> Those who are blessed with the pierce
> From my cry can understand.
> It is for them I sing my song.
> And it is for me that they too
> Shall now weep.
> For we are sisters and brothers.

As the final echo faded, Neera lifted her magnificent gray head to the heavens and returned her love-cry . . . so powerful and thrilling that all animals who heard her knew she had left the valley on a journey of great importance. They honored her in a forest silence—a prayer for her safety and a tribute to her unfailing wisdom.

CHAPTER TWO

WHEN THE BUFFALO received the request to join the Council of Beasts, he could barely stop laughing. His molting coat shook in dusty delight as he stomped his hooves and giggled a series of whimsical snorts. His first reaction was that he had been summoned by a simpleton's error or by some practical joker, at the very least. There was a weasel nearby who was constantly devising methods of foolish entrapments . . . .

"Me? The Great Council of Beasts sends their summons to *me*? Harrr!"

"It's true, Moko. They asked for you specifically. They want *you*," the Blue Heron said dryly as he casually checked the condition of an ailing talon.

"But, I know nothing of Council matters. In fact, I don't know much about anything. Why me?" Moko asked through his laughter.

" 'Why' is not my responsibility, Moko. I am chosen for my swift dispatch, not for my analysis of who is chosen or who is not." He shifted to one leg to rest the other. The Heron spoke with long, nasal tones to match his narrow, aquiline bill. He sniffed and turned his bill, regretting having landed downwind of the enormous creature.

"Harrr!" Moko laughed.

"It's not funny, I can assure you. The Council does not summon for laughs. You have two weeks to get yourself there. I'll explain your best route and your instructions." He was clearly anxious to continue his journey.

Then the buffalo asked, with less joviality, "What will be expected of me?" The seriousness of the Heron's message was finally sinking in.

"I told you, Moko, I have no idea. Just be there or *I* shall be accused of failing in my duty." As the Heron talked, he scratched out a rough map in the dusty ground with one of his good talons. "This way should be the easiest for you in consideration of your . . . a . . . well, your size. Stay close to the River of the North here and the place of the Council will be held just about here," he continued.

"But look at me! I'm molting! I look awful!" Moko moaned, looking back to his shabby, ragged sides.

"This is hardly a festive occasion calling for your finest winter coat, Moko." The Heron looked to the sky to assess the wind currents and the time and added, "Look at that sun! I'm hours behind on my schedule. You've taken enough of my time." He flapped his wings and eased himself into flight.

"But I wanted to ask you . . . " Moko called to the soaring bird.

"Save your questions for the Council. And don't be late!" the Heron called.

Moko watched him ascend effortlessly and then disappear into a cloud. Then, he looked at the map etched into the ground and he studied it carefully. "But, I'm so dumb," he groaned. "What would those Council Beasts want me for?" There was a hint of suspicion in his musky voice. "They'll laugh at me! I'm big, I'm ugly and I'm so duummmbbb!" He continued talking to himself as he took the first lumbering steps of his journey. "And I've never been that far from home!".

He had gone but a few hesitant paces when a tiny head popped up from a hole inches from Moko's powerful hoof. "Watch it, Moko! If you cave in this hole, it'll be your third one this week! How much can a prairie dog take? Now be careful!" the animal squeaked up bravely at Moko.

"I'm sorry, Little Paw. I wasn't watching where I was going,"

Moko said as he stepped back carefully to get a clearer look at the prairie dog. He lowered his head to sniff in friendship and to add, "Besides, Little Paw, I'm thinking as I go, and doing both at the same time is so difficult."

"You have me convinced!" Little Paw said sharply, but then added with a mischievous chirp, "So, are you going to stand there or are you going to tell me what is so important for *you* to be thinking about?" His tiny face was overcome with an enormous toothy grin.

"I don't know if I'm allowed to tell you," Moko stammered, slightly embarrassed.

"Oh. I see," Little Paw said, in a successful effort to sound slightly hurt. "Something you can't tell your best friend must be something indeed."

"Oh, now . . . I'll, well, I'll tell you all I know, then. I never know very much, you know, Little Paw," Moko said, with his head close to his friend.

"I know," agreed the prairie dog. "So tell me what you do know."

Moko took a long breath and exhaled heavily, causing a large cloud of dust nearly to blow Little Paw completely over. The tiny creature coughed, sputtered and said, "Aughhh! Must you, Moko? A breath to you is a tornado to me!"

"Sorry. I forgot," Moko apologized meekly.

"Don't mention it. Go ahead with your story."

"Well, I'm on my way to the Great Council of Beasts, whatever that is. They have summoned me. Me! Not just any buffalo, but me! Moko!" The buffalo pawed the ground next to Little Paw's burrow, trying to suppress an odd mixture of pride and embarrassed humility.

"Yeah, sure. And I thought I'd fly to the moon after dinner tonight," Little Paw said, rolling in laughter.

Moko looked away and said lowly, "It's true."

Then it occurred to Little Paw that Moko would not, could not conceive such a fantastic story. He stopped laughing and rolling and said diplomatically, "Then, Moko, you are indeed a buffalo among bison. And fortunate too. How were you informed of the Council?"

"They sent this long blue bird around. He brings a message. I hope they're not all like him at the Council. He was rude, you know?" Moko said, looking around to be certain no one else was listening. "Not at all like the birds around here."

"Are you in any kind of trouble or something? What do you suppose they want you for? Did this blue bird say?" Little Paw asked, a grave look of mulling concern on his wee forehead.

"No. That was what I was thinking on. What *is* the Great Council of Beasts, anyway?"

"All I know is, it's something special. I remember my parents talking about it once." The two thought in silence for a moment. Then Little Paw barked in excitement, startling Moko, "I have it! I'll go with you!"

"You? Oh, I don't think it's allowed, Little Paw. I mean, it would be nice to have you with me, but I really don't think it's allowed. I'll have to go alone."

"So, who has to know? There are some advantages to being my size, you know. Who will notice me next to a beast the size of you?"

"Harrrr!" The comparison in size was humorous even to Moko, who had never considered it before. "The bird didn't say I had to travel alone."

"There! It's settled then. I will tell my family I'm off to scout for another settlement. I won't tell anyone where we're really off to. And when we get to the Council, I'll hide and no one will know."

"Oh, but if they discover I've brought you with me, it might anger them. I'm not so sure about this," Moko hedged as he nervously began to pace about.

"Frankly, Moko, not only are you going to appreciate my company along this journey, but also my abilities to analyze problem situations," Little Paw said in and out of his burrow, as he prepared hurriedly to leave.

"What do you mean?" asked Moko.

"Well," said the impish creature, out of breath, "think of me as your bodyguard. Buffalo should not be traveling alone."

"Oh . . ." Moko pawed the ground thoughtfully.

"Great. I'm all set. I'll speak to my family as we pass through the end of the village. Watch your step now, Moko. No use starting off on a bad hoof by caving in anyone's home," the prairie dog warned, going ahead of his lumbering friend.

And so the two began. Little Paw dashed about excitedly ahead of Moko, who walked with slow, deliberate steps, choosing each one with careful concentration.

Moko was able to go for miles at a gentle lope. Little Paw had conceived the brilliant idea of riding on the great tuft of hair atop the buffalo's head. And when his navigations had brought them to the River of the North, they decided to find food and rest for the night.

They were tired from the day, yet excited with the expectations of tomorrow. After their dinner, they both lay silently on the cool, sandy riverbank. Soon, Moko's eyes closed as he fell into a deep buffalo sleep.

But Little Paw just watched the moon's reflection on the water and thought. "Yes indeed," he planned out loud in a whisper. "This could just be the biggest thing ever to happen to this prairie dog. They won't call me Little Paw now. With Moko as my powerful ally, I shall speak louder than even *I* ever dreamed possible. It's the chance of a lifetime. Yes indeed."

Then, he drifted to sleep, dreaming of the Council and his future path to glory.

CHAPTER THREE

N OW ... THE HARD PART," the Heron said to himself.
"A raccoon: name unknown. Living somewhere
between here and the River of the North. Captive, yet not a
prisoner." His thoughts lingered on his last words. He wondered
if this information the Council provided was merely a game-clue.
And, with time being the prime concern, the Heron needed to
examine the next summons very carefully. He drew the dreaded
conclusion that this raccoon must be held somewhere within
human boundaries. Just the thought of the smell of a human's
land terrified him.

Along the River of the North there were numerous man-farms
and the Heron concluded this raccoon must surely live among one
of them. So, he flew dangerously low and searched each compound for signs of a raccoon. He passed over pens and pastures of
the domestic ones and, as always, was saddened to see their
complacency. The Heron ordinarily avoided these sights. Being of
the free, he pitied the fate of those less fortunate below. It was
beyond his understanding how any animal could exist and actually prosper within these boundaries of space . . . a fence, a barn
. . . to go only so far and that is all . . . to constantly be stopped,
pulled back, tethered . . . to repeat and repeat . . . to be dictated
to . . . to be owned.

So, when the Heron finally found the caged raccoon and offered him the ultimate freedom of the Council, the raccoon's reply astonished him.

"I won't go. Tell your leaders I'll have none of it!" growled the raccoon, taking a disgruntled swipe at the Heron's tail feathers. His deplorable reaction stunned the bird. He had assumed that any captive creature would rejoice at the offer of being set free. The beast's totally unexpected attitude repelled the Heron, even though he himself had wanted to reject the Council's offer at first. But then, he was a free bird and would kill to remain so.

"Listen you . . . whatever your name is . . ." began the Heron, twirling around and vexed to the point of flashing his sharp bill in defense.

"I am called Iscariot," the raccoon interrupted. His razor teeth glared, welcoming a fight. His rich, thick coat bristled and the black mask surrounding his eyes made them appear blood-red, reflecting the sunset in them.

"Absurd!" snapped the bird. "Are you not disgraced? Only a man could have named you. Not only do you allow yourself to be kept by these humans, but to answer to such a demoralizing name."

"I don't normally enjoy bird's flesh, but if you are as tasty as you are unlikable . . ." Iscariot said, reaching out with his long fingers and hissing another warning. "Go tell your Council that I will not be among them! And if they don't like it, tell them to send a more worthy adversary for me to fight! Tell them long ago I chose to dwell within the humans' fences. I have forsaken my kind. Tell your lords that when I sleep I do so on warm straw beds and I dream of the constant delicacies my humans provide. I am neither hunter nor hunted. Tell them there is nothing I lack and then ask them their desires. Report to your Council that I am alive and very well and to strike my name from their registry. Find yourself another raccoon. I stay!"

During his speech, Iscariot paced the length of his small pen while the Heron glared down at him with contempt, feeling only partially safe on his perch above.

"Save your rhetoric for one who cares," the Heron replied in a low and menacing tone. "I don't like you, so don't think I'm trying to help you. I don't give a damn about you or your life or what you believe. Only believe this, my vile cousin: no animal has ever ignored a request from the the Great Council. Two weeks, Iscariot! Death is your only excuse if you fail to show, and death will surely be your reward if you do fail. Sleep well tonight on your fine warm bed and dream about your fate!" The bird's wings unfolded and he gave out an enormous screech and rose swiftly to a tree branch above. The fire of the setting sun behind shadowed him, making him seem much larger and more powerful than any heron who had ever lived.

"I hear my human coming. I hope he has his war-stick and we'll see then about your beast's tea party! Be gone, fool!" The raccoon spat in rage and clawed the air.

"And we'll see whose altar you worship! Iscariot! You are justly named! Traitor!"

By the time the human had reached the raccoon's compound to investigate the screaming, the Blue Heron was a small dot in the deep purple sky overhead and the raccoon was nervously stalking his pen, for the first time ever like a captive creature.

The sky at sunrise was a deep and glowing indigo, and the tall mountain pines that reached into it appeared like huge black fish spines. The songs of the day were beginning to resound from seemingly every direction, each bird rendering its own praise of the sun and the delight of a new day of flight.

By the time the Blue Heron had arrived, the sun was already halfway into the morning sky. The rise in altitude had made his journey more difficult and he felt ill at ease so far out of his own aquatic world. The Heron wondered how any bird in its right mind could live in such a desolate, mountainous climate.

"You there. Bird! Whatever you are," the Heron called, directing his weary voice to a wrenish-looking bird who had flown over to investigate the blue intruder. "Could you help me?"

"Whatever *you* are. I am me, but what are you?" the tiny bird called back, coming in for a closer look.

"I am a foreigner here, as you can see," began the Heron.

"And you're lost? Do you know how bad it looks for a bird to get lost? I had an uncle once who couldn't find . . ."

23

"I am not lost, my good bird," the Heron said, cutting him off. "I seek Lordjahn, the condor. Can you direct me to his nest?" As they flew, the Heron looked about the jagged cliffs below and grew uneasy, while his companion flitted about and dodged the tree tops effortlessly.

"Lordjahn?" the little bird asked. "What for?"

"For business concerning only Lordjahn and myself. Now, will you take me to him or must I seek help elsewhere?" the Heron asked icily. His feathers were still ruffled from the previous evening's encounter with Iscariot and he dreaded still another confrontation with this small, insignificant mountain bird.

"First of all, not just anyone gets to see Lordjahn, you know," the small bird said with careless cheerfulness, unaffected by the Heron's superior manner. "And secondly, by the sound of your breathing, you'll never make it up to see him anyway."

The Heron recognized some truth in his words. The air was thinner and he was winded. "How much higher is it?" he asked, trying not to puff.

"It's not far at all. But you have to understand that none of us can just bring anyone to Lordjahn. I mean, I live here and would have his wrath upon me every day for bringing a curious trespasser. Well, that would be more of a burden than a bird my size could bear. You see my point, I'm sure. I remember a cousin who did . . ."

"Right now, all I can see is a small ledge where I can rest myself." The Heron descended immediately, leaving his escort above, talking on to himself. But, before he had landed and caught his breath, the little bird was with him again, strutting along the edge, perfectly at ease and balanced.

". . . exactly the same thing," he continued. "You certainly have an annoying habit of interrupting a bird when he's talking. Didn't your mother ever tell you? Well, as I was saying . . ."

"Please," puffed the Heron, "save your breath."

"Humpf!" the bird snorted as he stopped his pacing and considered the weary blue foreigner. "That might be my advice to you, stranger."

"All right, let's start over." The Heron's breaths were coming easier now. "I understand that you don't want to take the respon-

sibility of bringing me to Lordjahn. So, how does one seek an audience with him?"

"Well, it's just generally understood that Lordjahn sees no one anymore. He's quite old, you know, and not in the best temperament. Perhaps if I could tell him your reasons for seeking him. But, no matter what, it's risky."

"You mean he'd hurt you?"

"Well, his talons are larger than the whole of myself. Does that give you a clue?" The little bird puffed out his breast to appear larger, but he laughed at his own bravado.

"I see your point," the Heron said, suppressing a chuckle himself. "But it's essential that I speak with him. So, what are we to do?"

There was a silence between the two with only the high wind's whisper passing between them, reminding the Heron again that he was dangerously far from his own precious water element and nearly totally dependent on this small bird for assistance.

"I wish I could help you, Blue," the small bird said.

The Heron knew he was taking a chance, but he realized his only option was to ask, "Then how shall I explain to the Council that I have failed?" He carefully watched his companion's reactions to his question.

"The Council? You mean, *the* Council? Is that what this is all about? As I live and fly, that *is* impressive!" He flapped his wings, lifting himself a few inches off the ledge.

"So, you can see the dilemma. I like you, little fellow, which is why I tell you this. I trust you and know you have a love for all bird-kind. I know you'll help me. First of all, you must swear to silence, for if many knew what was about, there would be needless concern. Even I don't know why the Council has been called. Nor do I know why they have summoned Lordjahn. But I do know he must appear. There is a reason. The Council does nothing at random," the Heron said, his bill moving gracefully as he spoke. His nostrils searched instinctively for the fulfilling scent of water, for he was becoming hungry and needed food.

"Well, that being the case, I shall risk it. You have touched my patriotic senses. For the Council and you, whatever you are, I shall risk the wrath of Lordjahn!" As he spoke, he flew upside-

down to impress the Heron with his cleverness and bravery, then he landed lightly on one leg as he finished his sentence.

"Thank you," the Heron said. "You really are quite a little flyer," he added, lacing his thanks with a compliment.

"Well, thank you. Prepare for take-off. Next stop: the Lordjahn Universe." The bird lifted off easily and the Heron followed him, feeling a definite stiffness in his wings, but grateful that his search was over.

The condor's lair was just a short distance away and the Heron had only a brief time mentally to prepare his message. Not since he was an infant had he faced a bird larger than himself, and that, combined with the condor's foreboding reputation, made the Heron doubly uncomfortable. He longed for the day to end, for a lower altitude, and a fuller stomach.

"Land there," the escort said, motioning to a rocky spot on a sloping ledge not far from the nest of the condor. "Wait here and I'll just fly by him casually and drop your name . . . I mean, announce you."

Before the Heron had time to turn about to inspect his perch, the tiny bird came flapping back, out of breath and feathers on end. "He's coming! He grumbled something about him coming to you! I have to leave now. It's been grand, Old Blue." And the escort-bird was out of sight.

The silence of the mountain was rattling the Heron's head with the excitement of expectation. Only then had he considered the supremacy of a condor. Never having seen one, he had only the mental visions of the creature to satisfy his curiosity. His throat was as arid as the thin atmosphere and the high sun was uncomfortable on his face. Then the sun suddenly disappeared as though a black cloud sealed it, and a foreign gust of wind wafted from every direction, and the Heron froze, not daring to look about him to behold the condor, Lordjahn.

Seemingly suspended in space just above the Heron's ledge, taking up most of the immediate sky, Lordjahn spoke. "Fly," he commanded.

Still not looking, the Heron obeyed and flew off the ledge. The condor remained above him in flight as if to test the stranger's courage and aerial abilities.

26

"So, Heron. You have news of the Council? I wondered when it would happen. Speak as we fly." His voice was majestically deep and he etched each word carefully and with a certain wisdom of his kind, his age, and his magnificent superiority.

"I have been retained to give you notice to appear before the Great Council of Beasts. You are to be there by the end of twelve days' time. Follow the River to the North until you come to . . ."

"I know where the Council will be held. I shall attend. You fly well . . . for a heron. Follow me and I'll take you to the top of my world."

And only then did the Heron witness the splendor of Lordjahn as the condor soared well ahead with no discernible effort in space.

The Heron, in a respectful awe of this great bird, forgot his hunger, lack of easy breath and weariness. He gratefully followed Lordjahn, privileged to fly with him.

For the day, the two flew together. The first hours were silent, then they began to speak of simple, essential things like wind, sun, and water.

What was a mere outing for Lordjahn, even at his advanced age, was an agonizing excursion for the Heron. But, as the day ended, and the evening chill caressed him, the Heron was exhilarated beyond words when the condor shared with him his song:

> When I fly, I fly in praise,
> And I seek Heaven and my Forefathers.
> Higher and higher still.
> When I soar, I soar in my expression
> Of power, for my wings are stronger
> Than the iron of the man-cousin.
> When I glide, I glide in a peaceful
> Mystery that not even I can solve.
> For my gift of flight comes from powers
> Unknown to me.
> The chill of the air caresses the fingers
> Of my wings and the gentle sound of my
> Flight inspires me higher, faster.
> I can spy the precious prey of fulfilled

Hunters before me from uncanny heights
And I am upon it
Unseen, unheard . . .
Swiftly and with respect.
I defend the remains of my fallen
Land-cousins.
And I consume with thanks.
I am Lordjahn, the Condor.

CHAPTER FOUR

THE BLUE HERON hesitated momentarily before speaking to the nest of caterpillars. The tree branch was alive in the sporadic movements of innumerable and seemingly lookalike little creatures. The throbbing tribe was oblivious to the great bird's presence as they fed voraciously on the leaves that held together their birthing tent.

Finally, the Blue Heron cleared his long, elegant throat and ventured forward with his announcement of arrival. "Pardon my intrusion, delectable ones, but would the caterpillar among you called Chanta please identify him or herself?"

The nest ceased its activity as each diminutive fur-head looked up in reverence to the Heron, each colony member feeling certain the intruder had stopped by for breakfast.

"A discriminating palate indeed! What makes you think I would taste any better than one of my colleagues? I am Chanta and wish to remain so. Who are you?" Chanta spoke as she bravely singled herself out, crawling slowly onto a branch dangerously close to the bird.

"Could we be alone?" the Heron whispered, hoping to avoid the ears of Chanta's countless siblings.

"I don't believe what I am hearing. Not only does this bird have the nerve to come here, single me out for his appetizer, but now he wants to be alone. Well, not me! You only die once and now is definitely not a good time."

"Chanta . . . here, come closer. What I have to say is not for the ears of anyone but you. I haven't come to eat you."

Chanta began backing down cautiously toward the nest again and asked suspiciously, "How do you know my name? What's all this about, anyway?"

"Could you possibly drop down to the ground? I really must speak with you alone," the Heron insisted, pointing toward the still silent, eavesdropping mass of caterpillars.

"I could, but I'd never recover. Furthermore, it's against my better judgment to come when the enemy calls." Chanta's flip attitude did not charm the Heron, who was, as always, clinging to his strict itinerary.

"I eat fish, who sport a chance with me, not defenseless caterpillars," he said impatiently.

"Ha! I've heard *that* before. I think you'd better leave now, before my mother gets home."

"Ha yourself, Chanta. And I've heard that before." The Heron laughed in an effort to appear less threatening to the fiery caterpillar.

"If you'll excuse me, I've got to be getting back," Chanta said, inching her way back down to the nest.

"It's the Council," the Heron whispered.

Chanta's head rose up immediately and her many legs ceased in mid-step. "The Council?" she asked.

"Now can we talk alone?" The bird looked around for a private place to explain. "That flat rock over there looks quiet enough."

"Well, if I start now, I could be on that rock by the middle of next week," Chanta quipped sarcastically.

"Oh yes, I see," the Heron said. Then, after a brief considera-tion, he added, "I've an idea. I'll place my bill on this branch, you crawl onto it, and I'll glide you down there."

"Kichish! Here goes my reputation! All right, I'll trust you, Heron. But only for news of the Council, you understand."

His plan to transport the small furry caterpillar worked and Chanta was safely delivered onto the rock.

"The miracle of flight amazes me so!" Chanta gasped excitedly.

"I hear that a lot. But Chanta, it's a miracle that you yourself shall experience, given time."

"If I live that long, Heron. So, now what about the Council?"

"I act as diplomatic courier for the Great Council of Beasts. I have been ordered to inform you that your presence is required at the Council. You have eight days in which to reach the meeting place."

"Now wait just one minute there, if you please, Mr. Diplomatic-Courier-Heron. Before you go any farther, why is *my* presence requested? What do I have to do with the Council? And where . . ."

"First, Chanta, I wasn't given any reason why one animal is summoned over another. It is your duty not to question the Council's orders, but simply to be there. It will be held several miles from here, where the River of the North meets the Great Sea."

"Again, the problem of my immobility raises its obvious head," Chanta said, almost with a pouty inflection in her small voice.

"Indeed. I'm afraid that's my fault. You see, there was a slight error in my calculations. I hoped by this time, you would have transgressed to a more mobile state."

"You can bet your pin feathers your calculations were off! I'm due to pupate this week sometime," Chanta explained to the Heron. The problem was suddenly growing in complexity at the same rate that time was running out.

"And how long will it take you to complete this process?" asked the bird, searching for a possible solution as he spoke.

"Well, with luck and the right circumstances, I could be done with it in twelve to fifteen days. Would the Council give me some extra time?"

The Heron sighed. "I don't know. Tell me, Chanta, once your cocoon is made, can you be moved?"

Chanta replied, "All I know is that it must be warm and dark and as quiet as possible. Most of all, my cocoon must be kept consistent." She paused, exhaled deeply and added, "I guess you'll have to find another caterpillar."

"No, there is an answer." The Heron walked about in silent

thought, then returned to the flat rock where Chanta awaited his solution. "Would it be at all within the realm of plausibility for you to attach your cocoon to me here, under my wing?"

The idea sounded preposterous even to the Heron as he listened to his words. Chanta laughed and as she did, she wiggled back and forth in absurd merriment and said, "So utterly ridiculous is that idea that the plan might be tainted with genius."

"Could we do it?"

"It's scandalous!"

"Yes, but can it work? It'll be a stable environment—warm, dark, and most of all, protective." The Heron's enthusiasm was picking up and Chanta's small face reflected an optimistic smile as she considered the plan.

"Yes, I guess it'll have to work. After all, a Diplomatic-Courier-Heron couldn't lead me astray. I'll try. And if it works, they'll sing a song of us forever," Chanta said, bringing nearly half of her body up off the rock.

The two looked at each other in silence . . . looking perhaps for a sign of doubt or mistrust or just sizing up the other's capabilities to carry out such a daring plan.

"Well," the Blue Heron said, craning his neck down to speak to Chanta, "when should we commence? I mean," he stuttered, slightly embarrassed, "can you cause this process to begin, or must you await instinct's leisure?"

"I will need some time to prepare. I must eat, first of all . . . to gain the weight I need to see me through my change."

The Heron plucked some leaves off a nearby branch and offered them to her. Chanta began to nibble while the Heron talked.

"I admire you, Chanta, for your respect of the Council and for your courage. I'll do my best to get you there safely." He looked upwards and saw a small blue patch of sky above the thick trees and was aware of his demanding schedule. He found he was slightly disappointed in himself for his personal involvements. For a Heron who was known for his supposed qualities of detachment and stiff air of superiority, he was certainly becoming overly imvolved with the animals he had summoned. He had originally intended to deliver his messages quickly and then fly off for some isolated fishing, far from Council matters. But, like it or not, he was committed and involved beyond recall now. Yet, the Blue Heron felt a strange pride in himself for coming this far. It confused him, yet it stirred him. Or, he thought, where does pride end and conceit begin?

A draft whisked down from above and slightly nudged the Heron's feathers, confusing his new ideas with the instinct to fly. Chanta, unaware of her companion's reverie, was still eating contentedly.

"How much longer, Chanta?" the bird asked, anxious to be on with it.

"I'm not large enough yet. You should leave and eat your fill too. You'll have to remain very still while I spin my cocoon. But you'd better return tonight, in case I start early. Then, while you sleep, I'll begin. The sooner the better for all this intrigue." Chanta munched as she spoke, as though unable to halt the sudden growth process. It was obvious she was excited and nervous about her future. But, the machine had already started and Chanta was resolved to see it through. The Great Council of Beasts and its impressive summons was almost as important to Chanta now as was the metamorphosis itself. The Council would, most hopefully, assure her safe arrival with the help of this beautiful bird.

This was adventure—a calling and a reason—and a chance to fly before her time.

CHAPTER FIVE

CHANTA'S TASK, once started, was a simple one, yet complex in its natural wonder. It took many hours of patience on the part of the Blue Heron, but he endured as best he could and dozed several times during the transformation. He allowed himself the opportunity to reflect on his career thus far as messenger and to consider the myriad paths that his future must surely hold. The Council would be expecting his return any day. But he still had one more summons to deliver.

By noontide the next day, all movement had ceased in the tiny, tight pocket under the Heron's wing. Chanta had succeeded in burrowing herself deeply and safely down into the soft, snowy undergrowth, and her cocoon enveloped her in a warm, secure crypt.

The Heron, feeling stiff yet confident that Chanta was safe, carefully lifted his wings. He stretched them first, then gently, cautiously, flapped them. He felt a vague feeling of tightness as a result of Chanta's thorough spinning abilities, but other than that, her presence was barely noticeable. Yet, he realized that he could never allow himself, even briefly, to forget that she was there.

Then the Heron gently eased himself off the rock and flew upwards to announce his late arrival into the day.

The water from a nearby stream refreshed him, and the fishing was superb. He experienced a savory fish new to him, and he vowed to return again someday to enjoy a leisurely summer's day when the only important issue cluttering his mind would be how far south he should spend the winter. But such simple, sabbatical days were far away.

"In time," whispered the bird aloud, staring at the fish darting capriciously around his legs. He was nearly mesmerized by the random movements as his thoughts caressed his next summons, perhaps the most challenging of all—Et Ska, the salmon.

The vast territory a salmon covers was already baffling the Heron. He had heard stories of their long aquatic voyages ending in their final freshwater ascent upstream to spawn and die. Where would Et Ska's life cycle be at this time? Where to begin the search? In the shallow mountain streams or in the depths of the ocean? And so little time remained.

From the altitude above, the Heron examined both the problem and the country below. He decided to follow his small fishing stream until it merged with the River of the North. Perhaps there he could pry some information out of a river-dweller. Surely someone there would know of Et Ska, on the assumption that a fish summoned by the Great Council must be a fish of some notoriety. At the very least it was a beginning, and already the Heron regretted his leisurely prologue into the warming day.

The beneficial winds were assisting his flight, and he reached his destination in half the usual gliding time. The heat of the day was peaking as he landed, and the cool breezes off the river were refreshing. Without a second thought, the Heron instinctively plunged his bill into a shallow pool along the bank in search of a snack. He abruptly pulled up short, remembering he was there to solicit information, not feed on his preliminary sources. But in the process, a small rock had been overturned in the shallow edge, and a crayfish of considerable size stalked forth, snapping his claws in willingness to fight.

"It is my right to defend my life!" said the crusted fellow, still snapping and blowing ambitious bubbles of air as he spoke.

"Of course it's your right, friend. But in this case, a needless defense," said the Heron, suppressing a slight urge to gobble the morsel up.

"I'll break your bill in half!" the crayfish threatened. "I'll cut off your foot!" He ventured closer and popped his head out of the water to examine his colossal enemy.

"I'm sure you could," the Heron said patronizingly and taking a dramatic step back. "But please, don't come closer. I only wanted to ask you a question." It wasn't easy for the Heron to feign fright, but it was apparently going to be necessary in dealing with the crayfish.

"I live under a rock. What could I possibly know that you don't?" The carapaced creature held his ground and snapped his claws as he spoke. The sun glistened off them, causing them to appear larger, redder, and more threatening. The Heron had to admire the potential repast before him.

"A few questions and I'll never bother you again. My bill is no match for your forward weaponry."

"Well, make it snappy, or I'll . . ."

"Do you know of a salmon called Et Ska? I have a message for the fish and it's quite urgent."

"Have you learned your lesson?" countered the crayfish, feeling twice his size.

"What lesson?" asked the Heron indignantly. "Now, see here you . . ."

"To never again disturb my slumber-rock," continued the crayfish, in his new-found arrogance. "Say it and I'll tell you what you want to know," he added.

The Heron exhaled heavily in exasperation and in wonderment at the lengths the Council's business required him to go. "I shall never again disturb your slumber-rock," he repeated flatly. "Now, about Et Ska, if you please."

The crayfish hesitated slightly. "Et Ska passed through here two years ago," he said, still displaying his claws.

The Heron flapped his wings and exclaimed, "Aaaughh! What luck!" Then he looked around him and estimated the vastness of the river and realized this was not luck, not coincidence, but merely the Council's wish. He understood then that Et Ska would be found and that he was somehow being guided by the tremendous Will of a Power far greater. He looked down at the crayfish, laughed and asked, "How is it you have had the luck to survive two years?"

"Because I remind myself that life under a rock is far better than no life at all." The crayfish clicked his claws a final time and sank beneath the surface and was quickly under his rock to carry on with the rest of his life.

Continuing his flight downstream, the Heron could smell the first tang of salt air. The sea was not far, nor hopefully would be Et Ska, and just beyond that the Council. With only a few days remaining, the Heron's timing had been, all in all, rather good. By nightfall, he would reach the shore, and the search for Et Ska would resume at daybreak.

The tide was temptingly low the next morning, which meant warm tidepools with captive sea creatures. The Heron's appetite had returned after his evening fast and he always had relished an easy catch. While walking along the shore, he was caught totally unaware by a gusty voice within the surf: "So tell me, Heron . . . how do I know you won't eat me on the way to the Council?"

The bird whipped around and searched the white-capped water, but could see no one. He called out, "Show yourself!"

"Answer my question first!"

"Et Ska?" The Heron waded out in the foamy water, still searching.

"I will put it to you one more time: How do I know you won't eat me on the way to the Council?"

"I eat defenseless caterpillars, not fish who sport a chance with me," he lied diplomatically.

"Very well, Heron. Here I am. Et Ska, the salmon you seek." She was magnificent as she jumped out of the water to prove her identity. Her scales seemed like quicksilver with the morning rays shining against them.

The Heron reverently watched Et Ska's display. She was much larger than he had expected and as beautiful a fish as he had ever seen. "So, how is it you have found me, Et Ska? I wish all my clients had been this easy," the bird said, stepping deeper into the sea.

"The funniest thing, Heron. You and I have met before," Et Ska said while she jumped high above the surface again, keeping a yellow eye on the messenger.

"Not to my recollection," said the Heron, silently searching his past.

"Yes. In my dream last night. All of what we are now saying and doing came to me then. I know all about the Council's request," Et Ska said smugly.

The Heron looked far beyond Et Ska and studied the possibilities in the horizon. He was too weary to question the salmon.

"Well, where shall I be and when?" Et Ska finally asked.

"You have four to five days to get there. We're lucky, because it's not far from here. North of the river a small stream flows into the sea. Go up that stream until you come to a special pool on the southern shore. Council delegates will be arriving anytime now, so you will know the place."

"*If* I can get past the river itself."

"Why couldn't you?" the Heron asked, dreading still another complication.

"My instinct to spawn grows daily and my home-river flows just over there. It will take every ounce of determination in me to pass the estuary. I can smell my birthplace. But, if I keep my wits about me, I can do it," she said, never for an instant staying still.

"I am sorry, Et Ska. This has come at a difficult time for many. Do your best. It's all the Council asks." The Heron, again restless for high flight, flew lightly above the surf.

"I shall leave now, while still inspired by my dream," Et Ska said with conviction.

"And sing your song, if you have one, Et Ska," added the bird, winding higher in the sky, above the rising salty mist.

"I do indeed!" she echoed in her highest leap of all. She swam north, at a great speed, ignoring the temptation of the river's fresh call to home-water. And in a voice clear and lovely, Et Ska sang her song:

> I fly underwater.
> I feel the vital, precious water
> Cleanse my body.
> I live for the rush
> And the power of the currents.
> I lose myself in the black, icy depths.
> I warm myself in the sun-blessed surface.
> I embrace the mountains and the valleys

Created by the Water-god.
When storms damn the world above
I carve my sea-trail in a safe, serene silence.
The exuberance of my youth
Becomes the integrity and courage I shall
Require in my last year . . .
As I bid farewell to the bounty of the Sea
And accept the Final Challenge.
I'll return to the nest of my birth
Knowing I am
Complete. Fulfilled.
And chosen.
I am Et Ska.
And I swim.

CHAPTER SIX

I N A PLACE OF SOLITUDE, in a forest clearing, flanked by a quiet pond, the Council Ground had been prepared. It was a place of mysterious serenity, a haven of calm, and as beautiful a sanctuary as had ever been created. It was perfected by the Will of the Council, hidden and secretive and virgin.

Neera the wolf was the first to arrive. She cautiously sniffed the clearing to assure her safety. Then, satisfied the ground was sacred, she rolled playfully in the lush, tall grasses, joyful to have been summoned and to have arrived at last.

But by the peaceful, viridescent pond, Neera suddenly wearied from her journey. It was almost as if a euphoric spell had been cast over the Grounds, compelling her to dream. So she picked a shady spot to rest atop a slight rise, so that she could easily see who arrived next. She circled around three times to guarantee her comfort, lay down gracefully, sighed deeply and fell instantly asleep.

Her dreams took her hundreds of years away to a time known to her only from the inherited song of her elders—running, laughing, hunting, sharing, and dying with the peace and calm of knowing your young will prosper. It was a dream such as no other she had ever dared to dream and she awoke the next morning with tears of exhilaration. She felt a power inside her as she yawned and stretched, locking the dream deeper inside her. She had never experienced such a power. It was greater than the strength she had felt after bringing down her first deer. It throbbed through her refreshed body and seemed to grow in intensity as she walked around. She knew it was a gift from her dream and she sang a song of thanks.

"No, please . . ." came a voice shortly after she had finished her last verse. ". . . do not stop. It's been years since I've heard a wolf sing. Where I live, you know, there are none." The voice came from high above her.

Neera looked up and watched Lordjahn the condor break from his treetop perch and glide in an easy circle down to her.

"There are few wolves even where I live," she whispered as she beheld him.

He landed gracefully with a gentle bounce and asked, "Are we the only ones here?"

"So it seems. Please forgive me if I stare, but to see you so close . . . I bow to your supremacy, Lordjahn." She lay down in front of him and placed her head on her outstretched paws.

"Please, get up, wolf. You must not bow to me when I myself bow to one greater," Lordjahn said, a flush of embarrassment crossing his face. "But, I'm flattered you know my name. This is a beautiful place, isn't it, wolf?"

Neera rose and replied, "Please, I would be honored if you called me Neera."

Lordjahn turned and smiled. "Neera."

To hear the bird speak her name sent a streak of bristles up Neera's back, and the power inside her stirred and increased. "Have you come far, Lordjahn?" she asked.

"Yes, very. When once I flew for days in search of food and adventure, I'm afraid I now prefer to keep my wanderings closer to my mountain home. But of course, a Council calling would inspire my flight to the stars and back." He sipped from the calm pool waters.

"I would gladly keep watch, so you might rest, Lordjahn," Neera offered, approaching him.

"My dear . . . this is the Council Ground. It is not necessary to keep watch. We have no enemies here except our own indelible suspicions from our lives at home." He spoke in a whisper to emphasize the magic he felt. "I will build a nest on the side of that hill and I'll rest there." Lordjahn walked to Neera and smiled. "Please continue singing as I fall asleep. It's been so long. It reminds me of the old days."

The wolf escorted Lordjahn up to the side of the hill and they spoke as if old comrades, smiling at each other's insights. The two old survivors had much in common.

Neera sat silently and watched as Lordjahn began fashioning his evening lair. As he walked about, adding wisps of tall grass and twigs to his nest, Neera reached around to her flank and seized a huge tuft of her silvery, shedding coat and placed it on the nest of the condor. "Here, Lordjahn . . . birds seem to favor my old winter coat for their spring nests. For whatever use it is, you are welcome."

Lordjahn accepted the offering and said, "I am honored, Neera. I shall use this to keep my feet warm. The older I get, the colder *they* get!" He padded his feet with the fur and lay down.

"So, I will leave you to your rest now, condor. Perhaps by the time you awaken, the Council will have begun." Neera walked back down the hill to explore the limits of the Grounds and to relish her talk with Lordjahn.

There was a warm fog forming on the far banks of the pond and she watched its silent crossing until the mist finally reached her and refreshed her. She closed her eyes and wondered how she had come to be chosen—for what purpose and to what end—and above all questions, who the Council Authority was. She drifted off with such questions and thoughts and returned to her dream of tremendous power. And with it, a new song descended to haunt her mind. Over and over she sang it in her dream:

A Will
To keep each other
Strong and Long.
A power
A knowledge
A truth
In accordance with the
Design
Long ago made.
We gather
We, the Chosen.
Semper et ubique.

CHAPTER SEVEN

OKAY, I'LL WAIT HERE and you go see if this is the place," Little Paw told Moko. "According to the Heron, this should be it."

The giant, cumbrous buffalo stared through the trees and didn't acknowledge his comrade's order.

"What's the matter, pal? Go ahead. I'll wait here," the prairie dog repeated. But Moko seemed transfixed. "Hey, what is it?" Finally, in desperate exasperation, the small creature bit into the buffalo's hock, taking an unprecedented and death-defying step at getting a reaction.

"Yeeeooo!" the buffalo cried, stomping back a step. "What'd you do that for?" he bellowed.

"What's with you? It's like you just turned to stone or something," Little Paw squeaked in his defense, feeling rather lucky he wasn't squashed into the forest floor. He knew that biting a buffalo, even a good friend, was risky business.

"I'm sorry. I guess I was just thinking," the buffalo said, looking about nervously.

"I told you to let me do the thinking. Now, you go on in and make sure we have the right place."

"Oh, this is the place. Can't you feel it?" he whispered down to Little Paw. "Strange, eh?"

"Feel what?" snapped the prairie dog. "Hey, you aren't going vacant on me now, are you?" he asked, raising his tiny eyebrows. "Just what I need, an intuitive buffalo!" he added, under his breath.

"Never mind, Little Paw. Okay, I'll go in and make sure this is the place." And with that, he started to snap his way through the bracken.

"Wait a minute, Moko! Be sure to come back here as soon as you can!" yelped Little Paw after his burly companion.

The buffalo looked back at Little Paw and said, "I will, I will. I feel so strange . . . it's like . . . can't you feel it?"

"You're just tired from the journey. Look, the forest is no place for either of us. You're just nervous. Go ahead. I'll wait here. But hurry," called Little Paw in his small, assuring voice.

In the dense quiet of the damp and foreign forest, Little Paw grew increasingly nervous as he listened to the slowly fading, crushing footsteps of his buffalo comrade. He realized his own vulnerability on the forest floor, and the unnatural sound of his giant cohort breaking through the trees and bushes made him uneasy. Surely, every animal in the neighborhood knew of their trespass and he was certain he felt countless eyes on him.

"They probably think I'm a squirrel. I hope . . . humpf! Disgusting thought!" he said aloud, nervously trying to quell his uneasiness.

The strange feeling that Moko had experienced was growing within him as he headed for the clearing ahead of him. He walked slowly and deliberately, as if summoned forth by a silent and beguiling enchantment. When he arrived at the Council Ground, he stopped and deeply breathed the warm, fresh air. Looking around the compound, he saw no one and he stepped into an arc of sunlight. He shook the forest dampness from his coat, sniffed the ground and took a mouthful of the plentiful long grass at his feet.

Moko could feel an odd and unfamiliar tingling in his chest and he stopped grazing, listening to what it was saying. He felt it charge down into his powerful legs and back through his body. He smiled as he traced the movement within him, causing no pain, but leaving every inch of him stronger. He had never realized the confidence that one's own strength generates and he was struck with the enlightenment so suddenly, that he had to laugh out loud. He snorted heavily, kicked his back legs and charged about the clearing like a calf. The ground echoed his steps solidly and as the thunder in the Earth resounded, so did the powerful energy resound within Moko's giant countenance. He felt he could have run forever, never tiring. And for the first time in his life, Moko the buffalo sang:

> I am a blessed power
> No force can stop me
> Faster and farther
> I am blessed.
> The Will above me
> Around me
> Within me
> Has blessed me
> By making me so.

His husky voice vibrated through the clearing and as the last uneven note dissipated, Moko looked around to see if anyone had heard him. As he sang and listened to his words, he could feel the Earth quaking beneath him as though each of his four sturdy legs sent their thunder down to the core of the Earth and it returned to him magnified, much like an ocean wave, gathering force as it rolls. And it was only after an hour's meditating vigil, standing squarely thus, that he remembered Little Paw.

He turned to find his path back into the forest, but he found Little Paw on the Council Ground's border. He was sitting on his haunches and was strangely silent.

"Little Paw! I'm sorry! I forgot you," said Moko, smiling sheepishly.

The small tawny animal was clearly awestruck. He faintly whispered, wide-eyed and meek, "I've been watching you, Moko. I've heard your song. This Ground is hallowed. It's changed you. I see a glow about your body. A glow I've only heard about. And now it's all around you."

"Harrr!" Moko gently laughed. "I've just had a good run and gotten a closer look at myself. Not a bad song, eh? It's my first, you know."

Little Paw remained oddly still, as if afraid to move a step closer.

"It's a grand song. But it does change things somewhat."

"Why? What do you mean?"

"Because I know you don't need me here. Remember? I came to help you out—to think, study, and solve for you. You won't be needing me here." His face was pale and his paws began to shake uncontrollably.

"That's not true, Little Paw. You're my friend. You're welcome. No one else is here. Come on in and see the color of the water in the pond!" he said with enthusiasm.

"I can't," the prairie dog said in a low tone.

"What? Why not? Come in, Little Paw."

"I can't! I've tried! Don't you see? Something is preventing me." He held his paws up and pushed against the invisible barrier. "I can't go any further than this." A small creature-tear escaped his eye as he spoke.

"I don't get it."

"Don't you think I would run in if I could? Don't you know me any better than that?" cried the prairie dog. "I've watched you! This Ground has given you a song! That was to be *my* song, Moko! I would have betrayed our friendship for a single note of your song!" He went down on all fours, wept openly and gasped for air between words.

Moko blinked as he listened, slowly absorbing Little Paw's confession. "But . . . you and me . . . a team, you know?"

"I would have done it, Moko! I would have dropped you like a hot rock!"

And as those words were delivered to Moko's heart, his own creature-tear cascaded down his dusty face. "Oh, I see," he said, unable to watch Little Paw cry. "So where does that leave the team?"

"Broken."

"No, it leaves one-half of the team in here and the other half out there, thinking of new ways to get in," Moko replied calmly. He sniffed and added, "See? I'm not as dumb as I look. Come on. Try coming in again."

The prairie dog crept forward and then was dashed back by an invisible Will forbidding his entrance. "I knew it! I'm being punished for coming where I'm not wanted."

"Then, if I were you, I'd start to burrow a home right now. You'll just have to wait outside until it's time for us to go home."

"Well, that was my original idea," Little Paw said, trying to recoup his confidence. Then, he started digging a hole with renewed energy.

"The sooner you have the safety of your burrow, the better I'll feel about it," Moko added, stifling a yawn. "I think I'd better go now and rest." He started to leave. "Good night, Little Paw, little friend." He lumbered off, disappearing through a passage leading to the other side of the Council Ground.

Little Paw watched him go, held up his right arm in reverence and whispered, "I've underestimated you, Moko. And what's worse, I've overestimated me." He sat on his haunches and stared into the Council Ground. Then, he smiled and added, "Oh so what? This beats hanging around the prairie all my life."

By nightfall, Little Paw was sleeping in the warm safety of his newly dug home, dreaming he was a mighty warrior being led into battle by an even mightier general.

CHAPTER EIGHT

WHEN ISCARIOT THE RACCOON escaped from his fire-consumed cage, his only fear was that the Heron's prophecy was coming true. And had he not had the foresight to learn how to slip the latch on his cage over the years, he surely would have perished.

At the wood's edge, he watched his humans running about his blazing cage, shouting and tossing buckets of water. The terror in Iscariot's eyes was magnified by the reflection of the dancing flames. They seemed to call his name as they crackled and consumed his bed. He stared, heart thundering, unable to tear his eyes away. It was only then that he noticed the deep sting in his right front paw. He examined and licked the deep burn as he mentally retraced his escape. He was angered when he recalled how he had swiped at the first spark of fire, as though he could destroy it.

He thought of the Heron and the summons he had delivered a week earlier. The threat of death for ignoring the Council was a vivid, sudden reality.

"All right! I'll go to your damn Council! I'll face whatever or whoever you are! One chance at the Heron. That's all I ask," he called out to the sky. Then, he added to himself, "I may be a traitor, but I'm no coward!"

With that, Iscariot began his journey. It was a long distance and he had to nurse his injured foot along the way. He traveled by night, avoiding the heat of the day, and he stopped only occasionally to eat and rest.

His once-beautiful pampered coat had lost its sheen and his well-kept belly growled in discontent. The price for his domesticity was high, he soon discovered, as he had lost many hunting skills. His reaction time was decreased and his heavy paunch slowed him down miserably. But, in four days and three nights, Iscariot finally arrived at the Council Ground border. His shabby and torn body ached as he sniffed the air wearily. Then, he fell where he had stopped outside the Grounds and instantly lapsed into a death-like sleep.

The Council Ground from the sky above looked just as magically beautiful as it did from within. The Blue Heron flew in a low circle to survey the sight in peaceful consideration before landing. He saw Moko kicking up dust on the eastern border and Neera was drinking from the pond on the opposite side of the compound. Standing not far from her was the exquisite Lordjahn, preening himself.

The Heron dropped in lower and circled the complete area in search of Iscariot. His heart began to race as his fears and expectations unfolded. The raccoon was nowhere to be seen. He landed, spitting and cursing Iscariot's name. "Damn beast!"

"I beg your pardon, Heron," said Lordjahn who had spied the messenger's return and flown over to greet him.

"I beg yours, Lordjahn," the Heron said, embarrassed for his transgression. "Be assured, I wasn't referring to you."

"I assume not." The condor turned to Neera and called, "Neera. Come. Here is our friend, the Heron."

Neera's head rose high and she trotted over to the two birds, smiling. "So I see," she said. "You look well, Heron, considering the distance you must have flown since last we met."

"And you look well also, Neera. I see you have met Lordjahn, and Moko the buffalo, I presume?" The Heron looked around the clearing as he spoke and sniffed for a trace of the raccoon.

"Moko? No, we've seen no one else," said Neera, also looking around and sniffing the breeze.

"See that dust rising above those trees?" the blue bird asked, indicating the air above them. "It comes from a great dust bin beyond. And in that dust bin, we will find our buffalo friend."

"A buffalo! How charming! And will there be others?" asked the wolf.

"Hopefully. Have either of you seen any traces of a raccoon? Perhaps during your voyages here? Anything at all?" The Heron looked at each, eager for positive news. But both the wolf and the condor shook their heads. "Well, that's it, then. One less for the Council and, I'll give you odds, one less for raccoon-kind."

"But there is still one more day," Neera said softly. "Perhaps this raccoon will arrive by tomorrow."

"For the sake of the Council and no others, I'll pray you are right," the Heron sighed. Then, he added, "Well. It's my problem. Not yours. Let's go meet Moko. I think you'll find him unassuming and kind, if nothing else. An interesting choice on the part of the Council, don't you think?"

Moko was still rolling blissfully in his cool, dusty paradise when he caught the scent of the three others. He rose quickly with an unnatural grace, shook the dust from his coat and addressed the Heron. "Oh, Heron. It's good to see you again. So, I am here. What do I do?"

The Heron flapped his wings to clear the air of the dust and said, "I'm afraid it's not as simple as all that. The Council won't convene until tomorrow. But, I want you to meet two fellow delegates—Lordjahn the condor and Neera the wolf."

Each animal took a respectful step toward the other to acknowledge the introduction. Moko was undeniably impressed by the company he would be sharing and said, "I still say there is some mistake, Heron. What do I, Moko, have in common with the widsom of Neera and the magnificence of Lordjahn? These are two of the greatest beasts known to me. I am honored."

"The Council has a reason, Moko," the Heron replied simply. "But I do have a job for you now."

The buffalo, eager to assist, pranced forward, leaving a trail of dust in his wake.

"The pond there is served by a small tributary coming from the sea. I am expecting a salmon to enter any time now. Her name is Et Ska. Once she has arrived, we will be complete. Or as complete as we can be for now. Wait and watch for her and let me know when she has arrived," the Heron instructed.

Moko stepped closer to the Heron and whispered, "I would be delighted. But, what is a salmon?"

The Heron whispered back, "Oh. My error. A salmon is a rather large fish. Have you ever seen a fish, Moko?"

"One who lives under the water, not breathing the air? Yes, I saw one once."

"Good. Then all you need to do is to place yourself next to the tributary until you see a fish. Et Ska will be the only one."

"Shall I bring her to you when she has arrived?" Moko asked earnestly.

The Heron swallowed a compelling urge to laugh, then answered, "No, I think she'd rather I came to her. Thank you, Moko." He smiled weakly. Then, to the condor and the wolf, he said, "I am going to patrol the perimeters of the Council Ground for the raccoon. If either of you wishes to help, I'd be grateful."

"Why does this raccoon give you so much anguish?" asked Neera, in her golden, soft voice.

"Anguish!" the Heron echoed, turning sharply on the wolf. "Not one moment of anguish, Neera! He is a vile creature, capable of little good. I do not let beings like Iscariot cause me anguish!"

"But, see your anger?" joined Lordjahn. "Are anguish and anger not cousins?"

"All right! I'm angry! He's ruined my record! I warned him, though. A poor Council choice!" The Heron was pacing nervously back and forth as he talked.

"Relax, Heron. If your raccoon is anywhere to be found, we'll find him. But, if he doesn't show, it's his fault. Not yours," Lordjahn said with the trace of a knowing smile.

So, they each parted in different directions in search of the raccoon. But it was Neera, with her great, sensitive nose, who found Iscariot. She called a signal to the condor and the Heron, then crept quietly closer to inspect the animal. He had not moved from the spot where he had collapsed the night before. The wolf carefully walked around him, sniffing his still body and looking for signs of life.

She spoke to the Heron as he landed next to her "Is this your vile creature?"

The Heron stared at the sickening condition of the animal. He was shocked and momentarily could not speak. Then, "Yes, that's him. Iscariot. Is he dead?"

"As close as I've ever seen an animal," she answered. Then Lordjahn arrived with a swosh of wings, causing Neera's fine coat to wave. "Lordjahn, here is the raccoon," she said compassionately. "You know best when death is near." She stepped aside to allow the condor to judge Iscariot's condition.

Lordjahn walked around the raccoon, tilting his head as he listened for signs of life. "He is all but gone. Is there nothing we can do?"

The Heron, who had not broken his stare upon Iscariot, muttered, "I don't understand. What good? What good?"

"But perhaps . . ." Neera began.

"Drag him in," the Heron interrupted.

"What?" she asked.

"Drag him in," he repeated. "Bring him through the Council border."

"An animal has a right to die where he has prepared his death-nest," Lordjahn objected delicately.

"He has come this far. Drag him in, Neera."

The wolf took the raccoon by the neck and gave a gentle tug. He was not heavy in his debilitated condition, and she pulled him along as easily as though he were one of her own errant pups.

Once inside the Council Ground, the three animals stood around him. Neera arranged him comfortably in the soft grasses and instinctively licked his masked face. "Look here," she said, "these hairs are fire-kissed. What do you suppose happened?"

"Come, Heron. Leave Neera to heal him while we fly. You look as though you could use it. I like flying with you. Come. Forget him. If the Council wishes him to recover, then he will recover. It's beyond your power now. So come. You need a change of altitude."

"Well, for a moment, perhaps. Do your best, Neera."

In a silent breeze, the two giant birds were through the clouds, high and gliding.

Neera, calling on all her healing knowledge and prayers, did what she could to see to Iscariot's comfort. Then, she lay down next to him to warm his body and to assure his sleeping soul that her life was just as near to him as was his death.

When the raccoon stirred and moaned, Neera knew it was more than just her powers which had inspired the animal's return. The Will of the Council had deemed his life necessary just as surely as it had inspired her new song just the day before.

Life slowly began to reclaim the tattered body. Iscariot stretched his legs, as if awakening from a long, grand sleep. When his eyes finally opened, he raised his head to speak to Neera. "Where's the Heron?"

"Hello, Iscariot," Neera said warmly. "I am Neera, the wolf. Welcome."

"I can see you're a wolf. Where's the Heron?" he snapped.

Slightly set back, but granting the raccoon a transgression out of his discomfort, she replied softly, "He's out flying. He'll be pleased you feel better."

"I'll bet he'll be just delighted," he hissed.

"Can I bring you food?"

Ignoring her question, he looked around and said, "So, this is the ever-popular Council Ground. Go tell the Heron and his Council I'm alive. Tell him there's a little matter of a fire I wish to discuss with him."

"I'm not here to act as your messenger," Neera growled.

"Then why are you here?"

"For the same reason you are. I have been summoned by the Council. And as far as I can see, that is the only thing we have in common," she growled further, in a gravelly, proud voice. She turned her back on him and began walking away.

"No matter. As long as you're not here to eat me. Where did you say the food is kept?"

She kept walking, head low in a growing contempt, and said, "Find it yourself, Iscariot. And when you do, gorge yourself and become fat." She stopped and looked back at him over her bristled shoulder. She raised her lips to display her intimidating fangs and snarled, "For we all have to eat sometime."

CHAPTER NINE

W HEN THE HERON returned from his flight, he commenced with Council business. His first concern was the condition of Iscariot. He turned to Lordjahn and said, "Thank you for the soar. It was exhilarating. But, now I must see how that raccoon is." They said goodbye and as the condor walked away, the Heron felt honored to have flown again, wingtip to wingtip, with the great Lordjahn.

The Heron walked around the deserted area where the near-lifeless body of Iscariot had been dragged. The grass where he had lain was still crumpled down, but the Heron could sense the raccoon's presence close by. His immediate feeling was of relief: Iscariot had survived, even though his next thought was the dread of confronting the beast again.

But before he could face this dread, Iscariot was upon him, attacking from behind. The Heron screeched in horror as he felt the beast's claws slice down his back. Flapping his wings instinctively, he was well above Iscariot before he could strike again. His anger from letting his defenses down so stupidly was greater than the stinging pain running down his spine. He grasped the nearest branch and glared back down at his assailant. Stuck between the raccoon's claws were remnants of the Heron's glorious dark blue plumage, and the Heron became incensed.

"Iscariot! You shall die for that!" he cried.

"Not before I kill you for burning me out! No one crosses Iscariot!" the raccoon screamed back.

"Idiot! What power could I possibly have to burn you out? The Council did it! To attack an animal within the Council Ground is sacrilege! You're finished this time, Iscariot!" The Heron was beginning to feel the pain crawl up his back and he knew his wound would need attention.

Neera and Lordjahn were aroused by the screaming from the other side of the Council Ground and each rushed to see what had happened.

"I smell blood!" cried Neera, rushing past the crouching raccoon and looking up at the injured bird.

Lordjahn flew up to the Heron's safety-branch and examined the bird's back, then said down to Iscariot, "Do you always back-attack, raccoon?"

Neera bared her terrifying teeth and approached the raccoon, who held his ground. "I would rip your worthless pelt off your body were we outside this sacred ground."

Iscariot growled, still low to the ground, ready to strike if necessary. "He sent a fire to kill me," was all he said in his defense.

Shaking from shock, anger, and pain, the Heron said, "The Council will judge and punish him. Come with me, Neera. I need your help."

"Can you fly?" asked Lordjahn.

"Yes, but I feel faint. Fly with me, Lordjahn."

So the two birds flew to the side of the pond, followed by Neera. Iscariot turned, lay down and watched them with neither feelings of regret nor remorse.

With the help of his Council friends, the Heron's wounds were cleansed with the clear healing waters of the pond. Attracted to the splashing, Moko wandered over to the triad.

"Excuse me," he said, meekly addressing the wet Blue Heron. "The fish . . . she's here now."

The Heron looked up and smiled. "Well, that's good news, at least. Thank you for your help, Moko."

"What happened to you?" Moko asked, trying not to stare at the Heron's bloodied back.

"A little run-in with a raccoon," the Heron replied, looking around for Iscariot.

"Do you want me to trample him?" Moko asked innocently. "I do it good, they say."

"No thank you. The Council will deal with the beast in Its own way," the Heron replied. "How does Et Ska look? Did she arrive without too many scrapes and scratches?"

"She looked fine to me. But she's my first salmon, remember. She's a flashy little thing, that's sure," Moko continued, looking out over the pond and wondering if she could hear him talk about her. "Well, if you don't mind, Heron, I'm hungry now." The buffalo slowly walked away, feeling accomplished in his first mission for the Council.

As the Heron carefully began to preen himself, Neera caught sight of a protruding bulge under one of his wings. "Heron, you've missed a spot. There, under your right wing. See? Something is stuck there."

The Heron then remembered Chanta's cocoon and he gasped out loud in horror that perhaps, between the attack, water, and preening, she might have been injured. "Look at it Neera, and, tell me if it seems harmed," he said urgently.

"Don't you want me to just pluck it out?" she asked, stepping closer and examining the object under his wing.

"No!"

"What do you have there?" Lordjahn asked, stepping closer.

"Quickly, Neera, is it harmed? Look closely. See? It's a cocoon." The Heron stretched his wing even farther to allow for a closer examination.

"Well, so it is. It seems intact to me. But I still don't . . ."

"Wet? Does it look wet?" the Heron asked, cutting her off.

Neera gently touched the silken pouch with her sensitive nose and said, "Ahhh! It moved, Heron! And it seems secure and dry."

The Blue Heron exhaled heavily in relief and slowly refolded his outstretched wing. "That's good. I'd forgotten she was there." His eyes expressed an exhaustion beyond description.

Lordjahn smiled and said, "Then we are to assume that whoever 'she' is, she is a Council member also? Or are you keeping a pet for yourself?"

"It's a long story," the injured bird said, reflecting on the weariness of his day. A giant fog of fatigue suddenly enveloped him—the flight with Lordjahn, Iscariot's attack, and the entire Council affair weighed him down, and the need for sleep was immense.

"You must excuse me," he said. "If I don't rest before the Council begins, I'll be as weak as a chick half out of its shell." He spoke softly, as if not to disturb his already quiescent mind. "Please give Et Ska my congratulations on her safe arrival."

"We will see to everything, dear Heron," Neera said soothingly. "Go off to your nest and sleep."

So, the fatigued bird limply took wing and flew ill-balanced, just barely off the ground. When he found a hillside place of rest, he landed awkwardly and folded his long legs under him. His thoughts ached as did his body. He reflected on the one success . . . they were all, all the beasts, now within the Council Ground.

"So, have I completed my task?" he muttered aloud, slurring tired words together. "Is everything to your satisfaction? Now that I have been humiliated, aggravated, and attacked, is it finished now? Just deliver Chanta and then let me go home." His voice grew smaller. "Please," he whispered. Then sleep mercifully consumed him.

CHAPTER TEN

T HE NEXT MORNING, each of the chosen animals in the Council Ground awoke at the same instant. Every eye opened as though it had never closed for rest, without trace of sleepiness or even that first, regretful blink in a temptation to fall back into slumber. The sun had not yet risen and the entire area was smothered in a dense fog, creating a stunning silence. Far above, the setting star tossed a few rays of iridescent light down into the Council Ground, but the heavy mist stubbornly refused to lift.

And so the animals each came from their sleeping places—the condor and the wolf, the buffalo and the salmon, the Heron and even the raccoon. They met without words at the side of the pond. They met and waited. The only movement was Et Ska's light shimmering along the pond's shallow edge. Iscariot stood much apart from the rest, but seemed as strangely compelled and drawn to the pond as were the others. Although no words were spoken, each one present grew more nervous, as the increasing morning brightness overhead finally began to seep its way into the rising mists. The scents of fear and anxiety reached each sensitive nostril and the Ground seemed to vibrate with each racing heart.

The Heron looked about, as curious as he was cautious. It was as though the entire compound was spellbound and he could feel his mind begin to whirl with the excitement. Whoever or what-ever the Council was, it was about to come forth. It was time. The great mysteries that had surrounded them were about to be unraveled.

Then, from the far side of the pond, lost in the fog, came the sound of something stalking through the still water. It was Neera who first caught the sound and when her ears focused on it, the other animals did likewise. As the sound approached them, there was barely a breath among them all, yet nothing could be seen through the fog.

When it seemed as though the sound was all around the transfixed animals, it ceased altogether. They looked about tensely as if awaiting an attack from an unknown, greatly feared enemy. Then, directly before them, with only his head discernible above the fog, was the One who had summoned the trembling congregation. Each animal gasped to behold such a creature. A slight breeze off the pond gently tugged the fog away from his body and he slowly became more visible.

In all of nature, there had never been one so powerful, so magnificent, nor one so wise as Athanasy. He stood three times as high as Moko the buffalo and twice as wide. His head was adorned with a set of mighty antlers that spanned a distance of nearly twelve feet.

One by one, the animals before him offered their stunned, silent respect. Each bowed or knelt, but could not for a moment take their eyes off Athanasy.

Then, when it seemed as though the silence could go on no longer, he spoke. His voice was deep and strong, and at once the Heron recognized it as the Voice in his dreams.

"I am Athanasy, the Elk that is no more." He remained in the shallow water and looked at each one present.

The Heron came forward to offer his welcome, but Athanasy spoke before the bird could summon the courage. "You have done your job well, Heron, although with some hesitancy. You are all here, so we can begin. Welcome, Lordjahn, Sky-God . . . Neera, Soul-Seer . . . Et Ska, Brave-One . . . Moko, the Mighty . . . Chanta, soon to be among us. And Iscariot . . ." The raccoon cowered to the ground, then slowly rose on his haunches to receive whatever deathblow the great creature might deliver. "And Iscariot, you are welcome also."

Although Athanasy did not smile, there was a calm, relaxing, and almost hypnotic quality to his voice. He surveyed the beasts at his feet and the serene Council Ground behind them and said, "I know your questons are many and, in time, I'll answer them all. On this shore will be our place of Council. Let us begin at the beginning. But remember, your time is precious. My time is never-ending, so therefore, my chosen ones, I shall serve you."

Then Athanasy finally emerged totally out of the water and showed his full size. His coat was ablaze with reds, golds, and browns melting together in regal harmony. His long legs carried his weight well and he was the very essence of elegant symmetry. His majestic antlers jutted forward from his massive head, then curled back and armored his entire body. They were thick adorn-ments, rather like those of the moose, with innumerable points of unquestionable authority. His neck and chest rippled in strength as he walked and they supported the weight of his antlers in absolute grace.

As is the case with most creatures, tales and superstitions and legends were passed down to every new generation. There were stories of the brave, the wise, the foolish, and there were stories of the lovers. Some were merely fables created to correct the errant young; many were true and cherished tales. But in none had there ever been any mention of one such as Athanasy. He was almost too magnificent to behold for a long period of time and the animals would have to look away to assure themselves of reality, only to slowly have their glances stolen back by the superb creature.

At seemingly the very moment Athanasy had arrived, the mys-terious fog had lifted, allowing the sun to shower down on the Council Ground. The multitude of greens, the creamy azure of the sky, and the metallic glints off the sparkling water all seemed magnified and even more glorious in the presence of Athanasy.

And with his arrival, it was time to begin.

Athanasy opened the long-awaited Council by sharing his song with his chosen. As he sang, his deep bronze eyes seemed to glow in a faraway fascination, as though he too were being inspired by his song for the very first time. The fine foreign melody of the song was as richly reverent as its words:

From centuries past, buried
In a time unknown,
I died one day.
But no one
Knew of my passing.
Until another day when some being
Turned and saw I was gone.
Then, he cried for me, as did they all.
Murderers, they. Now mourners with regret.
So, from their deeds
And from their tears
I rose again, reborn to know
That with my birth
The fallen souls from all the past
Came again to be
And now, reside in me.

Athanasy! Athanasy!
The sum of all souls passed.
I am Athanasy.
O Brothers and Sisters,
Be with me,
For I am Athanasy!

A silvery silence encased them all. No one moved. As it had been since Athanasy's arrival, the air around them was scented with magic, binding each creature into a spell of inspiration. The words of the song carried a different, private message to each Council member.

Finally, Iscariot, still protectively apart from the rest, stepped forward and demanded, "Why am I here? I have nothing in common with anyone in this place. What do I have to do with your great Council? If I am here to be made an example and punished, then get on with it!" He faced Athanasy, yet couldn't look directly into his eyes. Then, he turned on the Heron and added, accusingly, "I wanted nothing to do with it!"

The Heron spoke. "That's true, Athanasy. From the start, Iscariot has been difficult!" He stiffly walked forward, wings unable to fold into his swollen back. "I demand that he be punished for back-attacking me."

"You burned me out!" Iscariot hissed.

"I burned you out," Athanasy said, stepping between the two. "As you had every intention of staying in your secure, complacent cage, I simply destroyed it and gave you no choice but to leave."

"I demand to know why I was summoned in the first place!" Iscariot cried.

Athanasy, ignoring his question, walked among the others and said, "Disagreeable creature, is he not?" He turned and addressed the raccoon. "How very human."

Then the elk walked to the water's pebbled edge and lay down, folding his stately long legs under him. Likewise, the Council animals surrounded him and knelt. "The time has come," he began, "to consider our future. Of course, I speak of the future of all creature-kind, for our own lives are meaningless. Let us speak of our man-cousins. Let us speak of . . . extinction."

His last word pierced every heart to the soul. The terror of extinction was inherent in all animals.

"Neera," he continued, "let us hear from you. You are chosen for your wisdom. Tell us what you see in the future."

"In my song, I weep, as have my countless ancestors. And, although he may not know it, Moko the buffalo and I share the same tear." Startled, Moko looked up at the mention of his name and blinked in puzzlement. "How very sad, Moko," Neera continued, "as our man-cousins slaughtered the millions once among you, that he took as many of my own kind as well."

"I don't get it," Moko said, feeling a surge of embarrassment. "Say it so I can understand. Man-cousins? You mean one of those upright things?"

"Yes," she smiled, "an upright thing. But, didn't you know that, in the beginning, there were families of buffalo so vast that it would take many days for the entire herd to pass? Did no one ever tell you that one day a mighty machine with curious round legs and a head of smoke came forth, carrying the man-cousin and his war-stick? Were you not aware that, for mere sport, you now face extinction? So, without the sacred buffalo meat, where could my ancestors hunt except in a man-cousin's boundaries?

We are two of us slain with one arrow. Surely your father has told you."

Moko looked around to the others, who stared back at him. Their faces expressed sympathetic sadness as the buffalo learned of his heritage. He simply hung his head and quietly said, "No. My father always said I was too sensitive when I was a calf."

His sad honesty brought smiles to the gathering.

"And look at Lordjahn," the Blue Heron added. "He has flown for years without seeing another of his kind. Not one. If the wolf cannot hunt, leaves no carcass, whatever will the condor have to eat?"

"One can die of hunger only once, but one dies of loneliness each day. To know that I am one of so few is the loneliest thought in the universe. I try not to think about it. One can have countless friends, but unless one of them is his own kind . . ." He looked skyward, avoiding their faces, then added, ". . . no words can capture the emptiness."

Then, leaping high to express her point, Et Ska spoke. "I myself am one of millions. But our man-cousins affect our numbers incessantly. Between their polluting wastes, their fiery oil upon our water, and their constant nets which harvest us without mercy, one is lucky to make it home to spawn. The only reward I have ever sought for all my cleverness is to die a natural death, in my home-water."

"Millions of us have known the toxins of the man-cousins' vanity," Athanasy said. He looked out beyond his Chosen and appeared to be speaking into the wilderness. Then, he looked into each somber eye as he added, "We can no longer afford to let our extinction be our silent protests."

"A silent protest is no protest at all. The two words don't even belong together," growled Iscariot. The others, surprised to hear him speak, turned and looked at him. There was a brief period without movement, then Athanasy arose.

"You are right, Iscariot. Actions, not words," Athanasy said. "But hear me now, the man-cousins' trespasses on our evolutions have only begun. For now it is out of his hands and he has embarked on the final threat of all. The total devastation of all his wars combined cannot match the hideous threat upon us now.

Have none of you noticed in your travels a strange round mono-light reaching to the sky?"

"Yes," said the Heron. "I paused for a few days once and watched part of one being erected some time ago. It was a curious shape, even for the man-cousins' dwelling-places."

"If only the man-cousin would be content to war with himself and not with the whole of nature," Athanasy continued. "For with these structures, he does battle with the very essence of life." His voice grew in intensity.

"But, I don't get it," Moko sighed.

"You know little of the man-cousin, Moko," Athanasy continued. "But just trust me. What I say is true. The dome of which we speak is only one of hundreds of such structures on our land. The man-cousin calls these peace-time wonders, breeders of essential power. Curious words, I know. But, there is a place to the north that sends this power out in great ships to do battle. This power has been growing and growing for too long now, my cherished. We watch and wait, as is our destined nature. But no longer. The power has grown too great. This is our mission. We will be silent no more."

Athanasy looked lovingly at his Council animals, then added gently, "We . . . you and I, brothers and sisters, we are gathered here to demand that the man-cousin cease, once and for all time, this last attack on nature. We are here to see an end to what he calls advanced technology. As the man-cousin has so brutally taught us in the past, only the fittest of all shall survive. And we, my children, have never been so mighty."

There was a powerful silence. Then, Athanasy added, raising his head to the heavens, "Semper et ubique. Always and forever!"

CHAPTER ELEVEN

THE SERENE early-morning darkness which embraced the horizon hills was rudely broken by two harsh and glaring lights winding their way down and through the foggy foothills. From a distance the beams trespassed in silence, jaunting along steadily until they were joined by the low rumbling noise of an engine in need of repair.

As the sun began to rise suspiciously on the intruder, the vehicle ground to a halt under tremendous protest from the exhausted braking system. The contraption heaved a giant sigh of relief for stopping at last and the two bright lights went out slowly, as if two great, sleepy eyelids just drooped closed. Then the dawn was as still as before.

At first, the newly risen birds cautiously avoided the strange night-vehicle which now slept in harmless and silent immobility. The fog rose and transformed into a light mist, blocking the sun's first rays and blurring the dozing foreigner. Its color was unfamiliar to the circling birds and many were unable to contain their insatiable curiosity . . . such an odd land-beast, invading their land. Others similar to this had passed on occasion, but none with such strange markings. It was long, with eye-windows encasing its rectangular shape. Its color was rather like an angry sunset, all brightness and flaming hues of orange. Running down one of the sides of the vehicle were uneven stripes with more colors still, as though a drunken sloppy rainbow had fallen there to rest.

The mist was banished by the warm morning sun, the early shadows grew smaller and yet the intruder remained still and quiet, inside and out. By mid-morning, every creature in the valley had been warned of the foreigner and stayed well away. By noon, the bright orange box was nearly forgotten until the object moved slightly from within. Then, word telegraphed instantly that the object had finally awakened. With an accompanying screech, two flaps swung open and a four-legged creature leaped outside. At first, the animals who watched were relieved to see one of their own kind jumping from the intruder. But, as its scent traveled before it, the wild ones shuddered in recognition of the frightening smell. The animal was the dreaded man-pet, the low and unfortunate dog, disgustingly loyal to its master and never to be trusted in the wild.

The dog, delighted in being released from her confines, struck out joyously to explore her new territory. The animals spread the warning word of the dog's presence, gathered their curious children in and ignored the invader.

Unaware that she was being watched, the dog continued to widen her circle of exploration. She was well-gaited and carried herself gracefully as she galloped along, her nose constantly to the ground. The new area was full of deliciously strange aromas and just as she picked up a scent, she would cross another and follow it until the next. The result was an erratic, zig-zag trail of new delights, each scent more irresistible than the last.

The dog would have continued forever had she not heard and obediently responded to her human's voice.

"Fetchit! Fetchit-5! You expect me to wait breakfast all morning on you? Get on in here before your eggs galvanize!"

The dog joyfully leaped aboard the bus, climbed upon a chair and panted patiently, waiting for her meal to be served. Her alert eyes followed every culinary move her human made as he dished up breakfast. When the two plates were piled high with steaming, sloppy eggs, the plates were placed upon the table. Fetchit-5, in well-rehearsed courtesy, didn't touch her breakfast until her master was seated and had lifted his fork. Then, with one expert inhalation, her meal vanished. She licked her plate, her chops and then looked brightly at her human.

Charles Ellingson Sayble, at age seventy, looked more like sixty and, many times, acted only a third of that. His robust face, although weathered, glowed in sun-blessed health, and his eyes were naturally dark and dancing. In his youth, his hair had been a deep auburn, the envy of many women, but now it was faded and streaked haphazardly with white. He was not tall by human standards, but he had a barrel of a chest, making him appear quite large.

Very seldom having any place to go, nor anyone to object if he didn't, Sayble dressed in casual comfort . . . ill-fitting baggy jeans held up by an enormous silver and turquoise belt. He always wore one of several identical red plaid shirts, all of which were permeated with stale cigar odors and patched at the elbows. Sayble cherished his collection of bolo string ties, and each day he selected with care the one he would wear.

Fetchit-5 was the fifth in a continuous line of dogs all called Fetchit. There was little to know about the dog's ancestry: Fetchit-5 was a mutt. She was on the large size, weighing about ninety-five pounds, but her skin was tight and sleek upon her muscular frame, giving her quite a streamlined appearance. Her coat was blonde with crisp, well-defined patches of white. Her narrow, rapier-like tail was always in motion and seemed an adequate ballast when her nose was to the ground. Her ears were incongruously long and had the charming habit of folding themselves back. When this happened, her head would seem curiously off-centered as if she wore her "hair" high upon her head with a human-like femininity. Adding to her odd appearance was a chipped canine tooth which gave her a lop-sided grin when she panted contentedly after an exhausting romp. She was, in total, a human's animal with countless human traits. She was carelessly happy and had never allowed herself to separate the man-cousin's world from her own. They were one and the same.

Sayble and Fetchit-5 had shared eight years together and traveled wherever the road was passable for their conspicuous home, the converted school bus. Sayble's pension as a retired sign painter was minimal, but several wise investments made when he was younger deposited regular amounts into nearly thirty banks across the country. When funds in one bank grew low, he simply moved on to the next, healthier bank account. But, as he planned on living another forty years, he and Fetchit-5 lived frugally and in great enjoyment of life.

Their traveling home contained a vivid assortment from Sayble's past. The walls were covered with peeling postcards and faded photos of areas they had visited. There was a stack of oil paintings in various stages of completion leaning against the rear exit door. Sayble enjoyed his oils, especially when in the company of a bottle of wine. His painting talent was questionable, but his pleasure in landscape was immense, which was all that mattered to him.

Without a doubt, Charles Sayble lived in constant disarray, preferring his few, but precious, belongings to be tossed into a disheveled heap. All his earthly possessions were safely contained somewhere within the bus, and that was all he cared about—knowing they were there, somewhere.

Sayble had barely begun with the dishes when Fetchit-5 again started dancing about, her signal to go out.

"What? Again? All right, take your damn run and get back quick!"

She was gone in an instant, retracing her earlier trail. "And don't go far, or I'll leave for the river without you," he called out after her. Then, to himself, he added aloud, "That's no threat. She could outrun this old bus to the river."

Eventually, Fetchit-5 returned in her usual short-winded manner. She hopped onto an old milk crate next to Sayble as her human urged the hesitant bus down the deteriorating road toward the River of the North for some leisurely fishing, perhaps some painting, and, most assuredly, the greatest adventure of their lives.

CHAPTER TWELVE

THEIR RICKETY JOURNEY to the River of the North was relatively uneventful. Fetchit-5 dozed in and out of Sayble's repetitive verses of a ballad popular in his youth.

Following a dusty, forgotten road, Sayble navigated the bus through the undergrowth until he found a small clearing within view of the river's bank. Here he parked his home and prepared it for a long stay, which took him the remainder of the afternoon. By evening, he had settled in and Fetchit-5 was out on still another routine investigation of the area.

Sitting outside the bus in a folding chair, Sayble opened a bottle of wine and contemplated the sunset.

"Hey, Fetchit-5!" he called out into the darkness. "I'm tired. Let's turn in." He paused to listen for her return, but he could only hear the gentle shoreline lapping of the river waters. Without waiting any longer, realizing she would eventually return, Sayble stumbled up the bus steps, laid his tired and tipsy head upon his pillow and fell asleep.

Abandoning all elements of time and propriety, Fetchit-5 sailed through the tall waterbank grasses, her nose riveted to the ground, relishing the night scents. And so, in this fashion, nose down and tail up, did she wander dangerously far from her sleeping master.

The moon afforded much light and sparkled off the river. Stopping briefly on a sloping hilltop to survey her new territory,

Fetchit-5 took long, exploratory breaths. Then, as a sudden breeze from the north overtook her, she froze in the exciting terror of numerous strange scents. They were as powerful as they were scintillating. She tried to sort out each foreign one, but their odd combination confused yet excited her. Then, as swiftly as the breeze had developed, it ceased, and Fetchit-5's curiosity rose temptingly. She crept down the hill and carefully followed the origins of the compelling new scents.

She walked lightly and with caution, making certain to investigate each new sound and smell. She was so totally engrossed in her search, that not once did she think about Sayble. She continued through the night, resting occasionally, but far more consumed with curiosity than fatigue.

As the sun began to rise, she was far from the River of the North and had entered a damp, dark wooded area. It was there that one of the scents was most powerful and fascinating. It was only a matter of moments before Fetchit-5 was glaring into the terrified eyes of Little Paw, the prairie dog.

Neither beast moved.

Chasing squirrels was a favorite pastime for the dog and she was puzzled why this one did not take flight instantly as the rules called for. Then, to hasten the chase, Fetchit-5 took a slow, but very deliberate, step closer.

Little Paw panicked and struck out at a dead run to the sanctuary of his burrow. But in his confused terror, the prairie dog scrambled into the unfamiliar woods with Fetchit-5 nearly upon him. In his fright and disorientation, Little Paw was unaware that he crossed into the forbidden Council Ground. When he did realize where he was, he was not about to stop and wonder why he was able to enter . . . for not only had he entered, but so had the pursuing enemy.

"Moko! Help! Moko!" gasped the prairie dog, taking a swift glance back to see how close destruction was. But the dog had stopped abruptly. Little Paw whipped around to face his foe, but Fetchit-5's eyes were not on her prey. She stared up in frozen horror.

Following the dog's glance, the prairie dog turned back around and slowly looked straight up to the sky and beheld the giant Athanasy.

The mighty elk glared down at the two invaders. One by one, the other Council members arrived and stood behind their leader.

As Fetchit-5 saw each strange and powerful animal, she shrank closer to the ground, displaying subordination . . . a new emotion for the carefree mongrel.

When Little Paw saw Moko, he yelped with relief and looked up at him, trying to mask a sheepish grin.

"Little Paw! How did you get through?" called Moko, venturing forward.

"I don't know. But . . ." the prairie dog chuckled weakly, pointing over his shoulder, ". . . as you can see, I've brought someone with me."

"Athanasy, this is my friend Little Paw," the buffalo began carefully. "I can explain all this."

"It is not necessary. It seems, that in Its willingness to save your friend, the Will has also allowed this creature in," Athanasy said. Then, looking down at Little Paw, he continued, "You. You were not chosen. Your ambition was too great. But you are among us now. Perhaps we will find a use for your ambition after all, Little Paw. If the Will permits it, I won't argue."

"But the man-pet. What of that?" Neera asked, staring at her cousin warily.

"The what?" asked Moko.

"That creature cowering there. The one that chased your friend. It's commonly called a dog, an eternal ally to the man-cousin," replied the Blue Heron, stepping aside to avoid the unpleasant human scent Fetchit-5 had brought with her.

"But it looks like Neera and is called a dog like Little Paw," Moko continued, aching with confusion.

"It's a long story," snapped the Heron, impatiently. He envisioned the dog's trespass as still another complicated delay.

As the animals talked about her, Fetchit-5 clung to the ground and occasionally tapped her tail lightly, praying she appeared a hapless victim of circumstance, rather than an invader.

"What's your name, man-pet?" asked Athanasy.

"Fetchit-5," she answered meekly. "But I answer to nearly any name."

"Typically complacent," grunted the Heron.

71

"And," continued Athanasy, glaring at the Heron, "aside from the pursuit of your breakfast, how is it you came to be here, so far from civilization?"

"Oh, the squirrel wasn't for breakfast, only for fun! You see, I rarely ever catch anything. Honest. I've never even tasted a squirrel."

"Only for fun!" Little Paw yelped, turning on the dog ferociously. "Some fun! And, I'm *not* a squirrel!"

"Well, perhaps not. But, you run like one," Fetchit-5 said, trying not to break into a pant.

"Where is your human?" Athanasy asked.

"A . . . oh yes, him. Oh, miles from here. At our campsite. Unless he's already come looking for me. Sometimes we play this game, see. I run. He looks. Actually, he's not very good at it." She had the uncomfortable feeling that anything she said would be the wrong thing.

"One party after another," snarled Iscariot sarcastically, crouching under a large thorn bush.

"In fact, I suppose I ought to be leaving so you can all get back to whatever it was you were doing," continued the man-pet, slinking backwards.

"I'm afraid it's not as easy as all that, my friend," said Lordjahn, flying closer in.

"My god! It's a vulture!" cried the dog, cowering back down. "I know what that means!"

"Whoever told me that man-pets were educated?" asked the Heron with a disgusted flip of his bill.

Circling thoughtfully, Athanasy said, "Once inside the Council Ground, this place, you cannot leave unless the Will so desires. And we have many questions to ask you. So, perhaps, even you will prove useful to us."

"You think *you* have questions. Think what's going through *my* mind," Fetchit-5 mumbled to herself, daring to glance around at the animals.

Then Neera spoke. "But the human, Athanasy! Dogs are universally known for their fierce loyalties to their masters. And the opposite is true. She has said her human will come looking."

"But then again, maybe he won't," barked the man-pet. "It

depends on how much wine he's downed. You never know about a human, you know."

"So I've heard," said Athanasy. "But answer this: Would you betray your human? Could you live without him?"

"Well, if it's a matter of living at all, then you bet your rack, I could! And let's be practical here. There stand all of you and here sits one of me. I'll do whatever you say." Fetchit-5 flashed her lopsided grin. She may have looked and sounded buffoonish, but she truly realized the gravity of her situation and had every intention of surviving. "Besides," she added, "loyalty is for bloodhounds."

Lordjahn walked in closer and said to Athanasy, "She is, at the very least, prudent. Perhaps we can use her as a guard or something. I've heard there are many of her kind who are bred for just that purpose."

"And I've wandered so far, I doubt my human could ever find me. He's quite old, you know, and not long on patience or breath." She attempted to lace her words with nonchalance, but hearing her own voice speak so betrayingly of her beloved Sayble stung her heart. She realized her master would search only so far, finally give her up for dead, mourn appropriately and leave. Before long, there would be a Fetchit-6 and Sayble would be gone forever. Live tonight, escape tomorrow, she thought.

"Then we will be ten strong," Athanasy said, after moments of consideration. "But you will be closely watched, Fetchit-5."

"Don't trust the dog," hissed Iscariot, creeping forward.

"Why? Do you recognize some foul qualities akin to yourself?" the Heron snapped with contempt.

Disregarding their comments, Athanasy continued. "Our purpose will slowly be disclosed to you, as we witness your true loyalties. In this place, there are no desires or fears about a natural enemy. You will cease your chasing urges and food will be provided for you."

"Thank you. What did you say your name was?" Fetchit-5 jumped up, tail wagging uncontrollably. She was completely bathed in Athanasy's shadow.

"I am Athanasy." Then, the great creature lifted his head up high, caught a scent, and added, "Moko, take your small friend and this dog to Et Ska. Explain to her what has happened."

As ordered, Little Paw and Fetchit-5 followed Moko toward the pond. As the dog passed Neera, they briefly exchanged glances, comparing size and markings. Little Paw darted in and out of Moko's feet, yelping with joy at his sudden good fortune.

When the three were out of sight, Athanasy spoke. "I can read the questions in your doubting minds. But don't forget, this Ground has the power to change an animal."

"I have noticed this Ground merely magnifies an animal's own true nature, be it evil or good! I haven't seen Iscariot change for the better!" the Blue Heron said, flashing his long bill toward the raccoon.

"Heron, be still," cautioned Neera.

"If we are to function as a whole, then the integral components best fit together," Lordjahn said, glaring at the raccoon and the Heron.

"Well said, my condor," Athanasy said, smiling. "From now on, all our energies must be directed toward forming our plan. To prey upon each other's weaknesses would only destroy our united purpose. And under no circumstances must we fail."

CHAPTER THIRTEEN

FOR THREE DESPERATE DAYS, Charles Sayble searched for his dog. In the past, Fetchit-5 had vanished for a day or two, but never had she been gone for three days straight. Sayble's initial concern was that she had drowned in the river, yet the waters ran calm that spring and surely she could have survived a swim. By the second day, whatever tracking talents Sayble possessed deserted him and so he searched randomly, calling and whistling.

On the third day, he locked up his bus, put pans of food and water out should she return, and set out with his camping pack and rifle to search farther out. Among all the doubts and fears that ran through his mind, there was also the underlying old-man faith that he'd find his animal. Wearing his dog whistle and toting his backpack, he started out. The forest and river creatures watched him and silenced their voices to listen to him call, as if curious themselves as to what beast answered to the two-legged invader.

From the river, he slowly picked his way north until he could travel no farther. He set his modest camp next to the cooling comforts of a small pond, dined on crackers, cheese, and wine, and slept the night in his ancient moldy sleeping bag.

Early the next morning, there was a light fog rising off the pond as Sayble rose and prepared to continue his search. Then, off the

75

water, he heard an odd sound. It had a canine yelp to it, but it was a sound unlike any other he had heard from any animal. He held his breath, straining to hear the sound again. He seized his binoculars and through their magnification beheld the hazy forms of not only Fetchit-5 but several strange creatures along the opposite shore.

Stunned, he dropped his field glasses and squinted at the site, as though the binoculars were responsible for conjuring up such a vision. Convinced that he had found his dog, he scrambled through his pack to find the whistle. He gave three long toots, Fetchit-5's familiar call.

From the Council site on the other side of the pond, the chosen animals labored to arrive at their protest plan. The whistle that pierced their concentration startled all but Fetchit-5. Instinctively, she sprang to her feet, homed in on the whistle and leaped into the water.

No sooner had the dog's belly slapped the surface than Athanasy realized what was happening and called out, "Stop! Man-pet! Return at once or I will pull you under!"

Fetchit-5 stopped in the water, then obediently swam back to the shore. She crawled out and lay down, helplessly crying, "It's my human. Who would have thought the old man could find me? I'm sorry. I'm sorry for all of us! What will happen now?"

"Yes, Athanasy, now what?" asked Neera. "The human must know the man-pet is here. He'll follow, won't he?" She faced the whimpering dog and tried to feel her pain.

"The Will of the Council will not allow him in," Athanasy said calmly.

"And just how would a human react to an invisible barrier?" asked Little Paw. "It frightened me and I knew what it was for."

"It's true," added Lordjahn, flapping an itch out of his mighty wings. "His human mind will question. A man loves a mystery. Especially one he can take back to his brethren."

"Heron, fly up and see where the human is. See if he comes this way," commanded Athanasy. "Fetchit-5, does your man-cousin carry a weapon? A war-stick of any kind?"

"He has several weapons, but I don't know if he's armed now. What are you going to do?" The dog's voice cracked in sobbing panic.

Iscariot crept forward, faced the group defiantly and said, baring his razor teeth, "If you'll recall, I told you not to trust the man-pet. Now . . ." he smiled faintly, ". . . either you kill the human, or release the dog. Of course, you could kill them both."

"It should not have to come to that," Neera said, facing Iscariot. "But I agree that the dog must be released."

"Tell them, dog!" Et Ska broke in solemnly, staring at the dog from the shallow pool. "Tell them that you tried to escape last night!"

"What?" Athanasy demanded.

"When she was sure you were all asleep, the man-pet found she couldn't leave by land, so she tried to leave by water. She found even the simplest, easiest currents held her back."

Then the Heron returned, gasping, "He's nearly here! He's following the shore of the pond and will enter the Ground soon. He has seen us all, Athanasy! He has a war-stick!"

Athanasy looked quickly at each Council member to read their opinions, but before he could speak, Sayble was only fifty yards away. He was held, transfixed on the the border of the Council Ground. He seemed paralyzed, as he was unable to venture further. The same force that held the man-pet inside forbade his entrance. He held his rifle protectively close to his chest, and stared speechlessly at the gathering of creatures.

"Make your move, Athanasy," whispered Iscariot. "Kill him now. When the man-cousin's fright overwhelms him, he'll shoot."

"Can his war-stick penetrate the barrier?" Neera asked. A low, vicious growl was instinctively growing deep in her throat.

"I do not know," Athanasy answered, never taking his eyes off the bewildered human. "Fetchit-5, slowly come forward." The dog obeyed. "Understand what I am saying, man-pet. I am going to kill your master. I bear him no malice, but he has witnessed our gathering. And, if I have to, I'll kill you. So understand it, or die with him. It's your chance to show the true colors of your coat. Are all those present in agreement?"

One by one, each animal answered in the affirmative.

Then Fetchit-5 said proudly, "If my life could spare his, then that is my choice without a second thought. I have understood you, but quickly answer one question: A man is an animal . . .

why shouldn't a man be among your Council? With so many worlds represented, is it not presumptuous of you to ignore his?"

"But it is his world we are striking out against!" cried Et Ska.

"My human is a man who lives alone, who is more comfortable in my company than with his own kind. A man such as mine could help your cause," continued the dog.

All the while, Sayble remained where he was, only now he was crouching down, still holding his weapon. The foreign sounds from the animals, the ominous sight of Athanasy, and the unnatural combination of the others frightened him beyond action.

"Perhaps the dog has a point, Athanasy," Lordjahn said, slowly walking closer to the elk. "If we willed him in, gave him our speech and tested his loyalties . . . who knows how powerful an ally he might prove to be?"

"Kill him," Iscariot said.

Then Neera added, "But remember, his death will bring others in search."

"Who notices when a recluse dies? Kill him, Athanasy," Iscariot pressed. "And the dog."

"You're too anxious for blood, Iscariot," shouted the Heron. "Surely the man would leave something behind, something that would be missed, something to bring others looking."

"You are all too quick to change your minds. It proves our strength is less than I'd hoped. Moko, what do you say?" Athanasy continued.

"Me? You are asking me to help decide the fate of that harmless small thing?"

"The stick he holds makes him the most harmful animal of all," said Athanasy.

"There, you said it—'animal'!" ventured the dog. "Take your power and search his mind and see how valuable an animal he might be."

Athanasy weighed each opinion and realized then that he would have to spare the man-cousin. "According to your wishes, I will bring him in. But just as in nature we weed out the old, sick, and weak, be warned. I will destroy the man-cousin should I sense any inabilities or betrayals . . . the slightest weakness will be his last."

RANDALL BETH PLATT

He left the group and walked toward the man. As the immense animal approached him, Sayble stiffened and slowly rose, raising his gun to his eye. He was unable to identify the beast, but he realized it was prehistoric in size. The old man's heart ached from throbbing and his dry mouth was unable to swallow. His whole body shook as he tried to steady his aim on the approaching creature. Sayble blinked helplessly as he watched Athanasy through the rifle's scope. The crosshairs of the gunsight trembled in his shaking hands.

Athanasy stopped, lowered his mighty head to the ground, sending his seemingly infinite antlers skyward, then powerfully raised his head back to the sky, as though he had just drunk a potion of power. Assuming the beast was ready to charge, Sayble pulled back the bolt and waited. Athanasy's breathing became strong and his chest heaved in concentrating power. Then, in words Charles Sayble could understand, Athanasy spoke.

"Drop your weapon and step forward, man-cousin."

Denying any faith in his hearing abilities, Sayble looked around him to see who had spoken.

"I have given you the gift of my speech," the beast continued. "Drop your war-stick and come forward," he repeated.

The old man's face registered neither shock, fear, nor amazement, but rather levity. He lowered his rifle and eased it to the ground and said, "A man my age, who hears a fairy book animal talk, deserves to be mowed down by a giant elk."

"On the contrary, because you have heard me speak, you shall now live," whispered Athanasy. "Come forward and you might understand."

Sayble took several trembling paces forward until he was just inside the Council Ground. Athanasy was all aglow, as were the other animals just beyond who watched intently. "Am I dead?" was all the old man could utter.

"No. All of us here are very much alive. Can you tell me what you feel?"

"I feel stupid talking to a hallucination. My sister died talking to a picture on the wall of Lord Byron. God, what's happening?"

"How does your body feel? Come in closer."

Sayble looked at the formidable animals staring at him . . . the

79

wolf, the buffalo, the condor, the raccoon, and among them his own Fetchit-5. He took a few hesitant steps and, as he did, he felt much calmer. His legs seemed slightly stronger. "I think I feel lighter. Jesus Christ!" He put his hand to his forehead to feel for fever and added, "I must be delirious. Hallucinating!"

"You are neither." Athanasy examined the man's eyes for a moment. "You are old. Are you bothered by your heart?"

"If it still works after this, it'll work forever. What is this? What are you?" Sayble looked around the area. "Is this a joke or something? I know! Remote control! I've died and gone to Disneyland!" His ashen face creased in a weak smile.

Athanasy stepped closer and towered over the man. He lowered his massive head again and said, "In my eyes you will see this is no joke, man-cousin. Your doubt is natural to your race. I have spared your life by order of the others. But be patient with your questions, man-cousin. Just see and listen and believe."

"Do all you talk? Have you always talked? Who's going to believe any of this?" Sayble was finally becoming overwhelmed by his near-fatal discovery.

"You must prepare yourself a place of rest. Do you have all you will need to survive here?"

"What do you mean? Just give me my dog and we'll leave." He pointed to Fetchit-5 who was lying among the others.

"No, you are both here to stay. You may not leave the Council Grounds," Athanasy said, walking around Sayble as he spoke.

"Council? What Council?" Sayble demanded, fright again taking hold.

Athanasy studied the man-cousin up close, then faced him, bowed his graceful head and commanded, "Sleep, man-cousin."

Sayble fell instantly to the ground and for all appearances was soundly asleep. Fetchit-5 jumped to her feet upon seeing her master fall and ran over to his sleeping body, crying, "What have you done? We agreed not to hurt him!"

"Your human tired, so he is asleep. I'll send Neera to his campsite on the opposite shore to retrieve his belongings. Since it will make you both feel more comfortable, you may stay here with him. Be warned, though, you will not be able to share your speech with him until I so command. There have been enough interruptions now. If you and your man-cousin represent even one instant of a delay, one hesitant thought, I'll kill you both."

Fetchit-5 looked to her master, paused to gather her troubled thoughts, then said, "I understand. At times, I forget who and what I am. I'm truly sorry for following that damn squirrel in the first place. But my human will help you. I know he will."

The man-pet was as close to tears as she had ever been in her life. She lay down next to her master, put her head on his chest and waited.

Athanasy returned to the watching group and restlessly pawed the ground. "Iscariot was right. I should have killed him. I hesitated. I sought counsel."

"You did what the Will told you to," Neera said.

Athanasy smiled down at the wolf and said, "Today, he lives. Tonight, we'll tell him our purpose. And his actions will decide his fate."

CHAPTER FOURTEEN

ATHANASY'S MAGICAL SLEEP that descended upon Sayble lasted for several hours. While the man slept, the great elk walked the grounds and considered how his Great Council of Beasts had complicated and strayed miserably from its original purpose. The sudden addition of Little Paw and Fetchit-5, whether blessed by the Will or not, bothered him. And the man-cousin . . . how did such foreigners come to be woven into the fabric of his gathering?

His journey of recollections ended and he found himself standing once more over the sleeping form of the old man. Fetchit-5, curled warmly next to him, looked up, blinked sleepily, then began to tremble as she thought how quickly the beast could end their lives.

Athanasy looked down and heard the echoes of Iscariot's words of protest: Kill him! Kill them both! Athanasy shook his head and the words reluctantly fell away.

"Have your man-cousin's personal effects been brought into the Council Ground?" he asked the dog.

"Yes."

"And the war-stick?"

"There," she indicated.

Athanasy looked down at the weapon, studying its simplicity. His conflicting thoughts ranged from disgust to envy. Finally, he cursed aloud, causing the rifle to separate from itself, part from part. And when each piece was clearly sectioned off, they dissolved into the dust. Athanasy praised the powers of the Council Ground, turned and walked away, satisfied with his decision.

He trotted swiftly toward the pond, for in the very back of his mind he heard a faint calling. A voice beckoned him to the pond and the Heron's side.

He arrived to find the Blue Heron standing with one wing curiously outstretched, looking not only uncomfortable, but asymmetrical as well.

"Are you in any pain?" Athanasy asked the bird.

"Well, no," began the Heron. "It's just that I've been standing here like an idiot for over an hour. I'm trying to be as still as I can. I've never realized just how heavy this wing can be without the sky to hold it up."

Then, from under the bird's wing, the breathless voice of Chanta spoke: "I appreciate your patience, but I'll have you know it's no summerfest in here either. I'm exhausted and only one wing out! You really have no idea what it's like."

"I hatched myself once, you know. Just hurry up!" snapped the Heron.

"Whose idea was this in the first place? Just tell me that," Chanta snapped back. Then, in a more formal tone, she added, "I beg your pardon, Athanasy. I'll be out as soon as I can. Ouuufff!"

"Welcome, Chanta," Athanasy said warmly, walking around the Heron. Then, he said softly to the bird, "It will only be a few moments longer. You've borne your burden well."

"Well, I feel like a fool," grumbled the Heron.

"Here we go!" Chanta cried out in exasperated delight. "One more umph and I'm free. There! Okay, Heron, we've done it!"

"Now can I have my wing back?"

"No, not yet. Give a butterfly a chance to dry out."

"A few moments only, Heron," advised Athanasy, "and you'll be free of her."

"And all else," sighed the bird. "Free to go. Finally." A slow smile crossed the Heron's face.

"You would leave us now?" the elk asked, catching the Heron's golden eye.

A moment of silence accompanied the Heron's stare back. "What do you mean? Of course I'll leave. This whole mess is a lot more than I had bargained for and . . ."

"What bargain in the commands of the Will? You would see us this far in our mission and then just turn your back on us? Remember what happened the last time you turned your back? You were attacked."

"Athanasy!" the Heron cried. "What logic in that? I never would have been in the position of having that insidious raccoon attack me if I'd had the will to turn on that damn beckoning voice you cast about the countryside!"

"And now you fancy your own will is stronger than that of the Council?"

"I should have known you'd find a way to keep me here! How this time, Athanasy? Another demanding voice from nowhere or, perhaps this time, conventional ropes and cages?"

"I don't understand you at all, Heron. I've never known an animal so contrary to its own destiny, so able and so hesitant. So intelligent, so reluctant. We need you. It's essential to our cause that you be among us. Especially now, when we are so long at arriving at our plan." The level of Athanasy's voice did not change, but his breathing quickened.

"I'm not well-suited for heroics. I'm solitary. You must have known that."

"I have no power over you, Heron. You are free to do as you will," Athanasy said slowly, dropping his head. When he brought it back up again, he did so with the command, "Chanta! Fly!"

From under the Heron's wing, the lacy butterfly suddenly burst forth in a flight of brilliant, new-born color. She darted lightly in random movements as she learned to control her new powers. Wing, wing, wing, glide. Wing, wing, wing, glide. Her delicate weight made her prance upon even the slightest air current and she was caught on the draft of Athanasy's mighty antlers as they swooped upwards.

Momentarily, the Heron forgot the issue of his freedom as he witnessed Chanta discover hers. He flashed longingly on his own inspiring first flight—the fear, anxiety, the near-craving—then, the total trust in instinct as one bravely throws oneself into the air.

And the first glide when a breeze captures you, tosses you upward, around and then gently casts you about as though the wind itself were welcoming you with a laugh.

Chanta quickly tired and she rested on a tall, billowy flower to catch her breath. "Oh, Heron! It's everything I thought it would be. It's the purest power of all. I fly! I fly!" she cried with breathless exuberance. She flexed her bright yellow wings, feeling their fledgling strength.

The Heron, caught admiring Chanta, quickly busied himself by picking out remnants of Chanta's cocoon from under his wing and mumbled, "I'm delighted for you."

"There's no way to thank you for what you've done. My only attempt would be to say I'm glad you've decided to stay with us," she said, twinkling.

"No, you're wrong, Chanta. I'm leaving," said the bird with a tremendous, almost angry flap of his wings.

"Do not forget, Mr. Diplomatic-Courier-Heron, I've lived close to your heart and have glimpsed your soul. For all your talk of being alone, you respect and honor all animals. The only thing forcing you to stay now is your own conscience." She again took flight and landed directly on the Heron's long bill. She looked into his eyes and laughed. "And, I might add, that's some conscience you've got there."

"Is she right?" asked Athanasy, backing up as if to disappear.

The Heron, unable to sustain a serious cross-eyed stare, smiled at Chanta dancing along his bill. He simply replied in resignation, "Good God, Athanasy. Who knows anything anymore?"

"I need commitment. We can't afford to wake up one morning to find you've left us to seek out your precious isolation," Athanasy cautioned.

"Well, what's a few more weeks?" the Heron sighed, trying to focus on Chanta, still flitting up and down his bill.

"The remainder of our lives, perhaps," Athanasy whispered. Then he quietly slipped into the forest.

"I trust he was speaking symbolically," the Heron mumbled.

"Who knows?" sparked Chanta joyfully, not caring about Athanasy's verbal intent. "Come, Heron, let's fly!"

The bird reluctantly followed his tiny beautiful companion into flight and silently cursed himself for not leaving while he had the opportunity.

Sayble and his dog were awake and walking around when Athanasy reappeared. When the man saw the beast again, he ran his hand through his tousled thick hair and said, "I guess this means I didn't dream all this up."

"Not a dream, man-cousin. Come. Follow," ordered Athanasy.

With a slight hesitation, Charles Sayble looked at Fetchit-5, who merely returned his questioning gaze and wagged her tail blankly. "Well, come on, dog. You got me into this. You better start showing your old Sayble some loyalties. Guess we better follow that old moose."

They were led to the gathering site by the edge of the pond. Sayble walked cautiously into the circle of assembled creatures and felt immensely uncomfortable as the eyes followed his every move. He eased himself to the ground and sat cross-legged with Fetchit-5 next to him. The man nervously rumbled his hand over his dog's neck.

"On behalf of those who arrived late," Athanasy began, facing his congregation with a wry smile, "let us review our intentions here."

"Don't backtrack on my account, Athanasy. I've been able to absorb everything through the Heron," Chanta said from a flowery perch.

"Me too!" Little Paw barked with an enthusiastic grin, buck-teeth protruding. "Oh, that is . . . well, Moko has privileged me with a . . . well, he told me sort of what's happening," he added with an attempt at humility.

Sayble, confounded by the variety of voices, looked at each lingual animal. Then, he pulled Fetchit-5 closer to him and whispered in her ear, "What's this all about?"

The dog simply turned, licked her master's face and smiled.

"To answer your question, man-cousin," Athanasy said, "we are gathered here to put an end to man's desecration of our land." The beast towered over and stared down at the man.

"That seems like a noble cause. But, since man is the one with the guns, poisons, and every other conceivable tool of obliteration, what makes you think you few critters stand half a chance?"

"We are blessed with a Power. And a Will," Athanasy continued.

"A will, eh?" Sayble remarked, grinning. "In a man's language, a will is what's left over after someone dies."

"In an animal's language, a Will is something present before an animal is born," the great beast countered.

"A Will makes it so a man-cousin can talk to a condor," added Lordjahn.

"Well," Sayble laughed gruffly, "You've got me there. So, explain just how you plan on getting your divine message across to the other side?" He stretched his legs out in front of him. In the back of his mind, he doubted the reality of any of the conversation and longed for a strong cigar and a generous tipple of port.

"The plan has not yet been made. This is where we need you," Athanasy said, backing up slightly while addressing the man-cousin.

"*I* have a plan?"

"Being one, you are most familiar with the man-cousin. You, of course, know more of his weaknesses. So, tell us how *you* would force man to put away his toys of war." Athanasy lay down gracefully, not far from Sayble, eyeing him carefully. The other animals drew themselves closer, with the exception of Iscariot.

"Toys of war?"

"Blackness everywhere! Skies blackened in war's remnants; the sun weeps through a shroud of mourning; great forests blackened by the ignorance of greed; seas blackened with the spilled blood of our ancestors! These deeds are done and there's nothing we can do. But now the man-cousins strap their harness on too much power . . . power that does not belong to them. I speak of the place where man's war-power is fashioned to its last perfection."

"If you're talking about what I think you're talking about," Sayble said incredulously, "then good luck! Ha! Oh, my fine feathered hallucinations, thousands of man-cousins have been trying to put a stop to war for years!"

"The Will has seen beyond. It calls us to a place to the north, where the giants of the sea are fed this war-power," Athanasy continued.

Sayble tried to grasp the meaning between his words. "Just what war-power are you talking about?" he asked cautiously.

"The Will tells me nuclear power. Ageon power."

"You mean the Ageon Nuclear Submarine Base? You want *that* closed?" Again, Sayble gasped unbelievingly.

"It will die!" shouted Athanasy. It was several seconds before his echoes faded. His eyes seemed to glow in his prophesying, in his rage. "It is demanded! You will go among your brethren and tell them we demand a halt! We will not perish at man's hands any longer! It is finished! You will seek out the ones in command and call for a halt! You will tell them the Great Council of Beasts demands it!" The elk rose and stood staunchly above his animals.

"Why don't *you* tell them? From what I've seen, you carry the clout," Sayble snapped.

"I will tell them. Through you."

"Oh? I'm to go up to the folks in charge of the largest nuclear sub base in the world and tell them I've been talking to some animal friends of mine and they say to close the base or else?" Sayble laughed and nervously searched his shirt pockets for a cigar stub.

"He's right, Athanasy. Who would believe him?" the Heron asked.

"Does a man-cousin of your age not command authority? Surely the younger of your kind will listen to the wisdom of your years," Lordjahn said, lowering his head to catch Sayble's reply.

"Are you not dominant in your pack?" Neera asked, following the condor's logic. "Or have you already been expelled?"

"Of course he's been expelled, wolf! Look at him!" Iscariot growled, edging slightly closer into the circle. "I tell you, Athanasy, this creature will do no good! Why, I can hear him creak from here!"

"Now, hold on there!" Sayble protested, pulling his legs up as if to rise in his own defense. "What are you?" he demanded, squinting to see the half-hidden raccoon. "Jesus Christ! A raccoon! I'm sitting here being insulted by a goddamn raccoon!" He turned to

Fetchit-5 and asked, disgustingly, "Don't that bother you any? A raccoon! And there you sit!"

The dog exhaled heavily and looked to Athanasy, as if seeking permission to defend herself.

"Ah, don't let him get under your skin, man-cousin. Iscariot doesn't like anyone, least of all a . . . well, one of you," Moko said shyly.

"Let me get this straight. Before I came upon you, you were all set to convince everyone to stop this nuclear business?"

"It must cease," Athanasy repeated quietly.

"Yes, I know. You've made that quite clear. But I can tell you now, there is not one soul out there . . ." he said, rising to his feet and pointing to the far horizons dramatically, "who would believe me for even one instant! Any credibility I have left among my 'pack,' as you call it, would be smashed with one whisper of this place . . . or whatever you're calling this hoedown!"

"I think you'd better sit down," cautioned Et Ska, her silvery voice glistening off the pond.

Sayble strained to see where the words came from this time, but saw nothing but a slight rippling of water. "Don't tell me . . . a fish?" he asked, gaping at Athanasy. The beast nodded. "Well, now I've seen everything. . . ."

"Not quite," said Chanta as she appeared instantly in front of the man's flushing face.

Sayble looked about the gathering soberly. "Why me?" he asked calmly, casting his eyes downward.

"Because you are here," the wolf replied.

"Think of it as destiny," the Heron added dryly, glancing over to Athanasy.

"Each to his nest now," Athanasy ordered after a long silence. "The man-cousin will reflect on what he has heard. You will be guarded, so I caution you now . . . keep within the Grounds. Tomorrow, you will begin."

The animals each rose and left in various directions. Lordjahn remained behind and flew over to the bewildered man. "Do you have a song?" the condor asked.

"What? You mean, do I sing? Sure. Occasionally. Why?"

"But if you had a song, you would know it. Little matter. I've

just always wondered about the man-cousins' song, that's all."
The condor turned.

"Wait a minute," Sayble called after him. Lordjahn turned
back. "Is any of this real?" the man asked.

"Perhaps the only reality of your life. If you have a religion,
explore it tonight and discover which fate has brought you to us.
Resign ideas of coincidence, a disturbing human belief. If you are
graced with a dream of youth, as I often am these days, try to
grasp it momentarily and re-live the innocent joys of confidence."

"But . . ."

"I know you are bothered by your age," the condor continued.
"I recognize your fears, man-cousin. I am old too. Think back on
all the chances you've been given throughout your life. This
Council calling, man-cousin, is *my* last chance." The condor
gently rose in breezy flight above the old man, ruffling his hair.

The Council site was nearly dark. Sayble and his dog stood
silent and alone.

"Come on, Fetchit," the man said in exhaustion. "Let's turn
in."

"Right," the dog replied.

CHAPTER FIFTEEN

THE MAN AND HIS DOG walked in silence to their campsite. Fetchit-5 followed somewhat behind Sayble, pacing herself to his hesitant gait. Every few steps, Sayble would stop and look back to the dog as if to speak and Fetchit-5 would merely stop and smile smugly up at her master.

When they arrived at the camp, Sayble seized his backpack and rummaged through it, pulling out a large plastic bottle filled with wine. He drank half its contents, while Fetchit-5 sat and watched him, awaiting his next words. Sayble, feeling the warmth of the wine, stared back down at his dog.

"Want a drink?" he finally asked, showing her the bottle.

"I never touch the stuff," she replied.

"Too bad. It's great for chilly nights." As he exhaled, his breath clouded heavily and he realized how cold the evening was becoming.

"An animal's warmth comes from within, not from wine or other distractions," she said as she casually scratched her ear.

"Oh, not you too!" Sayble complained with disgust.

"Me too what?" asked Fetchit-5, wide-eyed.

"You too with all that spiritual, four-legs-are-better-than-two crap!" he snapped.

"You know, it's amazing how much humans take on the characteristics of their dogs. Your bark sounds just like mine."

Sayble glanced at his grinning dog, unable to supply a comeback. To ward off the encroaching chill, he built a roaring, crackling fire and sat next to it, wrapped in the warmth of his sleeping bag. He stared into the blaze and considered the situation, following the ascent of the embers and smoke as they curled upward, until they disappeared into the black, starless sky overhead.

Drawing a long twig from its fiery rest, Sayble lit a half-smoked cigar. Fetchit-5 was almost dozing as she welcomed the fire's security and the familiar aroma of the cigar smoke.

"Well, old girl," Sayble finally said, exhaling a cherished last puff, "so tell me who man's best friend really is." He looked over to his dog, who yawned and stretched out her forepaws.

"I'm not sure about other men, but your best friend is me. Just like the saying goes."

"And who is your best friend?"

"You, man-cousin," whispered the dog sincerely. Then she added, "I hope it won't be my undoing."

"What? Why?" Sayble drew himself closer to his pet.

"You can see that these animals are dead-serious. And what's more, they're dead-right." She put her head onto his lap. "Here. Scratch behind my ear, will you please? You do that so well."

Sayble obliged and as he ran his hand down the dog's neck, he felt her tremble gently under his caressing touch. "How'd we ever get into this mess in the first place?" he asked softly.

"A case of mixed loyalties, Sayble," she sighed.

"Say that again," he said, sitting straighter, causing Fetchit-5's head to rise.

"A case of . . ."

"No, say my name again."

"Sayble."

"Again."

"Sayble."

"Now say, 'Here Sayble.' "

"Here, Sayble!" she repeated. Then she laughed aloud when she realized why it caused her man-cousin's absurd joy. Together they wrestled, rolling from side to side, until their giggling ceased and they lay exhausted and entwined.

After a few moments, Sayble asked, "I still can't believe this. Are they really serious?"

"Yes, we are."

"Just remember, m'dear, man created the zealots," Sayble added with a voice low and faraway. "And the last thing the world needs now is zealous animals." He looked down at Fetch-it-5 and scratched her ear again. "You know, you've been a good dog to me, girl. Much better than Fetchits 1 through 4. Of course," he chuckled, "you're a mite more outspoken than your predecessors."

"Well, Sayble, after all the years I've really had only one complaint about you. That damn, damn song you sing. Day in and day out," she laughed. " 'Don't take your guns to town, son, don't take your guns to town,' " she mimicked in a low monotone. "I've heard moon-howling with more melody."

He rose and added more logs to the fire and caught the gleaming reflective eyes of a creature watching him. A grin spread across his ruddy face. He clicked his heels with a clumsy leap and sang with vaudevillian melodrama:

> Fee, fie, fo fum,
> I spy the eye of
> A creature-chum.
> Be he friend or
> Be he foe
> Step right up
> So we'll all know.

He turned back to his dog and bowed. "There. A new song. You like?"

The dog winced at her master's irreverent yet typical actions and said, "That should insure our privacy for the rest of the night."

"Oh. Might I have offended one of the hallucinations?"

"No, I'll just consider the source," said Neera. The wolf stalked quietly into the arc of firelight.

Fetchit-5 rose and wagged her tail in friendly, yet slightly nervous, welcome. "I hope we didn't wake you, Neera."

"No. I was drawn by the warmth. I've never seen a fire blaze up so close. Is it content to remain where it is?" she asked the man-cousin, cautiously sniffing the smoke and keeping her eyes on the spirited, dancing flames.

"No, I'm afraid not, wolf. It needs to be watched. Can't ever turn your back on a fire," Sayble said, seating himself back down on his bedroll.

No sooner were his words of caution uttered than Athanasy appeared and spoke. He also was engrossed and drawn toward the hypnotic warmth and music of the fire.

"It is the only thing that separated your race from ours—fire, man-cousin," he said.

They all turned with surprise at the elk's sudden appearance. Sayble, setting aside his fear of the immense creature, held out his gnarled old hands and said, "And these, Athanasy. These hands made it possible to contain the fire. While you animals were busy running from fire, man was busy evolving these." He spread each finger wide apart to emphasize his point.

"But can you seize a lightening-quick rabbit with your hands?" Neera inquired.

"No, but I got a dandy spring-trap back at the bus. Next question." He looked at each animal. They seemed to recoil at his words. It was then that Sayble sensed for the first time the animals' vulnerability, their fine intelligence, and their unsurpassed beauty. The generous firelight complemented the splendid coloration and strong physique of each being.

"You're all enjoying the warmth of my fire, aren't you?" Sayble asked finally. "Well, 'creature comforts,' as the expression goes. The more you enjoy it, the closer you are to becoming mine—if I wanted you, that is."

Each animal instinctively backed a few steps away from the man, his words, and his fire.

Then Athanasy said with a snort, "There are things a man-cousin does not have the power to possess!"

"Well, here we go again," Sayble sighed with exasperation. "Who are you to criticize me? Look, who or what *are* you, anyway? You look like an elk with a glandular problem! Did your mama feed you radioactive milk or something?" He laughed arrogantly, then grew silent as he realized what he had said. He hedged uncomfortably, then added, "I'm sorry there, Athanasy. I'm not used to anyone, let alone animals, taking me so seriously," he apologized quietly.

"I've explained to you all I can," Athanasy said, barely audible above the fire's nightsong. "All I dare add is, I am immortality, as close as any man-cousin can imagine it to be. Perhaps you will understand more later. Even I cannot fight the Will or I would have killed you at once. Good night, man-cousin," he added, disappearing back into the night, followed by Neera.

Fetchit-5 solemnly watched her master with a low-hanging head and a slow-wagging tail.

Sayble shook his head and muttered, "This is crazy."

"You're tired," said the dog with helpless compassion.

"You can say that again," Sayble sighed.

CHAPTER SIXTEEN

SAYBLE SLEPT IN PEACE, warmed by his bedside fire and serene boyhood dreams of sultry summer nights. Fetchit-5, who was unable to sleep, walked their campsite and restlessly considered her master's plight.

The old man awoke with the first hint of dawn and noticed immediately that his usual new-day stiffness was not present. Fetchit-5 trotted happily over to her master, delighted to have him awake at last.

"You slept well, Sayble," she said.

"Damn right I did!" he burst out, springing awkwardly to his feet and pulling on his boots with two simple tugs. "I feel great!"

"You were singing in your sleep," she continued.

"Same old song, eh? Sorry." He was examining several days' beard growth in a small, jagged piece of mirror. "Guess I'll shave."

"No, actually it was a song I've never heard before, man-cousin." She followed him to the water's edge and watched him kneel and begin his shaving ritual.

"Oh?" Sayble said, unimpressed. "Well, you never know what comes to you in a dream, eh? Ouch!"

"Nick yourself again?"

"As usual," he muttered.

"Why do you bother to remove your natural coat?" she asked casually, following the trail of a flea up her front leg.

Sayble stood up, holding a cloth to his wound. "Seems silly, don't it? I don't know. I guess to make me look younger. Don't you think I look younger when I'm cleanshaven?"

"Who cares how old you look?" she asked.

"Ha! So right you are! No one cares, plain and simple!" He gathered up his shaving implements and began packing his grip.

Fetchit-5 watched him, then nervously ventured: "So, what are you going to do?"

"About what?"

"About this!" she yelped loudly, unable to accept his nonchalant manner, as if he had no recollection at all of the Council and his role in the creatures' intrigue.

He turned and looked at his dog. "A mite tetchy this morning, aren't we?"

"You act as though you remember nothing of our mission! Just how far did your dreams take you?" she demanded, sitting down squarely.

"Just far enough into the no-no zone to make me realize it's worth a try. Swear to God, I don't know what makes me say so, but I think I have an idea. Imagine, at my age, an idea!" He laughed and finished rolling his sleeping bag and attached it to his backpack. He whistled vague melodic refrains while he worked.

Fetchit-5's ears recognized the tune from her master's dream and said, "That song . . . it's the same one you sang in your sleep."

"What's this thing all you critters have with songs? I tell you, sure is queer thinking about you guys being musically inclined," Sayble said, kicking sand into the fire. "Hey, where are you going?" he asked as Fetchit-5 started to leave their camp.

"To tell them you're leaving," she answered simply.

"Good. Bring everyone back here, why don't you?" He finished his packing, sat on the pond's shore and skipped rocks off the water while he awaited the Council animals. He ad-libbed the missing verses in his whistling tune and ignored the forbidding feeling which was etching itself into the logical perimeters of his mind. The words of the condor from the night before had surfaced continually throughout the night, assuming dream-like forms of people he had admired and respected. "My last chance . . . my last chance. . . ." The insanity, the adventure, and the extreme good fortune to be handed one last chance. . . .

"The dog tells me you have a plan," Athanasy said from the clearing, flanked by his Council creatures.

Sayble rose and walked forward with an embarrassed, lad-like awkwardness . . . as if called on to recite a neglected lesson. "Well, an idea," he explained.

"Then go see if it works," the great elk ordered.

"Just like that? You don't even want to know what the plan is?" asked the man-cousin.

"Would I understand?"

"No, I guess not. But I'll need a few things first."

"Don't trust him," Iscariot snapped, then turned and left for his nest.

"Someday, I'd be interested to find out how he got his name," said Sayble, pointing to the departing raccoon. "Okay, I'll need something from each of you animals—a feather, some fur." He pulled out his razor from his shirt pocket. "Shave, anyone?" he asked, laughing.

The animals looked at each other, questioning what possible need this could fulfill, but no one ventured forward to volunteer.

"Aw, come on, you guys. I won't take much. It won't hurt, I swear. Athanasy, you first." Sayble stepped closer, wielding his razor.

One by hesitant one, the fur-bearing animals stepped forward while Sayble took a small sample from each coat and carefully folded each in a scrap of paper. From the Heron and the condor a feather was begrudgingly plucked. Iscariot was commanded back and he was allowed to pull a tuft of his own hair, not allowing the man-cousin near him with the sharp weapon.

"But anything you take from me will affect my flight," said Chanta.

"Oh, I forgot about you," said the man, studying the problem.

"Heron, go find a piece of Chanta's cocoon and let the man-cousin have that," ordered Athanasy. The blue bird left and returned in a minute and placed the spun cream encasement before Sayble.

"And now you, fish," Sayble called out over the water. "I need some scales."

"Thereby causing a chink in my armor, man-cousin. But," she sighed, "here. Along my spine. Take a loose one, at least." The man reached into the water and tugged easily as directed. "Ouch! I said a loose one!" she cried.

"There," exhaled Sayble, pulling his hand out with four perfect translucent scales. "A while to dry and stiffen and these will be just what I need. Thank you."

He packed each specimen and tucked them safely away in a side pocket of his bulging pack.

"Tell us what you'll use your coat-scraps for. Are you making a potion?" Neera asked innocently.

Sayble laughed and said, "No, but that's not a bad idea. Any man crazy enough to believe animals talk might as well make a potion and drink it himself."

Neera didn't smile, but glanced carefully at the others, then asked the man-cousin, "Then why?"

"These are mementos, my dears. And an inkling of proof," the man replied. Then, there was another pause as the animals and the human looked at each other, assessing plausibilities, sanities, and intents. "Well," began Sayble at last, "I guess I'll be moseying along now. Come on, Fetchit. It's a long way back to the bus."

"Wait!" commanded Athanasy. "The dog stays here. As hostage."

"What?" Sayble bellowed, whirling around.

"To insure your return, which shall not exceed eight sunrises," the elk added forcefully.

"It's really for the best," interceded Moko gently. "The dog will surely slow you down."

"And time is our key factor," added Neera. "Your dog will be well-kept. She is happy here."

Sayble looked to his dog, who hung her head as she listened to her fate.

"And if I'm not back in eight days?" the man asked, turning his head suspiciously toward Athanasy.

"You think I will kill her. But she is ours now and she will always be among those touched by the Will. If you desert us, you'll never see her again."

The man considered this, then replied in arrogant, youthful confidence, "That seems fair enough. Well, no use wasting time on drawn-out goodbyes. Wish me luck." He knelt to pet Fetchit-5 and whispered in her ear, "I've got to be out of my mind."

She licked his ear playfully and whispered back, "You always have been. Good luck, dear Sayble. No matter what happens, I'll always remember you."

"You better, you bitch." His soft words carried deep affection. "After all, *you* got me into this."

"Return safely," said Athanasy, his own voice casting warmth.

The old man stood up and swung his pack over his shoulders, turned and left the Council Ground, feeling like a young man proudly stepping off to war.

It seemed to Sayble that the hike back to his bus was much shorter on his return trip. He was smugly proud of himself for immediately finding the direct way, whereas usually, several dead-ends would be encountered. He attributed his renewed tracking skills to a resurgence of that same ounce of ancient Indian blood which usually received the credit for his robust health, black eyes, and high cheekbones. And, as he briskly walked along, the tune he whistled became clearer and more defined.

By midday, the man could see the lonely colorful bus resting in its nest of greenery. He quickly examined the sun's position overhead and caught a glimpse of a large, winged creature coasting low in the sky. The Blue Heron spoke not, but merely followed the man-cousin. Sayble shaded his eyes to behold the magnificent bird's flight, then comically saluted the Heron as it glided lower down.

Without further delay, the man continued the last easy leg of his journey. The river sounds seemed louder to him as he neared his campsite, and it looked as though his bus's privacy had remained intact.

When he entered his musty, old friendly home, he took a quick survey of his precious belongings. After his initial feeling of relief, he was suddenly struck by the lonely silence in the vehicle without Fetchit-5's friendly panting and constant tail-thumping.

After a simple hasty snack, Sayble recommissioned his bus, encouraging its start with threatening vocal support. Without much coaxing, the engine turned over, held the shaky idle and was slowly eased out onto the bumpy road, returning, once more, toward civilization.

Once on the road, Sayble lit a cigar and looked out the windows to catch the Heron's position of pursuit. Seeing the bird not far behind, the man waved his hand outside his window, laughed and said, "Follow old Sayble, spy-bird! Tell your big old elk I'm on my way!"

He puffed his cigar and concentrated on the road ahead, then added softly, "Yep . . . Sis died talking to a picture of Lord Byron. Oh, hell."

CHAPTER SEVENTEEN

ITHIN AN HOUR, Sayble had rumbled into the outskirts of the seaport of Port Hartley. He had never traveled through the seemingly harmless community. It had all the typical touristy trappings of a small seaside town, artistically placed upon three small hills. Below was the harbor, maternally protecting the docks and ships from the sea beyond.

There was no need to ask where Ageon was. Just north of the harbor, sprawled out in neat rows and efficient angles was the facility. The most stunning of all was the cool black-gray of the submarine spines. Three of the whale-like giants lay in state, defying description and assault.

As Sayble looked through binoculars down upon his adversary, he felt a weakening of his spirit. Guarded by warriors, perfected by wizards, and sailed by commodores, he realized the subs were impenetrable.

He briefly explored Port Hartley, then settled his bus down in a roadside park for the night.

Early the next morning, after a rejuvenating night's sleep, Sayble again set out. With fire and brimstone, the rainbow bus began tracking up a long hill. But, as the evils of gravity took hold, the bus commenced to whimper its way up the remainder, suffering the indignity of being passed by numerous more ambitious contraptions, commanded by irritated Ageon workers late to work.

As he topped the hill and coasted into the harbor of Ageon, Sayble felt a grip around his throat. At such close range, the enemy which sprawled out before him was prepared to battle entire armies, let alone a single old man. The entire area was well-fortified—fenced and again fenced, guarded and again guarded. The cars in the parking lots suggested a battery of employees. The activity around the base seemed militarily orchestrated as each person went about his naval or civilian duties.

Sayble pulled off into a turnaround just before the guarded entrance and coasted to a stop. He stared at the sign:

AGEON NUCLEAR SUBMARINE BASE
AUTHORIZED PERSONNEL ONLY BEYOND THIS POINT

He re-lit his cigar and asked aloud, "*Now* what the hell am I going to do? Storm the gates?" He puffed thoughtfully on the cigar and looked out the windows.

From several cars away, a young woman approached the bus. Sayble watched as she came closer and was surprised when she knocked on his door, flashing a friendly smile up at him. He swung open the door flaps and returned her charming smile.

"Hi! You here for the march?" she asked, pointing to the main entrance gates. "They said some out-of-towners were coming in for this one. You one of them?"

Quickly assessing the situation and seizing an opportunity to begin his plan, Sayble replied, "Sure. I love marches."

"Well, good," she said enthusiastically, venturing a step up into the bus. She offered her hand and added, "I'm Alicyn Browne. Call me Al, most people do. And you are. . . ?"

"Charles," Sayble answered, taking an immediate liking to the young lady, comparing her to Fetchit-5's sparkling personality. Her dark eyes and hair accented the fairness of her healthy complexion.

"Where you from, Charles?" she asked, glancing about the bus, taking in its odd collections of time's passage.

"Oh, that way," he said, pointing vaguely over his shoulder toward the secret Council Ground.

Al was dressed in a sky-blue suit, very conservative, Sayble thought, for a protester. Indeed, it would seem that she had

103

stepped off the pages of a fashion magazine, rather than a liberal college campus where, Sayble had supposed, all these dissident types organically grew.

"Well," she said, feeling a bit ill at ease now as the stale old-man odors from within the vehicle reached her. "Here are some brochures. Offer them to anyone who looks at you."

He glanced quickly at the anti-nuclear materials, but before he could respond, she continued, "Are you going over?"

"Over what?" All he could think of was going over a prison wall.

"The fence, of course," she explained cheerfully. "They've sent some people in to go over the fence today. Thought I'd try it too."

Glancing at the armed guards flanking the gate, Sayble asked, "And what is it you plan on doing once you get over?"

"Getting arrested."

"Pardon an old man's ignorance, but why do you plan on getting arrested?" he asked, swinging his legs around and facing her directly.

"If we have to get arrested to prove our point, then that's what we're willing to do. Last month we lay down on the railroad tracks and blocked the supply train. I didn't get arrested, but I'll bet I do today." Again, her answer was brightly simple and Sayble wondered how the tiny lady could represent an ounce of a threat to anyone.

"I take it you haven't been trained for any of this," she continued. "Well, it doesn't matter. Happy to have you with us. See you on the line. Just make sure you stick with the group. The protest area will be clearly marked. And, like always, we can expect some trouble. Oh yes, and if you see any TV cameras, take advantage of them." She jumped down off the bus, gave Charles a chipper wave and walked toward the main gate, humming a song of protest.

In the hour that followed, Sayble went through the protest pamphlets and formulated his next step in the deliverance of the Council's message. He gathered up the few items he would need. He removed his various crumbling articles of identification from his tattered wallet and stashed them in a small manila envelope along with the bus keys. He stepped outside and lifted the bus's heavy, resistant hood. Looking around to insure secrecy, he removed the top of the air filter and placed the envelope in it. Working fast, he resealed the filter, feeling his heart quicken to a pace more befitting such espionage.

Back aboard the bus, Sayble took a quick glance around, feeling the rise of nervous excitement build. Attached to a smoky mirror was a crinkled picture of Fetchit-5. Her effervescent smile caught the old man's eye as he passed. Impulsively, he snatched the photo and carefully placed it into the pocket containing the coat samples from the Council animals. Then, feeling sufficiently armed to proceed, he pocketed the protest pamphlets and left his home for the slowly forming, gently milling crowd at the entrance gates.

As in any crowd Sayble had the misfortune to be caught in, the variety of people clouded his mind. Feeling not only uncomfortable but conspicuous as well, he edged his way along the outside fence. People chanted, babies cried, signs bobbed up and down, cameras rolled, and clenched fists raised in protest. There were several factions represented—peaceful, silent people smiling confidently, and solemn-faced, angry nonconformists who would welcome and relish a confrontation.

Struck again with the insecurities he always felt amid a large gathering, Sayble longed for the feeling of confidence which he had risen with the previous day. It seemed that the farther he traveled from the magic of his Council campfire, the greater his anxieties and fears had grown. In fact, amidst the sudden reality of the moving, breathing crowd around him, he was unable to conjure up one certain, vivid image from the strange, magical few days previous. Feeling his mind falter as he struggled to remember the words of the condor, he pulled out the carefully folded packets containing his only tangible reason for being there. Like an addict fumbling for a fix, he unwrapped the paper which held Athanasy's amber hairs. They seemed to glow under the morning sun and at once Sayble felt renewed and confident in his mission.

Grabbing eagerly at the arm of the first person walking by, he said, "Can you show me which one of you guys is in charge of the protest?"

"That man there, Matt Covello," the young man replied.

"Thanks, son," Sayble said. Then he began weaving his way

through several lines of people. Catching up to the one singled out as Matt Covello, Sayble said, nearly out of breath, "Excuse me, young man, but are you the person in charge?" He offered his hand and added, "Charles is my name and I have a much better way of getting this base closed down."

Covello seemed happy to meet Sayble and cordially returned his handshake, saying, "Pleased to meet you, Charles. So, tell me what your idea is. Come on. We have to keep moving."

At once, Sayble felt as if he were being patronized by Covello. At seventy, he had grown quite proficient in recognizing the signs—the genial smile, nodding head, and the manufactured "oh-really?"

"Well," he began, walking next to Covello, "all the people in the world can walk around this place talking about peace and energy and nature and those folks inside there won't stop doing what they're doing. Am I right?"

Covello smiled at Sayble's simplistic logic and said, nodding occasionally at acquaintances, "Well, Charles, I'm afraid that's all we can do at this point, while we wait for the politicians and the business community to agree . . ."

"Yes, at *this* point, perhaps. But I'm here to tell you this can all change."

Slowing down his step slightly to study the old man's face, Covello asked, "How so?"

"What would you do if I told you I had evidence, as in P-R-O-O-F, that the largest majority of intelligent life on this planet has come out against nuclear technology?" Sayble asked, grinning proudly, and stopped to catch the young man's reaction.

"Come on, we've got to keep moving. Now, tell me just what group, your majority of intelligent life, do you represent?" Covello asked, keeping an eye on the sloppily dressed man with the strange words.

"Well, I'll tell you, Mr. Covellano . . ."

"Covello," he corrected, smiling weakly.

"Covello. I represent the animal kingdom. Birds, fish, bugs too. All of them!"

Assured now the old man was a derelict, Covello, in compliance with his nonviolent beliefs, simply smiled and asked, "The animals? You represent the animals?"

"Oh yes," Sayble replied, picking up his step to match Covello's. He pulled out the packets and opened a few and flashed a wisp of Neera's silver-tipped fur. "See there? That comes from the wolf, and this," he said, holding up two elegant blue feathers, "this comes from the Heron. Oh, you should've seen his face when I asked for these!"

Covello stopped, glanced at the feathers and said, "Yes, I can see why he'd put up a fuss."

"Damn right! Oh, and look, this is from the fish. I know they look like regular salmon scales, but no salmon I ever talked to ever talked back! And here is a tiny bit of the cocoon."

"Uh . . . Charles, I find all this very interesting, but you see, I'm responsible for a lot of people here and really, I . . ."

"And I'm responsible for all the animals, don't you see?" Sayble said, sensing the mockery in the protest leader's voice.

"Sir, please . . . I'm sure all your animal friends are on our side. But I don't see what all this has to do with . . ."

"Well, now you don't have to march around anymore," Sayble explained, as if to a questioning child.

"I . . ." Covello began, embarrassed and unsure of how to handle the old man and his obvious delusions.

"Now, we go to whoever the Ageon honcho is and tell him that the animals are demanding a halt to all this nuclear nonsense."

"Mister . . . I appreciate your thoughts, but I really don't think you have any idea of what we're doing here," Covello said, breaking away and walking swiftly toward another group further down the protest line.

"Look at you. You're just a kid. What the hell do you know about nuclear war?" Sayble finally shouted, casting Covello a sad smile.

Matt stopped and faced Sayble. "I know we must never have one."

"Well, you're too late, sonny, it already happened. I was about your age when my outfit started to clean up Nagasaki. So now you just listen here," he called, waving the Heron's feathers. "All the animals have gathered now, see. And they sent me!"

Covello started walking away, giving Sayble no response. But others in the area had stopped their activities and were listening to him.

"The animals! They're holding my dog! Hostage!" he called out, this time helplessly facing the crowd which was slowly gathering about him.

Before he was able to sort his shattering thoughts, a force of people formed a semi-circle around him, speaking gently. Feeling defensive, but far from defeated, he began to show the people the feathers and fur samples. "Like I was telling your weak-kneed leader, there's been this animal Council, see, and they want me to tell these Ageon people to stop. Now, isn't that what you all want?"

Then, from within the enclosing crowd, the calm, almost condescending voice of the girl, Alicyn, caught the man's attention.

"Hey, Charles, what's going on? You know, we prefer the non-violent attitude." She walked in closer, keeping a careful eye on the edging man, like a trainer approaching a rebellious colt.

"Non-violent!" he echoed. "Don't you passive pansies understand what I'm trying to tell you? If *you* don't believe me, how in hell will *they* listen to me? I need your help!" he shouted, pointing the Heron feathers up toward the main gate.

"What is it you're trying to tell us, Charles?" she asked, smiling.

"The animals! They know what's happening!" His voice cracked as he pleaded, like an actor milking his audience for the ultimate empathy. "They've told me it's time to stop! Return nature's forces. We must learn our place! Ageon only represents our trespass." As he spoke, he beseeched his listeners for respect and understanding, but he found only pity, doubt, and that dreaded, fatal smile reserved for the repetitive, senile grandfathers. The condor was wrong, he thought, glancing at the faces around him—there are no last chances.

"You have no argument from us, sir," Alicyn said kindly. "But we are here to express peace. Shouting about your talking animals will only hurt our cause." Her words drew a few positive responses from the crowd. But now, walking toward them, were two uniformed men in search of the agitators. "Kiss my ass, you bleeding hearts! I'll take care of this myself! You and your damn peaceful protests!" Sayble hollered, heaving the stack of pamphlets into the crowd. He could feel his face reddening in anger and elderly zeal.

"All right," began one of the officers, taking Sayble by the arm, "what seems to be the problem here, sir?" He too spoke with professionally trained courtesy.

Feeling the officer's grip on his arm, Sayble instinctively pulled back, saying, "I'm sorry, officer. I don't want any trouble. I was just explaining a few things to these people."

"Officer Daily," Alicyn broke in, "this gentleman isn't a part of our group. I'm afraid he thinks he's been talking to . . ." She caught Sayble's eyes, then lowered her constantly cordial voice to accommodate only the officer's ears. "Well, I don't think he's all right. You know, mentally. Maybe Alzheimer's or something. But I'm sure he means no harm."

By this time, Covello had reached the scene and added to Alicyn's case. "Sir, I can vouch this man is not in our group. I don't know who sent him here, but he's nutzoid from the word go and we take no responsibility for his actions."

Catching his words, Sayble stepped forward, saying, "I told you who sent me! The animals! And I even showed you proof!" Again, he pulled out each packet and showed the policeman. "Look—condor, raccoon, butterfly, fish, heron—let's see, what's this one?" He studied samples of prairie dog hair. "Well, I forgot who this belongs to. But just look at this! This comes from a giant elk of some kind. Biggest you ever saw! He's their leader." He looked desperately to the sky, praying the Heron would fly down to his rescue, but his elegantly vocal savior was nowhere in sight.

After dispersing the crowd, the officers looked at each other, forming the silent, unanimous decision. "Sir, you better come with us," one said gently. "You can't stay here."

"Wasn't doing any good anyway," Sayble grumbled under his breath and casting a look of disgust toward Covello, the girl, and their passive, patient group.

"Sir, have you any identification?" asked the officer, ushering Sayble away from the protest area.

"Nope! All the identification I need are these," he said, proudly displaying the fur and feathers.

"What's your name? Where are you from?" continued the officer as they approached the squad car.

"Charles. From nowhere exactly and everywhere in particular. Heard that in a movie once," he snipped, feeling childishly truant. Then he turned and asked one officer earnestly, "But what would you have done? I tell you, it's true. These animals talk! Even my own dog! There's this place, see . . . kind of an enchanted forest place and, well, of course, I thought I was, you know, seeing and hearing things." They nodded patronizingly and opened the back car door for him.

"Oh, I have my bus up the hill. Thanks, anyway."

"Get in please, sir."

"You're not arresting me! I haven't done anything illegal, have I?" He backed up, but stopped when he felt one officer behind him.

"No, that's right, Charles. But for your own good, please come with us."

"Where?" he demanded suspiciously.

"I think you'd best stay a few days over at Greentree," the officer said gently, helping him into the squad car.

"What's Greentree? I don't need a motel. I sleep in my bus." The door closed and automatically locked.

"It's not a motel, sir. It's our county hospital. Sir, you appear to be a little disoriented. And, without any identification . . ."

Sayble settled back into the seat, folded his arms in resignation and said, "I was afraid of that."

As the police car left the parking lot and headed for the main road, the Heron lowered his altitude and followed the vehicle, damning the events that were pointing toward such an intricate and early failure.

Leaning his head back and looking out the rear window, Sayble wearily watched the vanishing Heron's flight and whispered, "There's never a heron around when you need one."

CHAPTER EIGHTEEN

Well, ATHANASY," the Great Blue Heron said, still out of breath, "I guess we all knew it wouldn't work."

"The man-cousin has failed? So soon, he has failed?" Athanasy asked, expressing both disappointment and anger. "Tell me what happened."

"There were many man-cousins at Ageon. Oh, the human stench was unbearable! Sayble spoke to several of his brethren. There was great shouting and this led to our man-cousin being taken away by wardens of some sort. I followed their transport until they delivered him to a large man-structure. That was this morning. It looks as though we are right back where we started."

"Was he hurt?" demanded Fetchit-5, who had crept in closer to hear of her master's fate.

"He seemed unharmed, but who can say about these creatures?" the Heron replied, preening himself after his exhausting flight.

Athanasy turned to the dog and asked, "You know more of the man-cousin's world. Where do you think they have taken him?"

"Was the building fenced and well-guarded?" she asked.

"Not nearly so much as Ageon."

"Good. Then maybe it wasn't a prison."

"You mean the man-cousin actually cages his own kind? In

111

addition to all our kind?" the Heron screeched with a horrified gasp.

"Incredible, I know," agreed the dog. "And for the strangest reasons. Sometimes to protect the whole and then sometimes to protect the one."

Within moments, the other animals had gathered. "Come be with me, brothers and sisters," beckoned Athanasy. They circled in closer and waited for his next words. "Our man-cousin ally has been captured. And yet, the importance of our mission grows daily, hourly. I feel the Will becoming stronger and stronger. We must return the man-cousin to this sacred place."

The creatures looked at each other and whispered their reactions as their leader spoke. "How do you know he hasn't gone to them for sanctuary?" asked Iscariot. "How do you know that he isn't at this very moment planning our destruction?"

"No!" shouted Fetchit-5, her hackles rising in Sayble's defense. "He wouldn't do that!"

"How do you know he wouldn't?" asked Neera, without accusation.

"Because *I* say he wouldn't!" Fetchit-5 growled, baring her teeth.

"Your loyalties disgust me!" Iscariot said, creeping forward and welcoming a fight.

Just as the dog lowered to spring for the raccoon, Athanasy thundered, "Enough! Dissension everywhere, but not here!"

They both backed off, but it took some moments for the chesty growl to subside in Fetchit-5's quivering throat. Then, in the quiet, Athanasy continued, "Sayble, the man-cousin, has shown himself to be a creature of courage. If we desert him now, it would be cowardice and betrayal."

"What is it you propose we do?" asked Lordjahn.

"Moko and his small comrade, the prairie dog, shall follow the flight of the Heron back to the place of Sayble's confinement and will bring him back," the elk stated, staring firmly at the mightiest and the smallest of the Council land-creatures.

"But I should go too, in case of problems with the man-cousins. I'm domestic. I'll look less suspicious," Fetchit-5 pleaded rationally.

"You realize you will have no power to communicate with the other man-cousins. Only Sayble. The Will forbids it," cautioned Athanasy.

"I've succeeded all these years without so much as a peep," the dog said, grinning. "And all any dog ever asks is a chance to save its master."

"Idiocy!" cried Iscariot.

"Opposition?" the elk asked the other animals. There was a silent glance about. "Good. Then they shall leave now," Athanasy continued.

"But wait," Moko said with a shaky voice. "How, I mean who . . . this is difficult, you know."

"Not to worry, old pal," Little Paw said, popping into the center of the ring of animals. "I've got a plan already!" The little creature's heart and head pounded with the excitement and glory of being chosen for such a mission as to bedazzle all animal-kind.

"Good. We'll talk on the way," said Fetchit-5, anxious to be on with the intrigue.

"Do you think they'll make it?" whispered Chanta, flying inches away from the Heron's ear.

"Oh yes, no doubt they'll make it. With all that near-sighted ambition, no doubt they'll stumble that old man-cousin right on back here. But what I'm worried about is what will happen then," he whispered back. Then, addressing the gathering, he said, "The sooner we begin, the better. I hate flying in the dark."

"Be swift then, and cautious," said Athanasy. "For time is . . ."

". . . of the utmost," the Heron said, cutting him off. "Tell me about it," he snapped. Then he smiled weakly and added, "All right. I'll fly low, so my air-tracks will be easier to follow."

The Heron took wing, followed by the buffalo with the prairie dog atop his head. Leading the menagerie was the dog, her nose to the ground and her tail in the air.

The admitting nurse had a cool, professional air about her as she asked the usual questions for admittance into the mental ward of Greentree County Hospital.

"Now please, Charles, we must have your last name for our records," the nurse said. Her tight thin lips were straining to smile.

"Sayble," he answered. "But you'll have a hard time proving it." He returned her smile with an earthy grin, wondering if the woman had ever known passion.

"Just as long as I have something to fill in the space. It'll do." Her manner was neither soothing nor compassionate. "S-A-B-L-E," she spelled. "As in the animal?"

"Nope," he groaned impatiently, "S-A-Y-B-L-E, as in SAY and BLE."

"All right. Do you have any family?" she rolled the pen in her long fingers and looked up at him for his reply.

"Yup."

"Good. Who are they?" She positioned the pen in the proper area on the admittance form.

"Got me a dog."

"Besides that."

"Well, let's see. I had a sister, but she died talking to Lord Byron." He looked up, rubbing his chin thoughtfully. "Got me a condor, a raccoon, a wolf, a buffalo, a prairie dog, a salmon, and a few other critters whose specific types escape me now. Oh yes, and an elk bigger than an elephant. Like I've been telling everyone, my animals were the ones who sent me here in the first place."

"Animals sent you to Greentree?" she asked.

"Well, of course not here!" he said haughtily. "Why would they do a stupid thing like that?"

"I don't know, Charles. That's what we are here to find out." Her attempt at sincerity was flimsy and offensive.

"Well, that may be what *you* are here for, Miss . . ." He squinted to read her identification badge. "Miss Grady. But I can guarantee you *I* have better things to do!"

"Oh? Like what?"

"Well, like stopping those Ageon people. What's so crazy about that?" he asked innocently.

"Nothing, of course. But most people would go about doing that in a more orthodox manner," she said, jotting notes down at a speedy rate.

"Yeah, like bombing the hell out of it. Hey, what are you writing there?" he asked, tilting his head in an effort to read.

"Just a few notes for the doctor," she replied. "So, Charles, how long have you been talking with your animals?"

"Look, Miss Grady, I know you think I'm hallucinating or whatever doctoring word you have for it, but I was just as normal as you are, up until a few days ago." He looked her over quickly, then added, looking away, "More so."

"That's when you first started talking to the animals?" she prompted.

Sayble got up and nervously ran his hands though his hair, then he massaged his neck. "Well, I've always enjoyed talking to Fetchit-5—she's my dog—but as near as I can recall, she never talked back . . . until lately, that is." He helped himself to a cup of water and continued, "I mean, not even after a whole bottle of wine have I ever heard her talk back."

"Then you drink?" she asked.

"Not as much as I'd like to lately."

"I see," she said, continuing her writing.

"No, miss, you do not see. Now, all day today, I've put up with young folks like you who look at me and make assumption after assumption. Assume I'm crazy, assume I'm senile, assume I'm seeing and hearing things, assume I'm drunk. Why can't anybody assume I'm right and that I know what I'm talking about? How come when you get older, no one believes you? Hell, I had more luck convincing my poor mama that story about the dragon living in our woodshed."

He crumpled his water cup and tossed it into the waste basket across the room.

Nurse Grady scribbled down every word he uttered. When he mentioned dragons, she looked up sharply.

"Now, don't go writing that down," Sayble said, pointing to her desk. "It's symbolic."

"Do you often think in abstracts, Charles?"

"Good God, woman! If these are the questions *you* ask me, what's the doctor going to have left to ask?" He lay down on the high, hard bed, feeling his power weaken and the grip of resignation approaching from behind.

"Are you tired?" she asked, rising from the chair and walking over to him.

"No, just get on with it," he said, exasperated.

"I think that will be all for now. I'll need your signature here, Mr. Sayble." Miss Grady attempted a softer, less professional manner.

"What for? Lobotomy consent?"

She forced a nasal laugh. "Hardly. These are your admittance papers. The police brought you in, so the county has the authority to put you on a 72-hour hold. This means, after our resident psychiatrist interviews you, he may or may not feel, for your own best interests, you should remain and be treated here at Green-tree."

"I can't stand how all you young people these days have everything memorized. So, what can I do to get myself out of here?" He rolled back down and stared at the sterile white ceiling.

"Well, a friend or relative could be notified and accept responsibility for you."

"No. Not likely you'd let a buffalo sign my release papers. Besides, I'm my own responsibility."

She patted his arm and said, "That's right. That's a very healthy attitude. Now, if you would, please sign here." She offered him the clipboard and the pen.

Hesitantly, he took them, clicked the pen dramatically, then scribbled where indicated. He handed them back to Nurse Grady as casually as a celebrity passing out an autograph.

She looked at his signature, exhaled impatiently and walked toward the door. "Thank you, Mr. Bonaparte," she snapped. "I'll send for the palace physician!" She left through the heavy swinging door.

"You can call me Napoleon!" he bellowed after her, in a thick French accent of royal cordiality.

Sayble shook himself awake and estimated that he had dozed for nearly an hour. His room was dark and it took him a few moments to remember where he was, why and how he'd gotten there. He switched on the bed lamp and rose to study his new environment. The view from his second-floor barred window was pleasant—just the sort of view a wacko needs, he thought. The lawns were well kept and were bordered with neat, symmetrical hedges. Sayble wondered how many gardeners had gone mad trimming them. And what better place to go mad than Greentree? The name itself suggested mental harmony.

He walked about the room, taking inventory aloud, "Your basic bed, your basic lamp, your basic sink, your basic bedpan, and your basic come-and-help-me-pee-in-the middle-of-the-night-buzzer." He held up the nurse's buzzer attached to his bed, considering pushing it to protest his incarceration, but let the buzzer swing from its wire.

Then he curled up on the bed to plan his escape.

CHAPTER NINETEEN

T O THEIR GOOD FORTUNE, the route the rescuing animals took was lightly populated, and they were able to follow the Heron with little difficulty and no detection. The powerful Moko was able to keep the sailing bird's pace with Little Paw clinging to his furry, bounding head. The few thoughts the prairie dog conceived for an escape plan were almost immediately tossed out of his head, after being knocked about from one side of his brain to the other.

Fetchit-5 was having some difficulty keeping up. So she put every ounce of her concentration into the plight of her man-cousin, and she forgot how her body and legs ached. When at last the Heron lit on an oak tree perch, the dog fell in her tracks, panting uncontrollably. So abruptly did she stop, that Moko had to quickly side-step the exhausted animal.

"Aaauuugh!" Moko hollered. "I almost squashed you to death, Fetchit-5!" He pulled up to a dusty stop and turned apologetically.

"A mercy killing, if ever there was one," the weary dog gasped. She looked up to the Heron and asked, "Are we there? Please say we're there. Please . . ." She ventured a smile, but found her tongue was hanging out too far.

"Just over that hill lies Ageon and the deadly whales. Just down this way is where they took the man-cousin." The Heron pointed straight ahead. "Perhaps you can't see the building from down there, but from here you can tell it's not far at all."

"Rather than climb the tree, I guess I'll just take your word for it," the dog said, beginning to get her breath back. "Okay, Little Paw, let's hear this plan of yours."

The prairie dog had jumped down off of Moko and scrambled over to the dog. The Heron flew down to hear the details and Moko walked closer and put his head down close to the ground, nibbling on grass as he listened.

"Yes," the Heron said, "what's your idea?"

Falling short on preparation, the prairie dog stammered, "Ah yes . . . well, the plan. Well, you see, it goes like this. . . ." He paused and looked into the small, but earnestly intent, eyes of Moko and continued. "Well, *my* idea was to infiltrate the building, after studying its composition, of course." He looked about for approval and he was proud of his fine wording.

"Eh?" asked the buffalo.

"Yeah. What?" The dog agreed wearily with the buffalo's confusion.

"Ah, I see there are some questions," Little Paw said, stepping slightly away from the others, strutting much like a wind-up toy soldier. "This is the way I see it: Fetchit-5 and myself—she, because she's domestic—your words, not mine . . ." she added diplomatically. "And me, because I'm smaller and therefore less detectable than Moko here. The dog and I will go to the building. She will create a diversion to anyone who might be guarding the man-cousin, and I will get into the building merely by the fact that I am so . . . uh . . . small."

The buffalo, dog, and Heron exchanged glances, but remained silent. Little Paw continued. "Now, then, the Heron can serve as look-out and will create a racket if there is a danger close by."

"What about me?" the buffalo asked, eager to learn of his heroic role. "What do I do?"

"I was coming to that, old buddy. You, sir, are a buffalo," Little Paw said, tapping his friend on the nose, "and buffalo around here are probably very scarce. Therefore, you shall remain hidden."

"Then what did I come here for?" he asked, disappointed.

"Well, do you think that old man-cousin will be able to run back and keep up with us? Have you no pity? Naturally, the man-cousin will ride you back to the Council Ground!" The prairie dog grinned with all this heart and soul.

"I don't know . . ." the buffalo hedged. "Makes my back itch to even think about it."

"You know, your friend here is right, Moko," the Heron said. "It's the only chance the man-cousin has of escaping with any speed. The dire essentials here are secrecy and speed. Little Paw's plan offers both. I suggest we continue. Do you have anything to add, Fetchit-5?"

"Well, I don't have a better idea, if that's what you mean," she said, rising and stretching her hind legs out to ease them back into action. "Let's be on with it. One thing, though—should any of us be caught, shouldn't we have a plan for the others?"

"At the first sign of an error, the rest will get back to the Council Ground as fast as they can. Agreed?" the Heron said solemnly. They all nodded and, as night fell, began to creep silently forward, eager for a glimpse of the man-structure which held their man-cousin, eager also for Little Paw's plan of deliverance to be successfully completed.

Sayble was allowed out of his room briefly, and he took the opportunity to explore the second-floor mental health unit. The intrepid Nurse Grady had mercifully gone off duty and was replaced by an elderly but equally starched nurse. Pulling together any fragments of charm he might have once possessed, he casually leaned on the night nurse's counter and asked, "How's about you and me blowing this joint and getting a little drink? You know, some place where just me and you can be alone?" He winked at her.

She looked at him and smiled the same, weak, patronizing smile which, by that time, Sayble had assumed was a new social custom.

"Well, you must be our new Mr. Sayble. I'd like to join you, but it's against the rules. And, of course, it would be difficult to get out of here in the first place. I'm afraid we are both in here for the night. Now, I can get something for you if you are having difficulty sleeping."

"No, I'll sleep when I'm ready. Tell me, what's to keep me from going right out that elevator?"

"Me. And a few orderlies, of course. But you just got here. Why would you want to leave so soon?" Her gray curly hair sprang out from under her nurse's cap at odd angles and Sayble wondered if it personified her wiry personality.

"Now don't tell me a little slip of a lady like you keeps an eye on all of us nuts, all night long?" he asked, prying for more information.

"First of all, most people here are delighted to stay. On the outside, they're not sure if they have a mental problem, whereas here, they're . . ."

". . . *sure* they have a mental problem?"

"Not at all," she said icily. "They're here because they know it's for their own good. And secondly, I have been in this business a long, long time and my record shows virtually no escapes."

The phone rang and she excused herself to answer it, keeping a constant eye on her charge. As he started to leave, she added, "Oh, and Mr. Sayble, the door to the stairs sets off an alarm when opened. Please go back to your room and try to get some rest. We have a big day tomorrow." She smiled and returned to her telephone conversation.

Back in his room, he looked at the pale blue pajamas and robe the hospital provided, then said aloud, "I'll be damned if I'm going to wear those!" He shoved them onto the floor and lay down on the bed. "You'd have to be pretty far gone to actually want to stay *here!*" he grumbled.

CHAPTER TWENTY

AFTER FINDING A well-treed area for Moko to hide, the dog, the Heron, and the prairie dog carefully advanced toward Greentree. As the moon rose and blessed their mission with silvery light, they glared at the hospital. Whereas it had only two stories, its length seemed endless.

"So how do you ever think we'll find him in that thing?" asked the Heron.

"That part hadn't occurred to me," the prairie dog whispered back. "I can't think of everything. Any idea, Fetchit?"

The dog, who had fallen slightly behind to explore some scents, caught up in time to hear Little Paw.

"Don't look at me. Nobody planned on this place being so huge," she said, studying its length.

"Well, can't you smell anything familiar?" Little Paw asked. "Aren't you dogs supposed to be good at that?"

Sniffing the air, she smiled and said, "Hmmmm . . . yes, now that you mention it, I think I smell french fries."

"French fries!" the Heron exclaimed. "What's that?"

"It must be food. Look, she's drooling," Little Paw said. "Come on, Fetchit-5, try harder. Anything?"

The dog raised her nose high in the air, continuing her search for whiffs of Sayble. "No. Sorry. Now what?"

"I know," the Heron began, stepping closer to his cohorts and whispering. "No doubt the man-cousin is wondering if any of us will follow him here. After all, he knew I was around until he was captured. So, it stands to reason that he'll be looking for us."

"And?" Fetchit-5 prompted.

"So what's unusual to anyone but Sayble about some stray dog howling at the moon? Wouldn't the sound of your voice bring him to a window or something?" the Heron continued.

"A grand idea!" chirped the prairie dog. "That was going to be my next suggestion. And, once we know where he is, I'll get in, find him, and lead him out to safety."

"How?" the Heron asked dryly, knowing nothing was ever as simple as the prairie dog made it sound.

"One ordeal at a time," Little Paw barked back, undaunted. "Heron, take flight and circle. Fetchit-5, go over toward those doors and start your song. Make it loud, long, and lousy."

"Where are you going?" the Heron asked, preparing for flight.

"I'll be close to the door there. And, as soon as you see the man-cousin and tell me which way to go, I'll sneak inside. Well, troops, this is it. Good luck. We'll all meet back where Moko is hidden." The prairie dog sat on his haunches and raised a paw as if to salute his comrades.

The Heron rose quietly as Fetchit-5 trotted over to the walkway near the main entrance to Greentree.

The young man who was overseeing the front desk looked up from his paperback and strained to hear again the odd sound coming from outside. The second howl was much louder and many times more piercing than the first, as if the dog had to work up to such a horrid pitch.

"What the . . ." the attendant asked aloud, slapping down his book and stepping over to the door.

Sitting on the front lawn, head to the moon, was Fetchit-5, delighted to be creating such a God-forsaken sound. The man unlocked the door and shouted, "Go home! Get away from here, you mutt!"

Fetchit-5 ceased for a moment, looked at him slyly as if to say, "Mutt is it? Here, buddy, have some more!" She set her head back and continued, louder and longer.

Now challenged, the man left his front desk post and walked

outside the door, this time shouting, "Get out of here! Go on! Scram!" He picked up a rock, tossed it at her, and walked back inside.

Thinking perhaps he had heard her call in his dream, Sayble rose slightly up in his bed, forgetful again of where he was. But before the next howl was barely out of her throat, the old man knew exactly who it was.

Leaping out of bed, he ran to the window and looked in either direction to detect the howl's origin. He fumbled in the dark for the light, then returned to the window. The security window only opened a few inches, but he called out into the night through the small opening.

"Fetchit! Here, girl! I'm here!" But there was no answer. Then, in a mighty draft, the Great Blue Heron swoshed next to Sayble's window. Unable to tread air for more than a second, the bird circled the area.

"It's you!" Sayble gasped. "Good God, you *all* came?" he asked, laughing aloud.

"No, man-cousin. Just a few of us. Are you harmed?" the Heron whispered as he again neared the window.

Before he could answer, the night nurse burst into his room and crossed to Sayble at the opened window.

"And just what is going on?" she demanded. Appearing in the doorway behind her was an orderly of immense proportions. "Why aren't you in your pajamas and asleep, Mr. Sayble?" she asked, taking a suspicious glance through the window. Seeing nothing, she closed and locked it.

She took him by the arm and led him back to his bed. "Now, get undressed and I'll order something to help you sleep."

Relieved the nurse hadn't seen the Heron, Sayble acquiesced dramatically, allowing her to assist him into bed. He gave a great sigh of exhaustion and said, "Perhaps that would be best. I guess I'm a little confused."

"That's right, Mr. Sayble." She called the orderly inside, saying, "Philip, would you please help Mr. Sayble into his jammers?"

"No, please," Sayble objected. "There are *some* dignities still left to me. I can manage. You've been most kind. Just a little pill to make me sleep."

"Very well. I'll be right back. You climb into bed," the nurse said in her soothing, I-knew-you'd-see-it-my-way voice. She and the orderly left, closing the door behind them.

Quickly, Sayble put only the pajama top on and hopped into bed, assuming a frail, fatigued position, pulling the covers up to his chin.

"Here you are," the nurse said, stepping lightly back into his room with a tray holding two small cups. "Take these and before you know it, it will be a sunny new day!" Her voice was cheerful, doting, and victorious. She watched him toss the two small pills into his mouth, handed him the cup of water and smiled. "There now, I'll bet you feel better already."

"You're too kind," he said, closing his eyes.

She turned off his bedside lamp and quietly stepped out of the room. The squeak of her rubber-sole shoes was the only sound as the door slowly closed.

As soon as he felt the dark upon his eyelids, Sayble sat up and spit the two pills and their bitter taste out onto the floor.

He quietly returned to the window and opened it, awaiting further news from the animals. He hadn't heard the clear, definitive howl from Fetchit-5, but he knew she wouldn't leave without him.

"A signal. They need a signal," he whispered to himself. Knowing that someone might detect his light going back on, he unrolled a wrinkled red bandana from his back pocket and dangled it from the window.

Waiting in a tree nearby, the Heron immediately saw it and, without any words to Sayble, flew over and snatched it away from the startled man.

Meanwhile, Little Paw, in his hiding bush near the entrance, was perplexed on just how to enter the building. He had seen the Heron fly down low over the dog a few minutes earlier and was angered that he was not informed as to what was happening. No sooner had the prairie dog planned his next move than the Heron landed lightly behind him, nearly frightening the little creature out of his nervous skin.

"Heron? Please say that's you," Little Paw said in a small voice.

"It's me. I've found him," the bird whispered back, feeling his own excitement grow. "Can you see me?"

"Yes. What is that you have there?" Little Paw asked, watching the Heron lay Sayble's bandana out flat on the ground. "What's that thing for?"

"Come closer and you'll see." There was a hint of pride in the bird's voice as he disclosed his plan. "Here. Sit in the middle of this."

"What? What for? Where's the dog? Do you mind telling me what's going on here?" Although the prairie dog's words suggested hesitancy, he did as he was requested.

"Good. Now, there isn't much time, so listen carefully. I sent the dog over to the side of the building. I found the man-cousin and I'm going to take you to him. I hope you aren't afraid of heights, Little Paw."

Then the Heron took each of the four corners of the bandana into his long bill and spoke with his mouth full. "Get the idea? Now, don't move. Ready?"

He gave a tug and straightened himself up to his full height, assessing the wing-power he would need for lift-off.

"But . . ." Little Paw protested, his voice muffled from within his bandana space capsule.

"It's too late for objections. Here we go!" With a hefty pull, the bird took flight.

"You know, this is how those nasty stork rumors get started," Little Paw quipped, clutching the sides of the bandana, panting in terror and delight.

Before Sayble had even taken the time to figure out his next step, he heard the flap of the heron's straining wings approaching his window again. Kneeling on the floor to afford a better glimpse of the bird, the man was able to squeeze his arms through the window. He waved his arms frantically to help the bird locate the right opening. At first, Sayble was astonished to see the bird carrying something in his bandana, but then quickly realized that, obviously, anything is possible.

"Here! Quick! Take this!" the Heron muttered through his clenched bill, helping the bundle into the window with his strong talons. Then, feeling the sudden absence of weight, the bird ascended at an enormous rate and flew off to locate the dog's new position.

Sayble pulled the wiggling bundle in to safety and quickly unwrapped it. He could feel the small animal's racing heart as he cradled the creature in his hands.

"Well, I know you're a prairie dog, but I forgot your name," Sayble whispered down to his quaking handful, gently stroking its back.

"If I never fly again, it'll be too soon!" Little Paw gasped, trying to quiet his pulse. "Little Paw. My name is Little Paw. I tell you, the folks back home will never believe this one." He took a few deep breaths, then continued bravely, "Well, come on. I'll get you out of here."

"*You're* going to get me out of here?" Sayble asked. "How?"

"By doing what I do best. Creating havoc. Put me down and follow me."

Sayble did as he was directed and then stood, his hands on his hips, smiling down at the ambitious animal. "You don't seem to understand," he whispered. "This place is guarded. We're locked in here. No one comes in. No one goes out."

"I came in," Little Paw countered simply. "Can you open that door?"

"Yes, but that's as far as we go."

"That's what you think. See if it's safe," Little Paw said, creeping toward the slip of light coming under the door.

Sayble tiptoed to the door and listened for the squeaky shoes. "All clear," he said, opening the door slightly. "What are you going to do?"

"You'll know when I've done it," Little Paw answered, peeking around the corner of the doorjamb. "Which way is the guard?"

"To your right," Sayble answered impatiently. "Do you mind telling me . . ."

"Is the guard male or female?"

"Female, by some standards. Why?"

"Ooooo, goody," Little Paw said, a wicked grin coming across his shadowed face.

"Little Paw . . ."

"Sssshhhh. Let an expert take over. You'll know when to move. When you do, make it fast." With that, the tiny creature slipped through the door.

Scrambling his slippery way down the shining, waxed floor, Little Paw positioned himself at the base of the nurse's station. The nurse was sitting on a stool, sipping a cup of coffee and reading a newspaper, oblivious to the intruder. But when the piercing squeal of the prairie dog broke the dead silence, the nurse jumped up screaming.

Little Paw, satisfied he now had her attention, stepped into her view, stood on his hind legs and increased the next bark threefold. He held his arms high over his head and continued his furious howl.

When the nurse saw her adversary, she screamed, "Mad rat! Mad rat!" and ran down the hall screeching for an orderly.

Sayble, watching through the crack in his door, figured he could have walked out right past her as she stormed down the hall. As soon as she galloped by, he quickly ran out.

As he ran down the hall, he pulled each fire alarm he passed, setting off stinging sirens. Then, as soon as he pushed open the door to the stairs, more bells rang through the ward, striking agonizing discord and causing, by this time, total confusion. He looked around the stairwell for his companion and was terrified to find no traces of the prairie dog.

"Damn!" he cursed. He bounded back up the stairs and looked through the small wired window in the door. At the opposite end of the hall, he could see the white uniforms dashing about. The heads of frightened and disoriented patients leaned out of their rooms for explanation.

Sayble quickly opened the door and called, "Little Paw!"

From around the nurse's station, the little fellow bounded, losing more traction the faster he ran. Sayble reached down and snatched up the prairie dog and returned to the stairwell. He took the stairs, three at a time, down to the ground floor. He charged through the exit and took a quick look around.

"Over here, Sayble!" Fetchit-5 shouted, peeking out from the shrubbery. "Quickly!"

The lights in the entire complex went on, inside and out, and in the distance, fire engines chorused a steady wail as they approached the assaulted Greentree.

Puffing as he followed the dog, who followed the Heron above, he clutched the prairie dog and gasped, "Guess it'll be a long time before they try to stable old Sayble!" He laughed as he sailed, almost deer-like, over the grass.

"Congratulate yourself later, Sayble. We're not home yet," called Fetchit-5 over her shoulder.

On the hill overlooking Greentree, the four rescuers and their man-cousin paused to catch their breaths and their wits. Looking down below at the chaos cheered them all. The fire engines had arrived and patients were being evacuated from every exit of the hospital. Red and blue lights flashed with carnival whimsy as the police arrived. Officials shouted orders, patients wailed, and those five who had successfully completed the daring escape each smiled in their own personal victory.

CHAPTER TWENTY-ONE

Q UICKLY! There is no time to waste, man-cousin!" the Heron whispered urgently, breaking Sayble's joy in beholding the havoc at Greentree.

"Right, you magnificent blue bird!" he exclaimed, feeling a pride vibrate through his veins. His entire life he had dreamt of such an escape. He joyfully threw his arms around the buffalo's neck, then his dog's, and he tousled the prairie dog's short coat affectionately.

"We have to get back to the bus," he said. Then, he stood up, remembering there was a healthy chance that the bus would have been impounded by the police. "Oh," he said thoughtfully, considering alternatives.

"What is it, Sayble?" Fetchit-5 asked.

"Heron, quickly fly ahead and see if my bus is still at Ageon," Sayble said, looking up to the bird in the treetops above.

"That has already been taken care of," the bird said, smiling smugly down at them. "While waiting for you to escape, I took a quick trip there and found your transport patiently waiting for you."

"But won't they be looking for you and try to follow the transport?" Little Paw asked.

"Yes. Perhaps we should abandon the vehicle and go straight back to the Council on foot," the dog said, looking to the others for their ideas.

"No!" the man objected. "This is my only chance to get my bus back. If I leave it now, I'll never see it again. And, strange as it might seem to you, it's my home."

"Oh," Moko nodded in agreement. "Like a turtle. Then hurry and climb on board, man-cousin. We have to hurry!"

"Huh?" Sayble asked.

"You won't have a chance of keeping up with us. Without extra legs or wings, you'll fall behind," Little Paw explained urgently.

Moko lowered his head and Little Paw jumped on top to assume his seat of high navigation. "See? Nothing to it!" he barked as the stately buffalo gently raised up with Little Paw in perfect balance.

"Well, how do I get on?" he asked, studying the height of the beast.

"I guess you'll just have to run and jump. But do hurry, man-cousin," the Heron said. "Every moment counts. You'll soon be reported missing."

So, with a long run and a yelp to assist him, Sayble threw himself at the buffalo's high, dusty back and was barely able to get his leg over. Grabbing at the furry sides, he pulled himself up higher. Moko didn't even sway under the man's weight, but merely stood patiently as Sayble dragged himself up to the most comfortable position possible.

"Now, how do I stay on?" He gripped tufts on both sides of the shabby mane, feeling unsteady. "The more I think about it, the more I think I do belong in that looney bin!"

"That's fine. Do just what you are doing," said Moko. "Lean forward so that you are flat against my back. Hold on as tight as you can."

"You can bet on that."

"And don't worry about hurting me," Moko continued with a glance back. "My coat is thick. I won't feel any pain until next week." He snorted a frisky laugh, delighted at last to be a part of the daring scheme.

As Sayble grew accustomed to the pace, the Heron flew further ahead and Little Paw watched the bird and directed Moko to the correct path. They avoided the man-roads, but took as direct a route as possible. Fetchit-5 ran alongside the buffalo and kept an eye on the bounding man-cousin.

They stopped on the hilltop which overlooked Ageon. The complex was lit with the cold blue of vapor lights, so much so that the area looked almost as bright as in the daytime.

"There is the bus," pointed the Heron.

"Oh good," Sayble remarked wearily, looking between the buffalo's horns. His brains, he was sure, had been jostled about to the point of idiocy and it took him a moment to sort out the real bus from the dizzy replicas which circled around it. Then he put his head on the buffalo's back and added with his last ounce of enthusiasm for the sport of buffalo riding, "Onward, James."

Before his words were shakily uttered, the entourage began the descent down the hill, following the trees that graced the landscape. The activity around the base was minimal and they reached the bus without a hint of detection.

Once on the pavement, Moko stepped lightly while Sayble slid off the beast with the same gratitude an acrophobiac gives when his plane touches ground safely.

Without allowing himself time to count his saddle sores, Sayble immediately opened the bus's hood and retrieved the envelope containing his papers and keys. The animals waited next to the vehicle, anxiously studying the sprawling size of Ageon as it lay in the man-lit darkness.

"It sure is scary," Moko said to the Heron.

"It's grown since the last time I saw it," the Heron replied academically.

When Sayble had started the bus, he called outside, "Okay, you guys. Everyone aboard!"

Fetchit-5 leaped aboard, in gleeful memory of old times, but the others were hesitant. "Come on! Get in here!"

"There is no need for me to ride in your transport," the Heron said, standing on the lower step and looking up at Sayble. "I'll fly ahead and alert the Council. Go on, Moko. Get aboard."

"No," Moko said, stepping back.

At that, the impatient Heron flew behind the hedging beast and poked him with his sharp bill.

"Whhooooaaaaa!" Moko yelped as he scrambled awkwardly aboard the bus.

Once aboard, Sayble watched the buffalo try to gather his

footing. He wasn't sure, but in the rear-view mirror, the great beast looked quite pale. "Talk about your bull in a china shop," he muttered. "Look, Moko, I think you better lie down."

With a mighty huff, the buffalo dropped to his knees, then pulled his hind legs under him and looked about with a snort of apprehension. Little Paw gently stroked his giant companion's head reassuringly.

"Ready?" Sayble called out, releasing the hand brake. "Next stop: never-never-land!"

On the voyage back to the river and the Council, Sayble listened to the news on the local radio station. He relived the escape from Greentree as the confused reports trickled through the media wires. The news made no mention of a Greentree patient escaping and he figured it could be well into the early morning before the hospital authorities reported him missing. And what of it? he thought as he turned off on a dusty road. As far as the uniforms were concerned, he still had not done anything illegal.

The animals who awaited their arrival stood in awe as they watched the colorful bus enter their sacred ground. The whimsical rows of color seemed to vibrate as the warm, rising morning mist consumed the vehicle, as if to offer it refuge and welcome.

Once inside the Council Ground, Sayble looked about and immediately felt renewed in the magic the place offered. All things were clear in his mind as Athanasy approached him, striding regally.

The elk walked down one side of the bus and looked into each window as if to satisfy a long curiosity about such things. When he had completed the circuit around the bus, he told Sayble, "Command your transport to stay and come with me. We must talk." Then, he walked toward the woods while the other animals crept in closer to examine the bus.

As ordered, the man followed Athanasy.

"I am glad to see you back safe, but tell me, why did you fail?" the elk asked.

"I knew I didn't have the chance of a snowball in hell anyway! I tell you, no one believed one word I said. For a while there, I had an idea . . . but I must have been crazy. I'm sorry, Athanasy. These things take time," Sayble said, looking out over the pond.

"We haven't got the time!" the beast thundered.

Sayble looked at him carefully and asked, "Just what do you know that we don't? How far into the future can you see?"

"Far enough," the elk said, turning as if to leave.

"Athanasy?" Sayble called. "What are you going to do now?"

The elk turned and replied, "Simple, let the animals now speak to Ageon."

"You mean, have them talk?"

"No, that is forbidden. We can speak without talking, man-cousin. We have ways. If Ageon's masters did not listen to you, perhaps they will listen to my Chosen."

There was a weariness in the elk's voice that Sayble found similar to his own. As the elk walked away, Sayble decided not to question the beast further.

He returned to his bus, climbed aboard and fell into a deep sleep.

After allowing the creatures to rest, Athanasy called them together.

"It's time now for you to go forward and make your protests known. If the man-cousin has failed, it is not for lack of loyalty. He is to be revered."

"But how, Athanasy?" asked Moko earnestly. "How can we protest?"

"You will be blessed with brilliance, my children. Instinct, that is your most powerful weapon against the man-cousin. Use it wisely. And remember, the Council's Will for survival surpasses your own. The Heron will watch over you and keep me informed of your successes. Come back safe and triumphant."

With that, he bid them farewell and watched them leave the Council site.

Overlooking Ageon, the animals stood in respectful awe of their enemy. To those who had already seen Ageon, it seemed to have grown in size as the daylight revealed even more buildings and the giant docks beyond. The man-cousins who tended to the needs of Ageon were countless, coming and going in their daily tasks.

With so much at stake, each animal planned its own assault on Ageon, knowing that, depending on their success or failure, the past would challenge the present, and the result would decide their future—the Will demanded it.

CHAPTER TWENTY-TWO

S LEEP, DREAM, AND SING until daybreak, brothers and sisters. Tomorrow we combine our powers," said Lordjahn, looking around the area for a place to sleep.

"Combine what powers?" snapped Iscariot, raising a lip. "None of us has any more power here than we did before this whole damn plot was conceived. Were you planning on casting an enchantment on this place? Listen," he added bitterly, "if there is magic to be done here, why didn't Athanasy himself, supposedly the King of Wizards, come with us? Why are *we* the ones who have to risk our necks?"

None of the creatures answered, but they exchanged looks of mutual contempt for the raccoon's words. "That's what I thought," Iscariot continued. "None of you can answer."

"I'll answer you," said Neera, approaching him and facing him squarely. "We have been chosen to represent the Will of all creature-kind. If you can't feel the honor, then that is your sorry business. If you can't hear your song, then I pity you! You are brilliant enough to be chosen, yet stupid enough to resist."

"So, tell me, how do you plan your sacrifices?" the raccoon asked her. "Look at Ageon! Look at the man-cousins! Count them! Smell their power!"

"Don't you understand?" Lordjahn asked. His voice was deep

and clear with well-balanced logic. "The man-cousin failed to convince his own kind. So now it is up to us."

"Look at us!" Iscariot shouted. "A handful of creatures. How far can we get before their bullets, gases, cages, and chains will stop us? If man's ultimate weapon is this, then all of us, even Athanasy, are helpless against it! If man can't convince his own kind to stop, then the idea of us doing it is idiotic and fatal." The raccoon's eyes grew red as he stared at each creature, from the butterfly to the condor.

"I hate to say it, but . . ." began Moko, looking around the others.

"Don't say it!" screeched the Heron. "Iscariot twists things until they make sense!"

"You're right, Heron," said Chanta, landing on his long bill. "Quite simply, this is how I see it. The man-cousin is so busy with this contraption, this Ageon, that a totally unexpected assault by us will make them listen."

"Listen to who?" demanded Iscariot. "Which one of us will speak? Athanasy himself said we have no power to speak to them outside the Council Ground."

"My man-cousin has already told them what our demands are. We are here now to prove what he said," the dog added, seriously.

Moko plodded closer to the raccoon and said, "The little butterfly is right. When do you suppose was the last time one of those Ageon man-cousins saw a buffalo . . . in the wild?"

"Yeah!" Little Paw chirped bravely. "Especially one with a prairie dog riding on his head."

"And I know for a sorry fact that no condor has ever flown these skies," Lordjahn added, stretching his mighty wings as he spoke, in a restless reverence for his children that never were.

"The man-cousin has always feared the howl of the wolf," Neera said proudly. "And here I shall freeze their hearts."

"So we have a circus act, a bird circling and a dog howling. I wish my heart would stop quaking in the utter terror of it all," Iscariot countered.

"You are blind, Iscariot!" Neera said, turning her back on him.

"You're wasting your time trying to convince him," concurred Fetchit-5.

Iscariot looked around the circle of Ageon-slayers. It was clear to him that either they knew something he didn't, or else their passions had finally overtaken them on to the suicidal end.

"What about her?" he asked, taking a swipe at the dancing butterfly. "What terrors will she create?"

"I may be small," Chanta said with resolve, "but I've more brothers and sisters than you would ever want to count."

It was then that Iscariot changed his strategy. He looked each one in the eye and said slowly, "Is it possible? Could I have lost sight of right and wrong? Look at me. In the midst of some of our greatest animals and still I falter." He crouched closer to the ground as though suddenly humbled and ashamed.

His turnaround silenced the group, until the Heron spoke. "What's that old story about the leopard changing his spots? As I recall, it can't be done."

Iscariot turned toward the Heron and said, "Since you're tossing out sayings, the one 'if you can't lick them, join them' comes to mind. Humans coined it. I suppose they're right."

"He's up to something," cautioned the Heron.

"Look, all I want is to get out of this damn Council business. So, the sooner we all work together on this ridiculous assault plan, the sooner I can get on with my life," Iscariot said, his voice now softer and logical.

"Then your heart has changed?" asked Neera.

Iscariot forced a smile and replied, "Only surrendered, wolf."

The sun began to set, casting Ageon in brilliant, golden sunlight. The times for dreams and songs grew closer.

"In my pack," said Neera softly, after the last rays had vanished, "we would sing our songs together. In so doing, we gained power and respect. But most of all, we learned the wisdom of trust and harmony."

So Neera started, raising her fine, massive head to the heavens. She closed her eyes and sung in her beloved fashion. Then one by one the others joined in, shy at first, for some had never sung before. But with Neera's powerful, beckoning voice to lead them, they all rejoiced in their songs together.

The eight-together song sounded curiously frightening, but the words were simple and clear:

The Will overtakes
Supersedes
Forgives and
Forms anew.
Ageon must die
The children of Ageon will
Never be.
The Will commands.
The Will survives.
WE are the Will.
Athanasy, Athanasy!
Be with us now.
Earth! Sky! Water!
Ours forevermore!

The song ended and the music of their thoughts slowly diminished until they were swallowed up by the protective trees, leaving them powerfully replenished. And, almost on cue, the sea of automatic lights flooded Ageon below.

"Uh . . . pardon me. But what was that I just heard?" The strange voice came low from the ground and had an odd lisp to it. The eight Council animals looked about, startled by the intruder.

"Show yourself or be trampled!" warned Moko, studying the darkness for the stranger.

"Hey, take it easy. I'm here soaking up leftover warmth from this rock. I've been here most of the day, but you all seemed too engrossed with Ageon and private wars to notice me. I don't normally eavesdrop, but you have to admit that a bevy of beasts such as yourselves raises a few eye-folds. Not that I care, mind you. It's just that we don't get many sightseers this far up the hill."

"What's he talking about?" Moko asked Fetchit-5.

The dog came forward and cautiously sniffed the rattlesnake. "Careful everyone!" she warned. "This kind can kill!" The dog stepped back slowly, keeping her eyes on the snake's mouth.

"Hey, listen . . . I can go home and get insults. All I asked was what was up." Offended, the snake rattled quietly as he prepared to leave.

"Wait," called Neera. "Please, the dog meant no harm. We are advised from birth to fear your fangs."

The snake smiled as he turned back toward the gathering. As the moon began to share its scanty light, the snake became more discernible. He was a long beauty, several years in length, with bright geometric designs decorating his back.

"What do you guys have against Ageon?" the snake asked. He had no need of mincing his words and deterring their meaning. "I mean, none of us was too thrilled when the man-cousin built it, but we've learned to adjust. That's what's special about us cold-blooders, you know. We adapt."

"What are you called?" asked the Heron, stepping closer.

"Rasslin. Mom always liked the name, but Dad lisps worse than I, so he never called me that. But, getting back to your chorus, I've never heard a song like that before. What gives?"

Feeling innately confident in revealing the Council cause and Its calling, the Heron stepped forward and addressed the snake formally. "Rasslin, have you ever heard of the Great Council of Beasts?"

"Hiss. Go away!" the snake said, smiling warily. "Didn't your mama ever tell you to never tease a snake?" But his serpentine smile faded as he perceived the solemn expressions of the others. "But, I thought that Council business was . . ." He paused, then laughed nervously. ". . . legend?"

"What else could make us sing together?" Neera asked, smiling toward Moko.

"You? You are the Council?" Rasslin raised his armored head. His eyes fell upon Little Paw and his tongue instinctively explored the air for scents of dinner. In response, the prairie dog shuddered and crept closer to Moko for protection.

Then, the Heron said, "Yes, we are part of the Council. To be brief, we are gathered to put an end to Ageon and its brethren. This tool of war is obsolete."

"Where were you ten years ago when we needed you?" Rasslin asked, arranging himself into a tighter, warmer coil. "I remember when this hill was a good place to live and raise our families. Then, Ageon came—piece by piece, layer by layer. Man is very clever how he begins with one stone and then, before you know it,

Ageon. So, we just moved further up the hill and invaded the lands of our distant friends and relatives. We tried to share what little food there was. But, we're only reptiles, you know. The strong lived, the weak died. But, after all this time, we have finally adjusted. So, if you've come to save us, you may as well go home."

"I'm sorry," said Lordjahn. "But our mission here is far greater than restoring your home. Ageon represents total devastation to all our kingdoms. We must make the man-cousins aware of the Will's dissatisfaction."

"Oh yeah. We get a lot of your type around here. Thousands of man-cousins have come, spoken their protests and left. Ageon thrives on it. Look, there was only one iron whale at first. Now, six. So, all I can do is hiss you good luck. You'll be needing it," Rasslin continued.

"In other words, you won't help us?" Iscariot snapped.

"Quite the contrary, consider me at your disposal," Rasslin said graciously, bowing his head slightly. "Even though you have a lot more to lose than I do. It takes a lot to wipe out a reptile, you know. Look, the only thing I fear right now is my wife's anger. The sun's long down and I haven't found our dinner yet."

He chuckled in harmony with his rattling tail and added, looking mischievously toward Little Paw. "We're nesting in a cozy little hole down the hill . . . feel free to drop in."

Little Paw stood on his hind legs and shouted, "Dinner jokes evolved out of my species years ago, Rasslin!"

"Just joshing, son," Rasslin said quietly. "I'd forgotten how easily ignited you prairie dogs are."

As the moon rose higher and the night-creatures' callings increased, the Council animals became aware of the hour and grew impatient to rest before their assault began.

Sensing their weariness, Rasslin said, "Tell me, before I leave to face my wife's wrath, what can I do to lend a hand, figuratively speaking, of course."

"I've been thinking about that," Lordjahn said. "Even if a snake is harmless, the man-cousins have long feared your crawling cousins."

"Don't you just love it? All I need to do is faintly rattle and a man-cousin nearby runs for his life! I could be in the best humor, could not care less about taking a bite, and I can smell the man-cousins' fear for a mile!" Rasslin chuckled.

"Well, if you could gather your family and friends and arrange to, at sundown tomorrow say, begin rattling all together, then the keepers of Ageon will surely become frightened," Lordjahn continued.

"A grand idea!" Chanta laughed.

"That would scare me right out of my skin!" Fetchit-5 howled. Then he caught Rasslin's eye and added, "No pun."

"Could you do it?" the Heron asked the snake.

Rasslin was slowly rattling to himself as he thought. "With a night and a day to spread the word, I'm sure it could be arranged," he said enthusiastically.

"Then it's settled. We add the serpents to our army," Neera said. "Rasslin, our plan is to meet back here tomorrow at sundown, so we'll be gathered to hear your chorus."

"Great. If I don't show, it'll be because my dear wife killed me tonight," Rasslin joked as he began to leave. "It's been an honor." He slithered a short distance, turned back and added, "The Great Council of Beasts. Well, I'll be damned." With that, he commenced his narrow path downhill, rehearsing his explanations and apologies to his wife.

The animals began to fashion their nests, keeping close together. "Who will keep the watch?" Moko asked shortly.

The animals stopped their nesting and looked about, considering. "Well," said the Heron, "I suggest we take turns."

"Right," Iscariot agreed. "And I'll take the first watch. I'm nocturnal anyway. It's not likely I'll fall asleep."

"Yes, but who'll watch you?" Fetchit-5 asked.

"Look, I said I'm with you now! Take me at my word!" the raccoon cried out in his own defense. "We've been through this. I give up! I'm with you. I'll take the first watch."

The wolf and the condor exchanged glances. But it was the Heron who spoke. "Very well, Iscariot. The dog was only joking anyway. We'll sleep. You watch. Wake me before the moon has gone behind those trees and I'll relieve you." He took a long, deep look into the raccoon's eyes, searching for a hint of treason.

Iscariot smiled back and said, "Good. Sleep well. You can count on me."

It took only a short time for the seven creatures to fall into a deep slumber. Iscariot, seated on a high rock, watched each animal bathed in moonlight.

An aura of peace filled their camp as each animal sank deeper and deeper into dreams of power and weakness, trust and betrayal, success and destruction.

Then, when the moon was at its fullest, Iscariot stretched his legs and softly jumped down from his post. Silently, he crept over to the dog, who was lost blissfully in paw-twitching dreams of Sayble. The raccoon lowered his head and spoke into the dog's ear, whispering barely above a thought. "Never take me at my word, you fool! No Will can ever weaken me!"

Without a last look around, Iscariot fled the camp with deceitful speed and disappeared into the black harborage of the woods.

CHAPTER TWENTY-THREE

A s SOON AS HE WOKE, the Heron knew that the raccoon had fled. He felt no anger for having again trusted the beast, but rather a smooth feeling of satisfaction knowing his dealings with Iscariot were, at long last, over. He realized no time could be wasted in anger or regret with so much at stake in the next few hours. So, when he awakened the others, it was with a calm, almost humorous explanation that Fetchit-5 had been right. Who would watch Iscariot watching everyone else?

"How could we have been taken in by that wretch?" growled Neera. "Deception!"

"He's gone and that's all," the Heron cautioned. "We can't waste time over him now!"

"Just as well, if you ask me," Fetchit-5 said, yawning.

"Yes, we're better off. But do you suppose he'll try to work against us? Take Ageon's side?" Chanta asked, flapping the stiffening, cool night air out of her delicate wings.

Emerging from his nest, Lordjahn said, "No, he's too smart to stick around. He's far away from here, you can be sure."

"Probably slinking back to his master's door," Neera growled.

Without wasting any more of their precious time on the raccoon's betrayal, their eyes fell upon Ageon below and their mission ahead became clearer.

"I wonder what songs the man-cousin sings before battle," Neera said softly. "Or do they sing at all?"

"They sing, all right," Fetchit-5 replied, rolling her eyes to the heavens. "Lord, do they sing!"

The others smiled at her human-like expressions.

"Well," the dog continued brightly, "any fleas who want to abandon ship better jump off now!"

The others laughed nervously. The Heron flew in front to face the rest and said, "I'll oversee each of you, assist where I can and co-ordinate from above." He paused. "Well, all I can say is, do your best, each of you."

They each looked to the other, drawing themselves closer for a prayer of safety. "Remember," the Heron added softly, "the Will commands it."

And so, each in a different direction, the Council animals descended the hill and approached Ageon, each embellishing their plans as they stalked the enemy.

That morning, Helen Forbes was, as she was nearly every morning, early for work. Long before she became affiliated with Ageon, she had nurtured the habit of rising before the sun to organize her thoughts for the day's work ahead. After driving down the oh-too-familiar road, she stopped at the check-in booth, then headed into the civilian employees' parking ahead and neatly pulled her late-model import into the spot prestigiously labeled "Dr. Forbes."

Before getting out, she twisted the rear-view mirror toward her to check her hair. At fifty-two, she used no make-up, thinking it was a waste of time in her all-consuming scientific world. She repositioned a few stray gray hairs and wondered why, after nearly thirty years of the same short-cropped hairstyle, did these same few hairs insist on wandering from conformity? "Oh, ritual," she supposed aloud as she returned the mirror and reached for her briefcase. She flicked off her headlights and got out, locking the vehicle behind her.

Her dress was simple, as she had never given in to flamboyant fancies. "Efficient and conservative," she wished to describe herself, while others might have referred to her as "neglected, but neat." She was on the heavy side, rather sturdy and short. She walked with determination, appearing almost top-heavy, facing the world nose first. Her low pump heels made hollow clops on the pavement as she approached the employees' check-in. The sky was lightening to a baby blue with the promise of a warm spring day.

Helen took a nonchalant glance toward the docks, failing to be impressed by the size of the nuclear submarines. She had worked around such naval fortresses nearly twenty years. But what did catch her eye was the immense wingspan of a bird which circled directly above the submarines. She stopped to watch the bird, mentally paging through species and phyla in an automatic effort to classify the creature. She squinted, fascinated in the perfection of its circling upward flight, and awed by its size.

Then, from out of seemingly nowhere, another bird, one which she immediately recognized as a heron, circled with the other. At first, she thought the two would fight, as though to regain a lost territory. Instead, the two giant birds simply flew together, almost as if aerial comrades.

Helen paused a moment longer, this time her scientific curiosity aroused. Then, abruptly aware of the formulas and tests awaiting in her lab, she slowly began walking toward the check-in point.

"Good morning, Dr. Forbes," the guard said. "Beautiful sunrise, isn't it?"

"Yes, it is, Jim," she answered, catching a last glimpse of the two circling birds. "Did you see those birds over there?" she asked, pointing toward the bay.

"Well, there was one huge one up there a few minutes ago. There's two now?" He poked his head outside. "I've lived around these parts for nearly fifty-five years and I can't ever remember seeing a bigger bird. What do you suppose that big one is?" the guard asked, returning to his post.

"Well, the smaller one looks like a heron. But that other one . . ." she paused. "Well," she smiled. "No matter, is it? Just enjoy it while it's around. It'll probably be on its way any time, now that the sun is rising. Have a good day, Jim."

Helen signed in and disappeared into the security entrance where she was obliged to undergo the detector systems. After she received clearance, she breezed through the long corridor that led past the general administration office and eventually to her small desk in the biology laboratory.

CHAPTER TWENTY-FOUR

Lost in the depths of the hillside woods, Chanta the butterfly called to the multitude of her brothers and sisters. And, answering the call, came countless others from countless families, so that, by noontide, virtually every color ever conceived by nature's palette was represented in the dark secrecy of the forest. A few spears of sunlight escaped the grasp of the thick overhead fir branches and the butterfly colors they caught were glorious. As their numbers grew, so grew the low, gentle hum as their wings moved incessantly. Chanta's calling ceased and still they arrived from every corner of paradise. It was as though they had all been awaiting the beckoning, as though the Will had touched them each personally, foretelling the event.

"And here they all are," Chanta whispered, smiling to herself. "Here they are . . . proclaiming me their general and ready to fly into battle."

It was an overwhelming feeling of power and Chanta knew then exactly why she had been chosen. She knew she was more than capable of leading her brethren.

When each wing finally came to rest, the forest floor was completely covered with their vibrant life. Each butterfly listened intently as Chanta spoke.

"Words fail," she humbly began. "I am Chanta and it is not within my power to express my gratitude. The Council praises your bravery in responding to my call. All you must remember is, together we are powerful. Separately, we are catalogued items in a collection, neatly pressed under glass. Follow me. Do what I do and by sundown, the man-cousin will have heard the thunder of our wings."

With that, Chanta flew above the rest, leading them toward Ageon.

From a distance, the Heron watched and listened carefully. He was proud of Chanta and he was moved beyond description at the powerful beauty of the gathering of butterflies. As the millions rose in flight, a breeze from their consolidated wings cleansed the forest and gently shook the branch from which the Heron watched, reminding him again . . . the power of the Will.

The Heron waited until the last one had vanished from the area, leaving the forest deathly quiet, as though the trees themselves were reflecting how, for one brief moment in history, they had experienced the entire spectrum of nature's colors. The bird shook away the bristling flash of inspiring awe, promising himself he would hold the memory for another day when the weather seemed endlessly drab and there were no Ageonic dragons to slay.

The Heron emerged from the treetops in time to behold the breathtaking sight of the thousands upon thousands of butterflies soaring toward Ageon. They seemed to move as one giant being, rising and falling with the currents, like coverlets of flowers upon a gentle sea.

Chanta led them on one circling voyage around the entire complex—appraising the enemy, planning the attack. It was the hour of the man-cousins' noon meal and many of those who tended Ageon had gathered to eat in a garden. Well-fenced, it contained benches and trails and, by the sound of the genial laughter, it was an area of great relaxation for them.

Chanta was the first to land, easing herself gracefully down upon the center of a picnic table. Two women who occupied the table seemed delighted to have such elegant company land so close. Then, one by one, and ten by ten, then hundred by hundred, Chanta's comrades followed. They landed on every inch of space . . . ground, fence, table, and finally the man-cousins themselves. Within a moment's time, the area was covered.

Screeching and swatting at the colorful beauties, everyone rushed back into the building.

"God, I've never seen anything like it!" gasped one soldier, watching the invasion from inside.

"I've heard of the seven-year locust, but this is ridiculous!" another person commented with a nervous laugh.

"Look at that! They're all over my lunch!"

"Oh, Sadie," the first woman responded, "don't be such a priss! What harm can butterflies do? Dr. Forbes, what kind of butterflies are those?"

Helen, who had been summoned to witness the phenomenon, seemed as perplexed as the others. "Well," she began, "obviously, it's a species of butterfly that swarms."

"*A* species?" Sadie asked sarcastically. "Must be a thousand species! They all look different to me."

The lunch bell rang, to Helen's relief, for she had no more answers to the barrage of questions.

One young man lingered, though, asking, "What do you suppose they want? Are they just hungry?"

The biologist sighed, indicating that she really had no idea at all, but answered with feigned authority. "No doubt they were attracted to the garden while migrating. That's all." She took a pack of gum out of her lab coat and absently unwrapped a piece while staring out the window. "Look there," she pointed, "they're starting to leave already."

"Just passing through, eh?"

"I guess so," Dr. Forbes answered, walking toward the entrance to the garden. She carefully opened the door with mythical Pandora memories running through her scientific mind.

As gracefully as they had arrived, so did they leave. Chanta rose first and was soon followed by great bunches of comrades. Their astronomical numbers grouped together like rustling fall leaves in an ill-kept country garden. It was, in all, a fantastic thing for Helen Forbes to witness, but also disturbing, for she, a biologist, had no explanation at all for such odd behavior.

When the last one had disappeared, she stepped out into the garden, hoping to find a few who had died in the swarm. She was a scientist who preferred to deal in tangibles rather than theories and felt that if she could only study one under a microscope, she could better understand the incident.

Her search proved fruitless . . . not so much as a wing fragment was left behind. She looked up at the sky, as though an explanation could be found written in the clouds. Then, she recalled the odd sighting of the two enormous birds earlier that day.

"Well," she assured herself aloud, "must be a full moon." Then, she smiled at her empty logic, knowing that nine out of ten scientists, when attempting to explain the unexplainable, jokingly blamed it on the moon.

When Dr. Forbes returned to her laboratory, she was greeted by Commander Howard Orinsky, Ageon's commanding officer and, in the strictest sense, upper naval management. Having risen to great military heights in comparatively few years, he was known for his cut-throat techniques in dealing with threatening sub-officers—a man who monitored his personnel, whether naval or civilian, more closely than the radiation levels in his own tastefully appointed executive office.

Helen regretted having to pass the man in the halls, let alone the prospect of dealing with him on a direct basis. She sensed that her own passive nature chafed his aggressive attitude toward naval affairs. She felt her own personal dedication to science was all that was necessary for a successful civilian career. Had she longed for the regimen of military life, she could have enrolled in that machinery thirty years ago.

She had been overlooked for advancement on several occasions, but with her complacent understanding of civil service, it failed to upset her. She was, after all, a scientist with the good of mankind to look after . . . why bother with such vanities as promotions?

But Orinsky had the Pentagon to answer to for the success or failures of his staff and he knew, of the thousands who tended the nuclear subs, Dr. Forbes's biology lab had tremendous public relations potential.

"Oh, Commander Orinsky," she said, attempting to sound pleasantly surprised to see him, "what brings you down from the War Room?"

"I'll get right down to brass tacks," he began. Helen fought back the impulse to cast her eyes to the heavens and carelessly laugh at his favored trite expression.

"Very well," she answered, this time attempting to sound scientifically serious.

"I assume you're preparing an explanation for all those moths." He looked directly into her eyes and Helen was sure that, behind his pursed lips, he was grinding his teeth.

"The butterflies? Why? They've left. But, if you need an explanation, I assume they were merely migrating in a swarm. You know, similar to the ordinary bee." Helen watched him as he considered her explanation. "If you wish, I'll do some extra monitoring, but I doubt if anything out of the ordinary will show up."

"I would expect you to do that," he commented. "You have to realize that the environmentalists are always chomping at the bit for quirks like this."

"I'm in my thirty-first year working as a biologist in nuclear science, Commander. I know all about the environmentalists."

"Good," he said with a snap. "And what do you know about buffaloes?"

She looked up at him, caught totally off guard. "What?" she asked.

"I just got a call from the guard at the front gate. He says there's a rampaging buffalo charging at cars!"

"A buffalo!" Helen cried in disbelief. "What's a buffalo doing around here?"

"That is what *you* are supposed to tell *me!*" Orinsky said.

"Have you seen it? Are they sure it's a buffalo? Well, obviously it's domestic," she stammered.

"You're the biologist, Dr. Forbes. I suppose we'd better go see." He stepped aside to allow Helen through the door.

They walked without speaking down the corridor, up a flight of stairs which led to an outside viewing platform. The warm, salty air was a relief to Helen as they walked to the rail where several standing sets of telescopes awaited them. From all appearances on that bright and warm spring day, everything seemed as usual. The low hum of the various machines in motion droned on unaware. From their vantage point and with the aid of the telescopes, nearly every sector of Ageon's acres could be seen. Orinsky wasted no time admiring the day, but seized a telescope and trained it on the front gate and the civilian parking lot beyond.

Likewise, Helen took a telescope and began searching for this buffalo intruder. "I don't see anything," she said.

"Me either," he agreed. Then, he walked over to a box, opened it and withdrew the phone inside. "Give me the front gate," he ordered. After a slight pause, he continued, "Commander Orinsky here. What's this about a buffalo? I'm on the viewing platform and I don't see any buffalo." Orinsky listened to the guard's explanation, then said, "Good. I want to know the minute it returns."

"What did he say?" Helen asked, squinting through the telescope.

"It was a buffalo, all right. Ramming the hell out of the gate . . . with some small furry thing on top of its head, no less! Obviously a prank. I tell you those damn protesters get crazier every day!"

Helen was intently watching the smooth gliding pattern of the giant bird, still circling over two of the nuclear leviathans. "It's a condor! I don't believe it, but that's what it is!" she shouted with an almost childlike enthusiasm. "Look, up there, circling over the water."

Orinsky looked through his telescope, took a brief glance at the bird, then said, "I thought those were extinct."

"Highly endangered, but not quite extinct yet and certainly not indigenous to this area." She looked at Orinsky and added, "Just like the buffalo."

Then, before either of them could draw a conclusion, a piercing howl came from the right. Another howl, nearly identical, came from the left.

"Now what?" Orinsky bellowed. "This is ridiculous! I have better things to do than to play animal lotto all day!" He placed his hands on his hips and paced the area while he thought, looking very much like a nervous ensign aching for his artillery team to finally hit the target.

Helen kept searching through the telescope for the possible sources of the canine howlings.

"All right," Orinsky began calmly, "tell the members of your unit that I want to meet with them in one hour in the Security Room."

"Yes, sir," she answered meekly. "Anything else?"

"There better not be," he warned. Then speaking back into the phone, he asked for Security and bellowed out his command to find the agitators and deal with them.

It was exactly 2:30 when Helen Forbes and five other members of the ecology/biology team entered the Security Room. There were uniformed guards sitting in the room along with Colonel Olsen, the Chief Security Officer. On each wall of the room were several closed-circuit television screens, each showing an area around or within the facility. The scientists were asked to sit at the long white briefing table to await the arrival of Commander Orinsky.

Orinsky arrived, followed by three other people, none of whom Helen recognized. Without formalities, he began. "For those of you who may not be aware, Ageon seems to be the target of a joke of some kind. Now, so far today, we have been assaulted, if you care to use that term, by an army of butterflies, a maniac buffalo, a giant bird, and two or more howling dogs."

"Has there been any damage?" someone asked.

"So far, only minimal damage to a few cars in the civilian parking lot and a couple of dents in the outer gates," he answered. "Now, Dr. Forbes assures me that the butterflies were probably just migrating and this I will dismiss as coincidence. But, these other animals have obviously been trained to howl and ram things as someone's sick idea of a joke or protest." He walked about the room and occasionally glanced up at the screens.

"Now then," he continued, "the reason I've called you together here is to inform you that we are already working on finding the people behind these ludicrous acts and dealing with them legally. Now, both the security and biology departments will be under scrutiny when the press gets hold of this one. And, in case you had any doubt, the press will get hold of this. Now, in order to second-guess any further damage we could suffer from bad copy, especially in light of the fact that we have two subs due in for re-fueling, the public relations department is working on a press release. They'll be in touch with you to tell you what our official response will be."

"Sir?" a guard said, pointing to a screen. They all turned and looked up and saw what appeared to be a wolf, digging at the base of Ageon's outer fence. They gathered around the screen.

"And here, sir," another guard said, pointing to another screen.

This time, it was a large dog, standing squarely on an expensive little car parked in the Naval Personnel Parking Lot, howling to the heavens. The convertible top sagged under the weight of the animal and the dog pawed at it urgently between howls.

"That's *my* car!" Orinsky roared, staring at the screen. He turned to Olsen and ordered, "Get a guard on that mutt. And I want to know how that dog got past the front gate in the first place!"

Olsen left the room, followed by two Marines.

"That will be all for now," Orinsky said, dismissing the group as he left the room.

As they were rising to leave, a team biologist turned to Helen and said, "That car cost him a bundle. Five'll get you ten we'll be dissecting a dog within the hour."

From his vantage point above Ageon, Lordjahn was the first to see several armed soldiers approach the area of the parking lot where Fetchit-5 was howling. In the swiftest of soars, the condor was upon the dog, gasping, "Run! Run!"

Fetchit-5 immediately jumped down, leaving the soft top miserably ripped. She ran with all her might along the fence toward the gate.

The soldiers were awed by the impressive sight of Lordjahn, but before they could raise a weapon or gain on the escaping dog, the condor was approaching them. The closer he dove at the men, the larger and more powerful he appeared.

The condor screeched as his wings tangled with the heads and arms of the guards. In their confused horror, they were unable to draw their weapons and Lordjahn rose for one more attack. He plummeted down, screamed with all the anger of his slain ancestors and attacked the men once more.

He seized one of their hats and, rising, tore it to shreds with his mighty, merciless talons.

And, before they had the chance to comprehend the sudden, savage attack, Lordjahn was above and gone and calling out to the dog, the wolf, the Heron, and the buffalo, "Run! Run! God, run!"

CHAPTER TWENTY-FIVE

EARLIER THAT MORNING, with Little Paw riding atop, Moko had made it to the hill minutes after the guard at the gate had drawn his weapon. The buffalo had not recognized the danger the rifle represented, but Little Paw instinctively screeched retreat when he saw the war-stick.

"Well, shouldn't we try to break through the gate again?" Moko asked innocently.

"Hey, that was a war-stick that man-cousin was aiming at us!" Little Paw said, jumping down off his furry helm. "Look, we did our best. What good are we to the Council if we get killed?"

"Oh. I thought we were expected to get killed if it meant getting the message through," Moko replied in simple calf-like tones.

"Well," Little Paw continued, "there's a difference between honest sacrifice and out-and-out suicide. Look, a target as big as yourself better stay in the woods. But you were grand, Moko, the way you charged the gate and all! How's your head?" The buffalo lowered it and Little Paw inspected a few gashes. "You better give your head a chance to stop throbbing."

"My head doesn't throb," Moko replied, shaking his head slowly.

"Well, it should. You better lay low. Since you're the only buffalo around."

"Lay low?"

"Never mind, Moko. Just hide. Understand?"

Moko sighed heavily and took a grudging snap at a tuft of grass. "Oh, if you say so," he said. "But where are you going?"

"Well, since I'm so much smaller, I thought I'd go back down there and see if I can eavesdrop on that war-sticking man-cousin at the gate. Maybe I can hear a snatch of a conversation they're having. At any rate, I'll see if I can find out what they're thinking and planning."

"About what?"

"Are you sure your head isn't throbbing? About us, of course! Surely we must have them talking by now." Little Paw sat on his haunches and pointed down into the valley.

"You'll take care, won't you?" Moko asked, taking a few steps deeper into the forest.

"Now, don't go looking so sad," Little Paw said softly. "This thing has only just begun and we can't afford to lose you so early in the game. I'll take care, you can bet your mane on that! After all, it'll be up to my own legs to escape now," he chuckled.

"Call if you need help?"

"No, I thought I'd scream."

"You'd better not come back with a war-stick hole in you," Moko added, disappearing at last into the thick woods with hesitant steps.

"Not me!" the prairie dog called back confidently. Then, he said to himself with an uncomfortable swallow, "Wouldn't be enough of me left to come back at all!"

On his brief trek back down to the armed keeper of Ageon, Little Paw had recollections of his life before weaseling his way into the Council plots. He thought about his modest beginnings and his constant longing for greatness. And now, he found himself treading beyond his greatest dreams.

He stopped as he considered his diminutive size next to the powerful Ageon and quaked slightly at the absurd comparison. Then, as he beheld the calm, constant flight of the great Lordjahn, circling high and steadfast above, he was comforted. "Good old Lordjahn," he whispered respectfully. "Circling your prey, allowing it the time it needs to die." Then, knowing his task was still ahead of him, the prairie dog continued on his journey.

When he arrived at the black macadam of the neatly surfaced road, Little Paw sniffed it cautiously, recalling nightmarish stories of flattened little creatures who failed to properly navigate such obstacles. There was a well-trimmed row of bushes next to the guard house and relatively little activity on the road. The little creature crept closer until he was finally able to hide himself in the hedge, just a few feet away from the guard's station.

When the guard's phone rang, breaking a dozing silence, the prairie dog nearly leaped out of his skin, but was able to contain a yelp which begged to surface. His tiny heart was racing and Little Paw thought for a moment he might faint. As the animal got hold of himself, he stretched closer to the entrance of the booth to eavesdrop on the man-cousin. It was a curious conversation, Little Paw thought, for only the one man-cousin seemed to be speaking:

"Yes, sir . . . I'm aware of that, sir . . . yes, sir. Yes, I did talk to Orinsky and I told him the same thing I'm telling you. A buffalo was down here ramming cars and my gate. There were several witnesses, like the people who are on their way to talk to you now. Yes, sir. It was their car that got the worst. Yes, sir, very angry. Yes, sir. Thank you, sir."

Then, as oddly as it had begun, the talk ended, leaving Little Paw distraught with curiosity and no more informed than before. He decided to wait in his hiding place for a while longer and study the situation at hand.

Minutes pass slower for smaller beings and it seemed like days before Little Paw heard the familiar howlings of Neera and Fetchit-5. He was comforted by their nearby, supportive presence, reminding him that he was not alone in the plot.

With the sun to warm his hiding bush and with boredom to convince him, Little Paw finally dropped off to sleep. It was an old habit, mid-afternoon naps, and one which had, regrettably, received little attention since the day of Moko's calling. But his dreams of dark, cool burrows and pups all heroically named after him were wiped away instantly when the prairie dog was jolted awake by Lordjahn's urgent warning, "Run! Run!"

Little Paw quickly snapped awake, immediately terrified and, for a moment, unaware of where he was.

"Run! Run!" the condor shouted as he zoomed low to the ground in search of his comrades.

Little Paw peeked his head out of the bush, looked about, then dashed across the pavement and headed up the hill toward the woods. He tried desperately to retrace his path, but realized in his racing fear that he was running in circles.

Finally, he stopped next to a large rock to catch his breath and get his bearings. Looking up, he saw no trace of either Lordjahn or the Heron and the skies were quiet. He looked about and saw the woods were still far away and he silently damned his faulty sense of direction. Then, the wind swooped by with the scent of even more terror. The prairie dog flattened himself low to the ground waiting for another sniff of the nearby danger. The scent was not altogether unfamiliar. Then, he heard footsteps from the other side of the rock. They padded closer and Little Paw could hear the creature's ground-sniffing. His heart froze. It was a dog. He forced his legs to move and he broke toward the hill.

The dog, much larger and bulkier than Fetchit-5, took chase, arrogantly oblivious to his master's hoarse entreaties to return.

"Casey! Casey! Damn it, get back here!" the man called out, running after his dog, waving his arms and a broken leash.

Heading for the woods atop the hill, Little Paw prayed if his heart were to give out, let it be before the creature was upon him. He was hardly able to utter a screech of terror, but gasped a few screams for help.

"Moko!" he called out, feeling the wind being pulled out of him. "Help me, Moko!"

He scrambled about as best as he could, knowing that his only hope would be to out-turn the dog, and perhaps, by some miracle, stumble into a burrow.

So utterly confused and exhausted was the prairie dog, that he barely recognized the racing form of Iscariot as he darted past him, diving for the dog's throat. When the terrifying sound of the dog and raccoon in combat reached Little Paw, he dropped to the ground, looking up at the two animals as they tore into each other's coats.

The dog, at first confused and frightened at the sudden attack, took on his opponent with a ferocious welcome. Large tufts of bloodied fur were tossed about; one landed not far from Little Paw. Horrified, he recognized it to be from Iscariot's pampered coat.

The dog's man-cousin had finally arrived, and he also stood, confounded and terrified. The sight of his pet battling the raccoon was sickening and the man watched as helplessly as did Little Paw. He screamed the dog's name over and over until his voice was practically gone.

Finally, the battle cries quieted as the dog and the raccoon tired. The dog had lost his challenging howl and was only able to utter pathetic yelps and seemed now willing to hear his master's pleas to stop.

Iscariot backed up a few steps, and nearly lost his balance as he took a last swipe at the whimpering dog's bloodied face.

Cautiously and with a gentle heave, the man-cousin picked up his wounded animal, keeping an eye on the raccoon, who faintly hissed victory at both of them. Then, summoning a last glint of energy, Iscariot ran past the speechless Little Paw and disappeared again into the woods.

Little Paw, eager to tell the other animals what had happened to Iscariot, began running toward their meeting place. He knew that he must bring the others quickly, for Iscariot, the warrior, had left an agonizing trail of blood.

Once the prairie dog caught the proper, familiar scent of his comrades' trail, his journey back was quick and direct. He arrived to find the others waiting impatiently for him and they welcomed his return with questions of their own.

"There you are, Little Paw, little friend," Moko said, trotting up to him. "I was worried. What did you find out?"

"Wait a minute! Wait a minute!" the prairie dog gasped. "Iscariot!"

"Iscariot?" echoed the Heron, feeling his back feathers rise in contempt. "You saw Iscariot?"

"Yes! He just saved my life!" he cried.

"Now slow down, Little Paw," Lordjahn said gently. "Take some deep breaths and tell us what happened."

Little Paw paused to catch his breath, then began in a shaky, weeping voice the explanation of how the raccoon had appeared from nowhere to challenge the dog.

"Where is he now?" asked Fetchit-5, ready to leave to find Iscariot.

"I don't know. He ran off into the woods. But he was bleeding something awful. We have to find him! He needs help," Little Paw pleaded.

"It's the last thing I would have expected from him," the Heron said, not sure whether to be shocked or angry for the delay. "All right, Moko and Little Paw, the three of us will go find him."

"And Neera," insisted Little Paw.

"And Neera," agreed the Heron. "Lordjahn and Fetchit-5 will stay here and wait for Chanta and Rasslin."

With Little Paw riding atop Moko, the four left, following the prairie dog's directions. They had not gone very far when Neera's keen nose picked up the blood-scent of Iscariot. The Heron, finding it too difficult to spot the raccoon through the density of the trees, landed high above the wolf, who had locked in on the fresh scent.

"How far, Neera?" the Heron called down. "I can't see much from here. . . ."

"Close," the wolf answered, keeping her nose close to the ground. "His wounds must be deep . . . so much blood."

Following close behind was Moko, crashing through the bracken to keep up. Little Paw finally jumped down to avoid being wiped off by the thick branches.

Then Neera paused, turned abruptly to the left and whispered, "He's there, under that bush."

"Iscariot?" Little Paw called, rushing past Neera. "It's us."

The bushes rustled slightly, but no answer came from within. The Heron flew down to join the others. They looked at each other with uncertain fear.

Then Neera pulled a branch aside and exposed the feverishly panting form of the wounded Iscariot. Little Paw was horrified to see the condition of the raccoon-hero and Moko turned his head away, unable to look.

Little Paw crept closer and whispered, "We're here now, Iscariot. That was a wonderful thing you did. But we're here to take you back to the Council Ground where Athanasy will care for you . . . work his magic and make you well."

Without lifting his head or opening his swollen eyes, Iscariot replied in a deep but trembling voice, "No . . . I'm beyond the Council. I always was beyond the Council. I feel no pain, so stop your weeping, Little Paw. Neera, Moko, take your friend away. Heron, I smell your presence."

"Yes, I am here," the bird answered solemnly.

"Am I absolved? Lying here, I thought of you. I knew you wouldn't miss my death, Heron. I knew you'd show up." Then, he paused and caught a precious gasp of air. "Oh God . . . how an animal's heart aches," he said, his voice lessening with life. He flickered an eye open for a precious last look. ". . . how an animal's heart breaks when it has felt . . . a human embrace . . . it feels so . . . warm . . . you can't hate me for that."

He stopped and Neera had to look away as the raccoon shed a bloody tear.

"Iscariot," cried Little Paw, "Please, don't talk . . . save your energy for the journey back."

The raccoon forced a smile and said, "No, no journey back. I journey from here forward—never back. . . ."

"Do you wish to die alone?" asked the Heron, pausing and looking away.

"Yesssss," came the thankful, gasping reply. His voice was almost gone. "All for a rodent . . . alone . . . yesssss." And he closed his eyes to the world for the last time and awaited death. Neera respectfully replaced the branch which concealed his death-nest while the others stood silent, unable to speak.

"It will be dark soon, Neera. We must leave," the Heron finally said.

"We can't just leave him here!" Little Paw gasped, rushing toward the death-lair.

"No, Little Paw," Neera said, preventing the prairie dog's intrusion. "Let him Complete."

Shaking, Little Paw looked up into Neera's eyes and understood. He looked over to Moko who, unashamed, let out a great cry.

"Come, Moko, Little Paw," Neera whispered, leading them away.

With sundown approaching, their journey back was quick and silent. Little Paw's only thoughts were of Iscariot, who was await-ing the peace of death . . . of the bravery the raccoon had found . . . of his curious smile when he spoke of a human's embrace.

In their camp overlooking Ageon, the Heron related to the others what had been Iscariot's fate. Chanta had yet to return and there had not been any word from Rasslin, the rattlesnake. The sunset was cloaked in silence and each animal felt ill at ease and restless. There was a breeze, which, like the silence, was uncharacteristic of sundown. They quietly stood, watching Ageon and reflecting on the adventures of that day.

Then, as the evening lights began to surround Ageon, making night into day, there came from every corner of the valley a concert of rattling, accompanied at first by a faraway thunder. Rasslin led the powerful symphony, having called his brethren to serenade Ageon at sundown with their most terrifying warning.

It was as though all of nature had silenced so that the world could hear the snakes and take heed. And indeed, every living creature in the valley fell briefly under the hypnotic spell of the thousands of serpents. Even the constant low hum of Ageon itself seemed to diminish, as if to listen to the snakes' song.

The rattling became louder, more intense and terrifying. Then, from the hills behind Ageon, Chanta returned with the millions of colorful brothers and sisters. As before, they flew gently as one, in a most unthreatening and beautiful pattern. They approached the high, proud foreheads of one of the nuclear whales and laced themselves around them. In symmetrical designs, the butterflies landed, wings touching, until they circled the deadly beasts several times over, adorning them with more color than ever could have been imagined.

Hundreds of man-cousins came out of the many buildings to witness the decorations and to define the continually increasing rattling. Then, as the final light of day left the valley, the snakes ceased their song and the butterflies left as harmoniously and as suddenly as they had arrived.

And the valley was as before.

The Council animals drew themselves together to share their stories of the day. And when a most agonizingly long rumble of thunder passed through the valley—they knew, each in their way, that this was the Will's thunder upon them—summoning the soul of Iscariot home and into the arms of infinity.

CHAPTER TWENTY-SIX

THE TALL, PROTECTIVE trees that graced the Council Ground barely felt the evening breeze that night, and the thunder that resounded through Ageon's valley was merely a muffled disgruntlement from the faraway clouds.

Charles Sayble had placed several lanterns around to afford his camp more light. Then, he set up his artist's easel and prepared the numerous old and cracking tubes of oils. His campfire encased Athanasy in warm, friendly light as the great beast watched the man with interest.

"Now, I want you to assume your most stately stance, Athanasy," Sayble said, positioning himself on a folding stool in front of his easel.

"Will this take long?" Athanasy asked with hesitancy in his voice.

"Not if you hold still," replied Sayble. "Ah, come on now, you agreed I could paint you. I promise it won't hurt you a bit."

The elk took his position, but then paused uncomfortably, as if listening to a distant whispering voice. He lowered his head until his powerful antlers pointed nearly straight up. Then, he said gravely, "One is gone."

Sayble looked up. "One what is gone?"

"I have lost one of my precious few, one of my Council animals.

Wait. Listen . . ." Athanasy brought his head up again and looked to the heavens. "We are now without one."

Sayble stood up, fearing for his own Fetchit-5 and asked, "Who?"

"Silence, Sayble! I'm listening to the death-cry." He paused, searching for the invisible sound. "It is Iscariot. Iscariot is dead," the elk said slowly and with solemn dignity.

"Do you know how?" Sayble asked quietly, as he mixed his oils.

"His soul has passed through me. I only know he died in grace."

"I never would have guessed *he'd* die in grace."

"He was chosen by the Will. He has served his purpose. He has completed his cycle."

"Well, you have an interesting view of death," muttered the old man.

"The firelight is going out. Do you still want to paint me?"

"Yeah, sure. Just stand where you are." They were both silent while Sayble sketched Athanasy's profile on the canvas. For nearly an hour, the elk stood motionless as Sayble painted.

Then, breaking the solemn mood, Athanasy asked, "Are you good at what you do?"

"You mean painting? Hell no! Oh, I can paint numbers and letters . . . you know, signs and all. Oh, maybe then again, you wouldn't know about signs. Anyway, painting made me a decent living for years and years. Now it's what I do for relaxation. 'Hobby', we man-cousins call it."

"Hobby," Athanasy repeated.

Again, the two were silent. Sayble added more logs to his fire to keep a steady light on his subject. Then, he said, "Tell me more about this cycle-completing. You know, what you said about Iscariot."

"It is our belief that every animal has a purpose to its life. When that purpose is realized or accomplished, the creature dies in peace knowing it has completed its cycle," the great elk answered simply.

"But what about the animals who are killed before they accomplish this?" Sayble asked casually, keeping his eyes on the blending colors on his canvas. But he listened intently for the elk's reply.

"Perhaps, Sayble, you have a specific instance in mind," Athanasy commented, looking deeply into Sayble's eyes.

"Well," he began, putting down his pallet and brush. "When I was a boy, not more than seven or eight, I killed a bird. I used my father's hunting slingshot and knocked that robin clean off a fence post. Never knew what hit him." Sayble paused as he vividly recalled the incident. "I can still feel that first . . . oh, what's the word? Well, it was a pain. 'Way down deep." He paused again, sniffed and asked, "So, how could that robin have realized its purpose in life?"

"Are you about finished, man-cousin? My legs beg to move."

"Oh, sure. I can put the finishing touches on tomorrow." Sayble took a rag tied to his belt and wiped paint off his hands.

"May I look at it?" Athanasy asked, stepping around the easel.

Sayble stepped back and watched as the gazed at the canvas. "Well?" he asked.

"Well, what?"

"Well, what do you think?"

"I think my antlers are too large."

"No, not about the painting. About the robin."

"Oh. Well, perhaps the bird's purpose in life was to make you feel the pain of regret . . . for taking its life so needlessly."

Sayble sighed as he capped some oil tubes and said, "Well, maybe you're right, Athanasy. But, regret is a hard thing to have at my age."

"Then don't have it anymore," the elk replied simply.

With that, Athanasy gracefully disappeared into the black woods.

Sayble looked around the empty compound and said in tones of sudden solemnity, "I see you. I talk with you. I even praise your mission." He glanced out over the heavy fog rising from the pond and asked, "So why don't I understand?"

From there his gaze fell upon the shadows on the canvas. He held his thumb up and closed an eye to calculate the proportions he had painted. "What do you mean your antlers are too big?" he mumbled to himself. Then he called out to the darkness around him. "Everyone's a critic!"

CHAPTER TWENTY-SEVEN

BEFORE SHE LEFT her lab that same evening, Helen Forbes, like her associates, looked outside the window to see for herself if it was nature's own thunder which rattled the rows of bottles on the shelves. A brief glance at the meteorological monitors on the wall assured her that a storm was passing. No, there hadn't been an explosive "accident." So she tossed a half-hearted goodbye to the night-shift lab personnel and proceeded down the hall toward the security area. She passed her radiation detection and identification badges in through the small opening in the thick bullet-proof window separating the personnel leaving Ageon from the main security area. Her day had been long, and she routinely and wearily paused through the radiation detection arch and awaited clearance. After a few seconds, a small green light blinked on, giving her sanction to pass.

"Good night, Hal," she said flatly to the guard at the door.

"Night, ma'am," he replied, holding the door open for her. "Are you sure you want to drive home in this storm?"

She looked outside, then said, "Where'd all that thunder sneak up from?"

"Just out of nowhere, I guess," Hal said.

Helen donned a folded plastic rain hat and secured it under her chin.

"Drive carefully," Hal added, holding the door open for her. "And watch out for those snakes." His grin covered his face as he waited for Helen to stop.

"What snakes?" she asked, coming to a complete halt.

"Well, if you watch where you step, you might make it to your car without stepping on one," he continued, smiling as he watched her reaction. Seeing that she refused to cringe like the other females he had bid farewell to that evening, he added, "Now, didn't anybody come tell you lab folks all about the snakes rattling?"

Helen, quite fed up with animal horror stories, was losing her patience. "Oh? Well, I monitor this valley every month and I happen to know for a fact that there aren't more than a handful of snakes around here. So whatever rattling you heard must have been coming from your head."

At that, Helen walked briskly to her car and drove away from Ageon and its multitude of complexities, intent on forgetting the baffling day for a few hours.

She flicked on the car radio and rummaged around the dial for some soothing classical work, but stopped instead when she heard an announcer say the word "butterfly."

". . . but now wait, folks, that's not all," the voice said, filling Helen's car with stereophonic hype, ". . . a lady called in saying she saw a buffalo trying to knock down the gate at Ageon. So, all you butterfly and buffalo owners out there . . . do you know where your pets are tonight? Well, maybe we'll be hearing more about this later on in our seven o'clock newscast. So, stay tuned for more on . . ." the disc jockey flipped on a reverberator, making his last three words echo dramatically. ". . . Ageon Animal Update!" Then, the announcer laughed and added, "Anything else weird going on out there, call us. And, on a serious, more personal note, I'd like to thank all those folks over there at Ageon. Because if it weren't for them, I'd have nothing to talk about on my show!" He chuckled professionally and Helen turned the radio off in disgust, continuing her journey home with only the reliable hum of her car's engine to comfort her.

Having listened to the same broadcast, Sayble thoughtfully put away his oils and set his painting of Athanasy inside the bus to dry

166

safely. After foraging around his storage bins for something to eat and pouring himself a second glass of wine, he lay down on the torn corduroy couch in his bus considering what hope there could be in achieving what this Council Will required. Then, he thought again about the disturbing broadcast he heard. Not only had the report revealed the "humorous" antics of the butterflies and the buffalo, but it also mentioned the large birds and the howling dogs. The report ended with the forecast of severe winds along with thunderstorm alerts.

Then Sayble drew the obvious conclusion. No doubt the people of Ageon will explain away these occurrences by the fact that animals always act odd before storms. "Ha!" the old man laughed, sipping his wine. "The animals in this joint act odd all the time."

He sat up, took a few more thoughtful tilts of his wine while staring at Athanasy's portrait resting across the bus. "Why, sure, everybody knows animals act strange before a disaster," he said aloud to the portrait. He slowly stood up as a look of astonishment grew upon his leathery face. Then, at the top of his lungs he shouted, "Everybody knows that!"

He bolted for the bus's door, remembered the last gulpful of wine and ran back to finish it. He laughed in praise of his genius and sailed out of the bus, calling for Athanasy.

From across the Council Ground, the great elk heard the man-cousin calling him and with clean, long strides, was soon standing before the puffing man.

"What is it, Sayble? Why are you laughing so?"

"Because, you fine whatever-it-is you are, old Charles Ellingson Sayble isn't quite the fool some people, or animals, might think he is," he bellowed joyfully.

"Congratulations, Sayble," the elk said, smiling.

"No, no, no," Sayble replied. "I mean, all your philosophy, that's all well and good, but listen for a minute to some of my own."

"What are you talking about? Have you had a vision?"

"Have I! Listen, is it not a well-known fact that, before almost any natural disaster—you know, storms, earthquakes, hurricanes—that animals know beforehand?" Sayble asked, squarely facing Athanasy.

"How did you know that?" the elk asked suspiciously.

"Hell, we figured that out a long time ago. Anyway, what would you do, that is, if you were the average man-cousin, if all of a sudden, all the animals—every damn one of them—deserted the entire area around the Ageon Nuclear Submarine Base?" Sayble stepped back to take in Athanasy's reaction to his plan. His broad grin lost some of its bravado as the silence between them drew on. Finally, Sayble asked, "Well?"

The elk turned around, lowered his head and returned it to the sky as if sniffing the night winds for an answer. Finally, the beast spoke solemnly. "So, what do you propose we do?"

Now Sayble spoke with the gravity that his plan deserved. "I propose to go back to Ageon, tell them to cease . . . or, by the next day, all the birds will leave the sky."

"They will take you away faster than they did before."

"Perhaps not now, Athanasy. At least now we have them listening. The people are beginning to talk about the strange things we've done to Ageon. It was on that radio you've heard me listening to every night. So what if they do laugh at me? What do you think they'll say when, with the help of Lordjahn and the Heron, all the birds *do* leave?"

Again, the elk stood in silence as he comprehended the plan. "And if they don't close Ageon, then what?"

"Then I go back and tell them that all of the insects will leave!" Sayble's voice grew hoarse as he enthusiastically elaborated on his plan. "If the voice of the Will could bring your Chosen to you, then surely it can help Chanta summon the insect realm to leave. Then the fish, then the domestic animals, the mammals, every one of nature's own!" Sayble shouted with growing passion for his plan.

"In an hour I will return with an answer," Athanasy said while walking away to his feeding ground. "Such a plan takes great power."

"Good," Sayble called after him. "You go talk with whoever or whatever you talk to! I'll be waiting!"

Exactly one hour later, Athanasy appeared at Sayble's bus. "Sayble?" he called out gently, as there was no sign of the man within the vehicle. "Sayble?"

"Well, what's the verdict?" the man asked, appearing from the darkness by the pond.

"The plan is good, man-cousin. I have called our comrades back. When they arrive, we will take it to head and heart."

"Thank you, Athanasy. I'm sure they'll agree it's the only way, short of causing a disaster of our own."

"Sayble?" the elk asked while turning to go. "You would die for us, wouldn't you?"

The man, caught off guard by the elk's question, wondered if it were meant as flattery or forecast. But, Athanasy did not remain to hear the man-cousin's answer. So, into the darkness Sayble replied, "Well, I suppose I have to die of something."

CHAPTER TWENTY-EIGHT

EARLY THE NEXT MORNING, just as the sun began to rise, the Council animals returned to the sanctuary of their beckoning leader. Each animal crossed the boundary weary with the exhaustion that follows defeat and loss. They had journeyed back in but each shared the regretful thoughts of having to face Athanasy with their tales of failure. Leading the pack was Fetchit-5, who had put her exhaustion aside as she searched for Sayble. She found his scent and bolted ahead and was soon in a wrestling embrace with her master.

After each creature had exchanged words of welcome with Et Ska, Sayble, and Athanasy, they refreshed themselves. Then they settled down to explain their adventures and express their fears.

The prairie dog shared the story of Iscariot and how the raccoon had died to save a life. Athanasy nodded quietly with the affirmation that Iscariot's cycle was complete and that he had died in grace.

Then, the Heron told the story of Rasslin the rattlesnake and the terrifying, purring roar of the snakes. Chanta explained how the millions had flown as one. Then Moko, Little Paw, Lordjahn, Fetchit-5, and Neera each told their stories of smashing gates, fine howling haunts and circling Ageon with encasing death-wishes.

It all sounded magnificent to Sayble, who smiled in delight and pride as he listened to each. Then, he abruptly rose and excused himself, for there was much to be done.

170

In his absence, Athanasy explained the plan Sayble had conceived. The animals, although weary and discouraged, nodded in acceptance.

"But, you look a bit doubtful, Heron. What's on your mind?" Athanasy asked the bird, who was thoughtfully poking at pebbles at the water's edge.

"Well," he began, carefully choosing his next words, "won't the man-cousins at Ageon recognize Sayble as the dissenter from before? The same one they took away, and the same one who escaped their place of confinement? They might even still be looking for him."

The condor looked up Athanasy and said, "An interesting point, Athanasy. They say a man-cousin never forgets, especially one who escapes their trusted institutions."

The elk paused and studied his animals. "The man-cousin calls his plan inspired. No doubt he has thought of this and knows a way to avoid detection." The elk smiled on his animals and continued. "You have all done well. Please go to the sanctuary of your nests and rest, for as you sadly know, it is not yet finished and we are one less."

So, anxious to dream of trouble-free days, the animals each left in different directions. Only the wolf paused. When the others had vanished, she cast her magnificent golden eyes up to Athanasy and said softly, "You are tired too, Athanasy."

"Neera, soul-seer," the elk sighed with soft, grateful tones, "how difficult it is to hide my weariness from you. They all know I am Athanasy, the never-ending. How can I tire, knowing I'll never rest?" He paused, then continued in a whisper, "But I do tire. I do."

"Does the Will not refresh you, as it does us?"

"I have been Athanasy for so long, *I* am the Will now, Neera. I cannot separate and say, 'Refresh me,' for only in death does an animal find rest, and I have no death."

Neera tried to understand. As she listened, she noticed a pain in Athanasy's velvet voice. She backed up respectfully, then asked, "Will I ever be permitted to understand you, Athanasy?"

Athanasy laughed. "I doubt it, Neera. But you'll keep trying, I know that. It is your nature, Neera. That is why you were chosen. Go rest, wolf."

Fetchit-5, eager to talk to Sayble, returned to the bus and the warmth of the old sofa inside. She hoped her man-cousin would be there, for she was anxious to discover the full depth of his new plan to overpower Ageon. When she leaped aboard the bus, she could hear Sayble toward the back, rummaging around in some old crates stuffed with articles of the past—seldom used, always present.

"Sayble? What are you doing back there?" the dog asked.

Sayble jumped around and said loudly, "Damn it, Fetchit-5! Don't ever sneak up on a man! Especially an old one!"

"It never seemed to bother you before I was able to talk to you," Fetchit-5 quipped. "So, what are you looking for?"

"Oh, just some things," the man said, pulling out an old leather briefcase. "Like this," he added, proudly holding up the dusty relic.

"What's that for?"

"You'll see." He started to clean the case off, wiping years of dust out of the folded corners. "What do all you beasties think of my idea?"

The dog seemed more interested in Sayble's use for such an object, but answered, "Oh. It's a grand idea, the exodus and all. But we did have a few questions. We were wondering . . ." the dog continued, ignoring Sayble's monotonous whistling.

"Ah hah. I know what you were wondering, old girl," Sayble broke in.

"Yes," Fetchit-5 said, patiently ignoring his joyful abruptness, "and then I wanted to know . . ."

"Tut, tut," Sayble interrupted again, shaking a finger toward the dog. "Didn't your mother ever tell you that curiosity killed the cat?"

"Okay, so find me a cat and I'll kill it!" the dog snapped, weary of her master's flippant attitude. "Really, Sayble, in light of all this failure, you certainly have developed an arrogant manner!"

It was one thing getting used to his animal talking, but being admonished by the dog was another.

The old man stopped what he was doing, knelt down next to Fetchit-5 and said, "Why don't you go rest?" He stroked the dog's head and she warmly responded by habit to his touch. "Give me an hour to pull together the loose ends of this fiasco."

Fetchit-5 yawned, remembering her fatigue and walked toward the couch. She looked up to Sayble and said, "I'll be on my couch."

"Pleasant dreams," Sayble said, smiling down at her and commencing with a quieter version of his humming tune.

A slight breeze had picked up around and through the Council Ground as the creatures slept and dreamt away their weariness. Sayble continued working in the rear of the bus and was careful not to disturb his sleeping dog.

When he was finished and ready to confront the rest of the animals, he called out from the back of the bus, "Oh Fetchit-5? Wake up, girl. Go and get the others and we can answer those questions now."

She didn't budge.

"Hey, you going deaf?" Sayble asked, poking her in the shoulder.

The dog opened one eye and said, "Dogs don't go deaf. They simply learn to ignore." She then yawned and stretched her sinuous body, front paws extended on the floor with the remainder of her body still on the couch.

"Well, go get the others," Sayble repeated with a boyish enthusiasm.

Obediently, she hopped out of the bus.

After giving the animals enough time to congregate, Sayble assumed a straight and confident stature, and walked over to the meeting place. He wished he had a camera to record the expressions on each face as the animals watched him approach. In fact, he was sure that if it weren't for his scent on the easy breeze forecasting his arrival, the animals wouldn't have known it was him until he spoke. He swayed in closer to the group and smiled wildly at their astonished expressions. He turned around to give them the total effect of his attire. He was dressed in a dark conservative suit, not altogether the fashion of the day, but it appeared clean and well-pressed and it fit him nearly perfectly.

Fetchit-5 came over to her master, wagging her tail warily and sniffing. For the first time in her relationship with Sayble, she could smell boot polish and a curious sweet fragrance upon the man. She looked him over carefully, wondering if she had ever seen him with so much beard growth. And his hair . . . less gray?

The group was speechless at how a man-cousin could change his appearance so drastically in such a brief time.

"My friends, allow me to present myself." He reached into his vest pocket and pulled out a small business card and read, "Signs by Charles Ellingson Sayble." He then held the card to his heart, sighed and looked to the heavens, adding, "Ah, Mama, if only you'd lived to see this."

The Heron was the first to speak. "Man-cousin, what is this folly?"

"Folly? Indeed!" the man snapped, jokingly. "This is masquerade, not folly, my fine critters. You don't think I'd be foolish enough to sashay back over to Ageon looking the same way I did before, do you? Hell, no. They'd slap me into irons, bypassing the luxury of the mental ward. So, what do you think?" He held his polished briefcase in one hand and, with the other, thoughtfully gripped his suit coat like a promising politician. He grinned insanely.

"What about your transport?" the Heron asked, looking beyond him. "Surely that will betray you."

"A good question, my fine feathered bird!" Sayble answered, still using his affluent-statesman voice. "I agree the vehicle is a bit . . . well, it's downright noticeable, that's what it is."

"Did you want me to give you a ride back over to Ageon?" Moko asked earnestly.

"God, no! I had in mind a much more conservative means of transportation."

"What?" asked the wolf.

At that point, Sayble pulled his tattered wallet out and extracted from it several bills of large denomination. He flashed the money toward the animals and said, "Money won't buy everything, but it will buy one slightly used vehicle."

Athanasy remained silent and assessed the new Sayble. Then, he stepped forward and asked, quite simply, "How shall we begin?"

Sayble then spoke in a voice more familiar to the creatures. "Well, Fetchit-5 and me will need some time at that town, Port Hartley, to pick up a car. I plan to take my bus part-way there, hide it somewhere and walk the rest of the way. We'll get a car and plan on being at Ageon by, say, three o'clock tomorrow afternoon. I'll deliver my message to Ageon and leave. We will give them until midnight to desert Ageon. Then, if they don't, Lordjahn and the Heron will command their fellow birds to leave."

"Just like that?" the Heron asked doubtfully.

174

"Just like that," Athanasy answered. "The Will shall carry out during the night and they'll be ready. All birds will await your commands."

"Then, if all the birds being gone doesn't do it, and Ageon still ticks, I'll go back and tell them the fish will be the next to go, and so on, until our meaning is perfectly clear," Sayble continued.

"One problem," Fetchit-5 said.

"*One* problem?" Sayble echoed sarcastically. "I can count at least four, maybe five."

"The dogs, the cats," the dog continued, "the domestic ones. They'll be hard to convince. Can the Will charm a dog into leaving its master?" She looked at Athanasy for an answer.

"You did," Lordjahn countered.

"Yes, but my man-cousin is still here with me. Who knows what I would have done if he weren't allowed to join us here?"

"You would have stayed as the Will so commanded," Athanasy replied. "Even Iscariot came and then finally died for us."

"As you say, Athanasy. I'll do my best to help convince the wary ones," the dog said, bowing slightly.

"Well," Sayble said, sighing heavily to check the rising swell of excitement once again present in his body. "Here we go again! Any last words of wisdom, Athanasy?"

The great elk cast his eyes down to the man and answered the question: "You must now decide whether it is better to judge an animal by a human's standards, or to judge a human by an animal's standards."

Sayble hesitated before responding. Then he smiled and replied, "Ask me when it's over."

The elk turned toward the Heron and the condor. "Fly now. Ready all those you meet. For the sun after next will rise in silence. Speed your winged brethren safely away."

So the Great Blue Heron and the condor rose regally above the others and were soon up and away, spreading their songs to all they met, calling the news of the exodus, and they, in turn, touching lofty wings with the countless brothers and sisters who occupied the complex valley of Ageon.

"Guess we'd better get started . . . again," Sayble said to his dog, appearing almost lost in thought as he cleared the failures out of his misty past and planned the future's successes. "The bus is ready to go. Let's do it."

Then, Athanasy, speaking from the center of the other silent animals, said, "Goodbye again, Sayble. And, this time, take the Will with you."

Sayble hedged an embarrassed cough, hoping this send-off wouldn't develop into a long, prophetic farewell. "So, do you each know what to do?" he asked the group.

"The Heron and Lordjahn will report back to us on your progress. We will know from them what is to be done next," Athanasy answered. "Go and succeed, man-cousin."

Sayble stared briefly at the elk, suddenly unsure of his own emotions. "Right," he said. "Come on, Fetchit, let's go."

The old man turned and gently slapped his leg to urge his dog to hurry. Then, he waved his hand high in the air in silent farewell to the creatures of the Council.

So, once more the colorful rainbow-bus was started up. It hesitantly rolled from its Council Ground keeping place. And Sayble, not looking back, thought only of the battle ahead.

Once on the road, Fetchit-5 found she couldn't take her eyes off her master.

"All right," Sayble finally said. "What is it?"

"You look so different. So . . . groomed."

"Well, I had to do something to improve my appearance."

"And those clothes. Where is your lucky bolo tie?"

"Too flashy. Basic black is better," he replied, loosening the awkward knot. "Almost forgot how to tie one of these damn things."

"Where'd that awful black suit come from, anyway?" she persisted.

"Hey now, watch how you refer to my one and only funeral suit," he said, not nearly as offended as he tried to sound.

"Your what?" Fetchit-5 gasped. "You've never known anyone long enough to go to their funeral, Sayble."

"No, no. This is *my* funeral suit. You know, burial togs. What every well-dressed stiff is wearing this year. It's all the rage," Sayble said, enjoying his dog's expression of ghastly disgust.

"A special suit in which to die? Just what are you planning at

Ageon? Suicide?" Her voice became a little shaky.

"Good God, dog! You sound more and more like a scaredy old woman the more I know you. First of all, just because I put these clothes on does not mean I'm off to die, and secondly," he paused, slowing down to study the road signs ahead, "well, there is no secondly and there sure as hell ain't going to be no suicide or funeral. Now, go have a dog biscuit or something and let me figure out what I'm doing here."

By nightfall, they had found a hiding place off the main road into the town of Port Hartley. Fetchit-5 took a run and ate, Sayble drank some wine and broke into his last cache of cigars and neatly laid his black suit out for the next day. They talked as the moon rose until all there was left to say was "Good night."

CHAPTER TWENTY-NINE

I T TOOK THE BALANCE of the following day to procure a new vehicle. The transport, well-chosen, was an antiquated military jeep, several wars old, whose color and personality blended well with Sayble's secretive mission.

"How much did they pay you to take that thing off their hands?" was Fetchit-5's sneer when Sayble first arrived in the jeep at the hidden bus site.

"The only problem with talking dogs is, they never know when to keep their mouths shut. And, they don't know diddly about cars!" Sayble snapped back. "Now, come on. Get in this thing." He grabbed his briefcase and a pack of food and added, "Let's go start a fire under Ageon!"

Taking advantage of the four-wheel drive, Sayble took several off-road short-cuts, pulling out finally, to Fetchit-5's relief, on Port Hartley's border. They stopped and overlooked the valley of Ageon. Sayble asked himself how he could have forgotten how impregnable the fortress seemed. In his conquering dreams at the Council Ground, Ageon had appeared much smaller and he, much larger, and ages younger.

Eventually, he bounced the jeep into a parking lot with a phone booth in a quiet corner. He instructed the dog to remain and he entered the booth, fumbling through his pockets for change. He remained there for quite some time. When he finally reappeared, he strolled over to the waiting dog with his familiar smug expression. Even through his snow-white stubble, Fetchit-5 recognized his smirk.

"Steps one and two, done and done!" Sayble said triumphantly, climbing back into the driver's seat. "Now, the fireworks begin!"

"Why? What were you just doing?"

"I just made two very important phone calls. First, I now have a four o'clock appointment to see . . ." He held the note paper outstretched to clarify the name he had scribbled down. "Doctor Helen Forbes . . . part of the Ageon biological team. Hell, if I'd known it was that easy to get into Ageon, I could have saved myself a trip to the mental ward."

"And the other phone call?" she asked quietly, looking around the parking lot to insure their privacy.

"Well, then I called the local newspaper, anonymously, of course. I told them I have inside info . . . that by this time tomorrow, the only thing that'll be flapping around the sky will be a few lonely airplanes." He started the jeep up and listened to the engine's uneven breath.

"Of course they thought you were crazed!" Fetchit-5 laughed, conjuring up the expression on the face of the person taking Sayble's prophetic phone call.

"I'm getting used to that. But, if I have to call them back tomorrow, they won't hang up quite so fast." Sayble chuckled also and, as they drove off, the sound of their combined, contagious laughter nearly drowned out the groans of the jeep's ailing engine.

With only an hour remaining until the four o'clock appointment, Sayble drove directly to Ageon. He stopped in the visitors' parking lot and allowed his dog a necessary run.

"Now, since I don't imagine they allow dogs in there, you stay close to the jeep. I don't have any idea what sort of hasty retreat I might have to make, so I don't want to have to stop to look for you." He scratched her behind the ears affectionately and took his briefcase. Then he cradled her head in his hands and whispered into her eyes, "Lunacy. Sheer lunacy." He affectionately flipped her ears back and added with a snort of old-man laughter. "But what the hell, right?"

Then he began walking toward the visitors' information center.

He turned around and called out to Fetchit-5, "And don't talk to strangers!"

Sayble had found it easy to procure an inside appointment with an Ageonite, but he certainly had not reckoned with the security measures taken to deter one from keeping that appointment.

Upon presenting himself to the visitor's desk, he received a chilly, professional reception as the guard suspiciously inspected Sayble's meager identification. Then, the guard excused himself while he phoned Dr. Forbes' office to receive an authorized clearance for the gentleman. He spoke in muffled tones and Sayble prayed that the rising nervous sweat he felt was not visible. He was Charles Ellingson Sayble, identified as such and totally implicated now. The guard returned his identification and said flatly, "Dr. Forbes is expecting you."

"Thank you," Sayble replied, smiling to cover his relief, appearing cordially professional himself. "Where do I go from here?"

"I must inform you that, in order to enter Ageon from this point on, you must submit to a full hands-on search. Your briefcase will be thoroughly inspected and you'll have to pass through our metal and explosives detector, similar to those found in any major airport." The guard didn't look at Sayble while he spoke his cool, rehearsed speech, but rather he kept his eyes on the many closed-circuit security screens in front of him.

Sayble's heart thumped when he realized the extensive security procedures ahead. He ravaged through his mind to classify what old papers they might find in his briefcase. And it'd been over twenty years since he'd even been near an airport . . . what metal detectors? What explosives detectors? What incriminations? Good God, he thought, I don't want to blow up the place, I only what to shut it down.

The guard handed him a bright yellow helmet, several sizes too large. "For the fallout?" Sayble jokingly asked as the guard led him to the main security area.

Once inside, another guard took over and blandly instructed him to remove his jacket and place it and his briefcase on the conveyor belt for X ray. Then he himself passed through the arch of the metal detector. Again, he feigned familiarity, hoping to appear as though such procedures were everyday occurrences for

RANDALL BETH PLATT

him. He wondered if the apparatus could detect his rapid pulse, his nervous sweat.

Then a tall, bulky female guard instructed him to stand with his feet apart and arms outstretched while she searched him. When it was apparent he was unarmed, he and his belongings were reunited and he was told to wait for an escort to Dr. Forbes's office. The solemnity of the procedures made Sayble's mouth dry with anticipation and dread. Thus far, he had seen no less than twenty heavily armed Marines. He realized the gentle stroll of the antinuclear war protest a few days' earlier was a child's romp compared to the austere, shoot-to-kill expressions of the protectors' faces. Machine guarding machine.

It was a short walk back to Helen Forbes's office in the biology lab. Sayble thanked the guard for showing him the way and was immediately relaxed by Helen's welcoming face. His first reaction was one of simplistic ease, for her smile contained not an ounce of threat to his mission and was, by far, the friendliest face he had seen all day. No uniform, no guns, no icy stares.

"This is some place you have here," Sayble said, offering Helen his hand. "I'm Charles Sayble."

"Glad to meet you, Mr. Sayble. I apologize for any inconveniences our security systems might have caused you. But we all have to go through it." She motioned toward her desk and continued. "Let me start off by saying that I don't usually do the supply ordering for the lab. But your offer over the phone piqued my curiosity."

"Yes, it usually does," he said, imitating the grin the used-car salesman had applied when he bought the jeep. He opened his briefcase and pulled out one of his cards. It was bent and he flattened it out before offering it to Dr. Forbes.

She looked at the card blankly, turned it over, then read it again. "I'm afraid I don't understand," she began apologetically. "Signs by Charles Ellingson Sayble," she read. "What makes you think I need a sign? You should be talking to the people in maintenance. They're in charge of all the sign-making at Ageon. This is the biology lab." Her voice became chilly as her suspicions rose.

"Oh, I'm sorry, Dr. Forbes," Sayble began. "I can see you are confused."

181

"Confused and busy," she replied, a harsh edge rising in her voice. "If this is some sort of a joke . . ."

"Oh no, no, no, Dr. Forbes. My card refers to signs. You know, foretellings—billboards of the future, you might say."

Feeling annoyed and angry for allowing the man into Ageon, Helen drew herself up straight and began to reach for the phone on her desk. Sayble placed his hand on hers as it reached the receiver and said gently, "Please. I've gotten this far. Hear me out, Dr. Forbes. Please."

She looked at the clock upon the wall and said, "You have exactly two minutes to tell me who you are and what you want."

"I can read the signs," Sayble began enthusiastically. How could he explain in two minutes? "The butterflies, the condor, the Heron, the snakes—we're all in this together."

Helen's own heart began to throb louder with the mention of each animal she had been watching in and around Ageon.

"If you're referring to the dribble in the local newspapers . . ." she began nervously.

"No, ma'am, I'm referring to the plot all these animals hatched against this nuclear submarine facility. The events of the last few days are only the beginning."

"What is it you're trying to say, Mr. Sayble?"

"I thought, as a member of the biological systems here, you'd want to know what the animals will do next." Sayble rose, feeling power from his words as he walked casually about the lab.

"Your two minutes are up, Mr. Sayble," Helen said stiffly, again reaching for her phone.

Sayble turned and said harshly, "You're a scientist, damn it, Dr. Forbes! You know full well something strange is happening in this valley. Where is your biological curiosity?"

"Strange things will always occur where there's anything using plutonium. That's what people want to read so that's what the press will write about!" she said, speaking louder in defense of her livelihood. The words were exact echoes of Commander Harold Orinsky's statements.

"Exactly . . . strange things will occur. Now, before you have me thrown out of here, listen to this: If Ageon does not begin dismantling by midnight tonight, all birds will leave the sky by sunrise."

182

"What?" Helen gasped, breaking into an incredulous smile.

"That's all I have come to say."

"And just how do you propose to take away all our birds?" she asked, holding in her laughter with folded arms.

"Right now, they carry the word to each other. By sunrise, they will be gone. I have no control over it," he replied quietly. He gathered his briefcase and headed for the door.

So sudden was Sayble's change in manner, that Helen was speechless as she watched him leave. The old man did reflect a quality of genuine sadness when he spoke of the birds. Crazy or not, he presented a feeling of honest endeavor. Sayble turned at the lab entrance and said with a smile, "Curiosity, Dr. Forbes. Take your academic assumptions to hell and just be curious. That's all it takes." Then, he left the lab and returned to the security area for clearance out of Ageon.

Helen was not able to absorb Sayble's parting words, for a phone call broke her thoughts.

"This is Dr. Forbes," she answered.

"And this is Orinsky," came the irritated voice at the other end.

"Sir?"

"I have just received the most annoying inquiry from the local reporters."

"Yes?" she asked, dreading what her superior would say next.

"Now they say some looney has tipped them off. Something about all the birds leaving." The mocking agitation was quite definite in his voice. "And would I care to make a statement. . . ."

Helen cleared her throat, wondering if Sayble had left security by now. "Yes sir," she began, "I just spoke to the 'looney.' He just left my office." She closed her eyes instinctively, anticipating the rage Orinsky would release.

"You mean to tell me Security let him in?" he bellowed.

"He appeared quite harmless. An old man."

"And what did he say? Why did he see you?"

"Well, he said the same thing. That all the birds would disappear by sunrise tomorrow if Ageon still operates. And I guess he came to see me because I'm the only biologist around today."

"Well, he's a professional agitator! An actor hired by one of those groups!" He slammed down the receiver.

Sayble's exit from Ageon was much quicker than his entrance. He was, in fact, surprised to see that he was able to leave at all. Just as he was leaving the visitors' area, though, the guard behind the desk was talking on the phone.

"He's heading for his car. Right, just a minute. Shall I have Lowell at the front gate detain him? Yes sir."

Sayble reached his jeep, tossing his briefcase hastily into the back, ignoring the questions his dog was asking and immediately started up the engine. He popped the clutch and headed for the parking lot exit and the last security gate. He was allowed to pass through the gate without incident, but, in the rear-view mirror, Sayble could see the guard writing down the license number of the jeep.

"Let's get out of here!" Sayble said to Fetchit-5.

"Well, what did they say?"

"I'll tell you later. Hang on, girl. This ride may get a little rough."

"Why? Where're we going?"

Sayble was not followed, contrary to his initial foreboding. He took the first available side-road that led into the hills overlooking Ageon. From there, he urged his jeep off-road until he was in a lightly forested area. His dog directed him to the same hiding place that the animals had previously chosen. And from there, the old man and his dog watched the activity of Ageon below.

From seemingly nowhere, the condor and the Heron were upon them, landing gently on the hood of Sayble's jeep. "What did they say?" asked the Heron.

"I talked, but they didn't listen," Sayble answered, studying the machinations of the sprawling base down below. "Are the birds ready?"

"From miles out they are already beginning to leave," answered the condor, with a proud sadness in his voice. "The word is spreading tenfold by tenfold. Tomorrow's sunrise will not be cheered by bird-song," he added. "Can you hear them now?"

Sayble listened and, as evening fell, indeed the birds seemed louder than usual. He looked up and the silhouettes of thousands of retreating birds graced the reddened setting sun.

"You're right, Lordjahn," Fetchit-5 commented. "It's begun."

By dusk, Helen Forbes wearily checked out of her office and

walked toward the employees' parking lot. The smell of spring fragrances cheered her momentarily, until she remembered her encounter with Charles Sayble and his chilling words of promise.

She looked about the valley and was keenly aware of the night-songs of the countless birds as they soared toward the hills. "Disappear indeed!" she said aloud. "More birds than ever up there."

Then, content that the valley of Ageon was calming its way into nightfall, she drove home in silence, trying to bury the memory of Sayble.

Long after nightfall, in the black before moonshine, the birds' exodus continued. Their concerted music sang praise to the Will in all animals. Ageon, man-lit for the evening's work, continued as usual, oblivious to the thousands of wings leaving the valley from every direction, radiating out, until by dawn, not a bird was left for miles around.

CHAPTER THIRTY

HELEN KNEW, Sayble knew, the animals all knew upon opening their eyes the following morning, that the birds had vanished. The cherished birds of spring were gone as the old man had foretold.

From his hilltop hiding place, Sayble watched the sunrise which was, for the first time in all of history, silent. There was only the sound of the gentle, lonely breeze tugging at the deserted treetop homes. As the sun rose higher, so did the feeling of power rise within Sayble. He examined the skies for signs of birds and, finding none, he turned his gaze on the giant whales of steel at rest in the bay below and he was angered at Ageon's blatant ignorance. He felt justly revengeful in beholding the empty skies.

"It's only the beginning! Do you hear?" he shouted down the hill.

"I'm sure they can't hear you," Fetchit-5 said with a parental sniff.

"They can't hear me when I'm talking right into their faces," he snapped, turning away. "You hungry?"

"I'm a dog. Of course I'm hungry," she replied logically.

"Come on, let's drive to Port Hartley. I know this little coffee shop."

"Do you think it's safe?" Fetchit-5 asked, hesitating.

"Greater courage hath no man than when he's hungry. Besides, it's early yet. Come on."

The cafe itself brought back memories for Sayble, who had spent many a morning before work in similar ones. The smell of bacon and coffee inspired his hunger as he took the last available stool at the counter. If Sayble looked out of place in his dusty and wrinkled black funeral suit, no one noticed.

When his meal came, he ate half, savoring every bite. Then he requested the remaining half to be wrapped. He had eaten in silence, keeping mostly to himself while straining to hear the topics of conversation from those around him. No one said a thing about the curious absence of the birds. Just as Sayble was maneuvering his way through the crowded, bustling cafe, Dr. Helen Forbes entered. Carefully wielding the boxed leftovers, Sayble met her before she took a seat by the window. "Well, hello there, Dr. Forbes," he said cordially. "Nice day, isn't it? Little quiet, perhaps, but nice."

She was caught in an uncomfortable cross between surprise and fear at seeing Sayble and was unable to reply.

"Some advice, Dr. Forbes," Sayble continued. "Try the hot-cakes, they're superb. Keep away from the coffee, though. It's a killer," he whispered down to her. Then he smiled and began to leave.

Then, he turned and added, "Oh, one more thing, Dr. Forbes. By tomorrow, all the fish will be gone."

She stared at him, still unable to speak. By now, several people had overheard the curious one-sided conversation and had stopped eating to listen to what the unkempt man was saying. Sayble opened the door and said in melodic tones, "So, best tell the Pentagon to pull the plug."

Fetchit-5 immediately detected the powerful glow on Sayble's face as he exited the cafe. So intense were his eyes that her first question was not one concerning her breakfast. "What happened in there? You suddenly look . . ." She stared closely at him. ". . . odd."

"Bad coffee. Here you go," Sayble replied, offering her the plate of food. Hunger winning out over curiosity, the dog inhaled the offering in no time.

By the time they arrived to their hilltop hiding place, the Heron and Lordjahn had been waiting for them nearly an hour.

"Where have you been, man-cousin?" the Heron asked harshly. "You should have told us you were leaving."

"I would have, but you weren't around yourself. For a while, I thought you two had left with the others," Sayble said, literally smoothing the bird's ruffled blue feathers.

"What's it like up there, being the only birds?" the dog asked.

"Like home," the condor replied sadly.

"Strange. But I rather enjoy the solitude," the Heron commented.

"Reflect later, you two. We have a lot to do," Sayble said, pointing downhill toward Ageon.

"We leave now to release Et Ska from her pond," Lordjahn said, preparing for flight back to the Council Ground. "And to tell Athanasy Ageon still breathes."

"Good. And tell Athanasy I've warned them twice. Tell him I'm prepared to take this to the last living animal." Again, the glow of energy surrounded Sayble, and the two birds and the dog stood listening with a certain awe. "Tell Athanasy the Will within me and the Will of the Council have met eye to eye, soul to soul. Godspeed, Et Ska. Take away the fish!" His voice called out over the valley and echoed off the bay beyond as the two magnificent birds took flight.

"Beware the power, man-cousin," Fetchit-5 growled quietly.

Sayble turned and looked down at the dog resting behind him. "For the first time in my life! Power! Up to here!" He gruffly indicated his neck.

"Yes, and if it chokes you, we're all doomed."

Sayble, considering her admonishing words, knelt next to her and said softly, "Don't you worry." He gently stroked her, rose again and cast his eyes back out over Ageon and whispered, with clenched teeth, "You will cease! By the God in all of us, you will cease!"

CHAPTER THIRTY-ONE

E T SKA THE SALMON had suffered considerably during her days of confinement in the crystal waters of the Council Ground. Her day of spawning had come and gone without fulfillment, for she had ventured a freshwater stream other than her sacred home-waters. The inspiring atmosphere and Athanasy's divine mission had not been enough to sustain her, for her season of change was upon her and the intimate Will inside her slim body begged Et Ska to return to her home. So, each day she paled. Her once-playful jumps were no longer high and daring and Athanasy had noticed with anguish that her song was now seldom heard.

But, when the word arrived from Sayble that it was finally Et Ska's turn in working the Council's magic, the graying fish sprang high out of the water, crying, "At last! A chance for me after all, Athanasy!"

"You look weakened, Et Ska. Are you sure you can travel as far and fast as the Will demands? Have I held you too long?" Athanasy asked, touching her listless soul.

"For me to quit now would mean I would die without a purpose. The strength I'll need will come. I feel stronger already."

It was true, for as she jumped and spoke, Athanasy noticed a trace of silver-glisten return to her back. He watched her swim with escalating speed around the pond and silently acknowledged the Will for replenishing the salmon.

Then Et Ska called out as she neared the pond's exit, "I'm ready, Athanasy. Release me!"

"The Heron will follow your trail. Through him, I'll watch you. My song praises you," the elk called out as he willed the power to open the invisible gate which had kept the pond's privacy. He watched her leave, looked sadly over the stilled and silent pond, and then he rejoined his remaining Council comrades.

The word spread from fish to fish with the contagion of a prairie fire, and it was not long before the fish from every stream, river and pond within miles of Ageon began to depart. The streams swelled with fish in all directions away from the valley, biologically contrary to everything mankind had ever discovered about nature. Even the fish which were contained either by man's cement-fashioned boundaries or by nature's land-locked ones, miraculously disappeared. It was the Will working its finest artwork. And leading them all was Et Ska, calling her brethren and urging the hesitant along. Her beguiling song was heard in every direction. It had never echoed so beautifully. Her strength and her speed increased tenfold.

By the day's end, the waters below were as silent as the skies above. The sun set upon the empty waters with the same eerie silence with which it had risen that morning.

The Heron had quite a difficult time keeping track of Et Ska, for her underwater speed challenged the bird's water-skimming skills.

"Don't you think we ought to be heading back now?" the Heron asked. "It's getting dark, Et Ska. We've come a long way."

The salmon slowed considerably and, leaping up, said, "No, Heron. Athanasy released me. I'm not going back."

"Why?" the Heron asked, landing on the shore.

"Because I'm dying," she answered with soft, simple honesty.

The Heron paused respectfully, then lowered his head close to the water, saying, "You can't die now. It's not finished yet."

"Oh, Heron, don't be foolish. You know I'm far beyond my time. I prefer honest death to superficial life, which is all my life would be now in the Council pond."

"But Athanasy . . ." the Heron ventured, ignoring her flawless logic.

"He knows I won't be back. My children have died within me. But the Will kissed my broken heart. Now, even the Will is draining from me."

The Heron, fighting off the pangs of sorrow, remained silent.

"Take my thoughts of love to the others, Heron," she continued with a cheerful voice. "You have no right to grieve for me. So go. Fly away."

Finally, the bird spoke. "I am a Heron. Above so many others, I am aware of your life's precious cycle. I've been fond of you from the start, Et Ska."

"You'd better leave now. I know how you hate to fly at night."

"Yes. Yes . . ." the Heron said, taking flight. "Goodbye." He circled over the salmon twice and watched her last but highest leap of all. Then, she was gone, plunging deep into the black water to die a silent and undisturbed death.

The early edition of the newspaper the next morning devoted a large corner section to the disappearance of the birds and the fish. It disclosed the premonition they had received by the anonymous caller. Then, as Sayble fumbled through the back pages of the paper, he found an article containing some statements that Commander Harold Orinsky had released concerning the birds' disappearances. It was a trite, patronizing article indicating absolutely no relationship at all between Ageon and the birds' migration. It didn't make mention of Helen Forbes or the fact that Sayble had paid the facility a threatening visit. It did mention that a team of biologists were "working with the community" in order to explain the sudden migrations. Sayble tossed the paper down, startling Fetchit-5 at his side.

"What is it?" she asked, yawning.

"Come on! We're going back to Port Hartley."

The dog grudgingly rose. "Are you sure it's still safe to be seen there?"

"Well, according to that article, we're *all* safe around Ageon. Idiots!"

Contrary to what the article said, Harold Orinsky was very

concerned with the disappearance of the birds and the fish. Helen had told him of Sayble's forecast about the fish the previous day and she, along with all available laboratory personnel, had worked through the night, monitoring the soil, air, and water from various testing sites in and around Ageon. Helen herself viewed the fish as they migrated in every direction away from Ageon. She caught several specimens and had them thoroughly tested and re-tested for any explanation. The entire team of scientists was totally baffled. They considered everything from subterranean activity to solar disturbances.

"This is ridiculous!" Commander Orinsky shouted at Helen after he read the final lab report. "Some deranged old man waltzes in here and says all the birds and fish will leave if we don't go play somewhere else. Then, by some quirk of nature, it happens. I don't buy it! There *is* an explanation! And you're going to find it!" He handed the report back to Helen.

"Only so much can be attributed to natural migratory habits, sir," Helen explained, feeling a deep, worrisome pang in her stomach.

"I know that, Dr. Forbes. It's probably only a matter of minutes before the whole country hears of this!" He exhaled heavily and thought. "I'm preparing an extensive memo to the Pentagon. We need help and we need it now." Orinsky spoke calmly now, for through his concern, he still held staunchly to the fact that Ageon, or any other nuclear installation, could not, in itself, cause such behavior in birds and fish.

"What should I do if that Sayble calls again?" she asked, anxious for him to take her share of the nightmare.

"You keep him on the line for as long as you can," Orinsky replied. "We've turned on the central trap line. Believe me, we'll catch this character. Our guards'll be on him before he even hangs up the phone."

"Our guards? Why not the police?" Helen asked.

"Really, Dr. Forbes. You have more than your share to worry about in your lab. Leave the politics of this to me." Orinsky himself was beginning to look slightly worn, even in his fine, crisp naval uniform.

Helen returned to her office and seated herself at her desk to study the results of still more tests. But she found her eyes wandering to the phone and the clock on the wall. It was nearly mid-morning. Perhaps Sayble wouldn't call and her part in the mystery would pass without further involvement. Maybe it was over, the entire thing was a mere coincidence of nature, a quirkish practical joke that, only by absurd odds, toyed with Ageon.

The sounds of the laboratory apparatus and scientists conferring became blurred as Helen tried to concentrate on the seismograph report in front of her. Then, with deafening clarity, the phone rang. She let it ring a second time, considering not answering. The workers in the lab watched her and she realized she had no alternative but to pick it up.

"Dr. Forbes. Can I help you?" she asked quietly. Before he spoke, she knew it was Sayble.

"Why, yes, Dr. Forbes," he began cheerfully. "You can answer a question for me."

"I'd be delighted to. Who is this please?"

"My question is," he began from a phone booth, "with no birds around and with no fish around, why would any insect want to hang around?" He waved casually to Fetchit-5, who was staring anxiously at him from the jeep, half a block away.

"I don't understand what you mean . . ." Dr. Forbes stalled.

"Don't be naïve, Dr. Forbes. You know exactly what I mean."

"Is this you, Mr. Sayble?"

Then, Sayble sensed something was wrong. She knew perfectly well it was him. He immediately hung up the receiver and listened to his change drop into the machine. He felt foolishly obvious in the confines of the small telephone booth.

He wasn't able to get even halfway to his jeep when the Marines approached him. Sayble knew it was useless to run or argue, so he himself initiated the conversation. "Howdy, boys. Want to see me for something?"

"Commander Harold Orinsky requested you come and see him," one of the guards answered.

"Good. Because I've got a few words for this Orinsky honcho myself. In fact, get the President on the line. To hell with Orinsky!"

Fetchit-5 froze in terror as she watched the guards take her

Sayble away. But this time, he was to be delivered into the hands of Ageon's own master.

It was only a few minutes before Sayble found himself being escorted through the security house. The guards remained with him during the entire process. Sayble didn't speak to anyone, but he went over in his mind how he would confront Orinsky. The rage within him grew so, that by the time he was presented to Harold Orinsky, his eyes blazed wildfire.

"If you have any special gift, Mr. Sayble, don't you really think it would be a benefit to all mankind to share it?" Commander Orinsky said with patronizing sarcasm.

"I thought that was what I was doing," Sayble answered, shrugging his shoulders.

"I beg your pardon. I'm Commander Harold Orinsky. And you are?" Orinsky walked forward, offering his hand to the disheveled old man.

"Charles Ellingson Sayble," he replied proudly, cautiously accepting the handshake. "But you knew that already, didn't you?"

"You're right." He smiled, looking toward the guards who stood on either side of Sayble. "I think Mr. Sayble and I would prefer to speak alone." Immediately, the area cleared and the door closed.

Once alone, the two men stood silent, assessing each other briefly. Then, Orinsky came close to Sayble and looked him carefully in the eye. When he spoke, Sayble knew it was through clenched teeth, for the blood vessels on his neck seemed to bulge right out of his collar.

"What's this all about?" Orinsky demanded, sharply controlling each word.

"Ask your biologists. I never got past eighth-grade general science."

"One phone call to Greentree Hospital and you'll be spending the rest of your life in a padded room," Orinsky cautioned, walking around his immense mahogany desk, as though to make the phone call. "Another call to the FBI and then one to the CIA and they'll both fight for whatever remains there might be of you if the Greentree mental ward spits you out."

Sayble did not falter. "One carefully worded thought from *me*

194

will take away every insect from within miles of Ageon," he countered, steadily intent on his mission.

"You don't expect me to believe for an instant that you or anyone else has the power to control these animals?" He spoke from across his desk, as if to appear more powerful from behind the elegant furnishing. Behind him were photos of the entire nuclear submarine fleet, backing him up.

"Well, of course not," Sayble said gently. "Who would believe a stupid thing like that? Do you mind if I sit down?" Orinsky nodded cautiously and Sayble wiped the dust from the seat of his funeral pants before sitting. "So, you run this place," Sayble continued. "I noticed a helicopter landing pad at the entrance. That for your quick escapes? How much time do you think you'd need for safe clearance if something goes . . . wrong?"

Orinsky's eyes throbbed with anger releasing inside. "I'm tired of explaining the safety of Ageon and the vital necessity for our nuclear fleet. That's not why I brought you here."

"Well, the only reason I came was to deliver the message about the insects." Sayble rose, feeling a sudden burst of strength in his legs.

"I can see to it you will never be seen alive again! I can arrange it so that Charles Ellingson Sayble never even existed!" Orinsky threatened, pointing a gold ballpoint pen at him.

"You're not very used to losing, are you, Commander? Don't you understand that it doesn't matter a tinker's damn what happens to me *or* you, for that matter? The animals decide now. They're in charge! I'm only a convenient speaking tool for them," Sayble said loudly. Then, his voice softened as he stared at Orinsky and added, "You and me—we're rather alike in that way."

"You *are* mad," said Orinsky, as he watched the old man before him go into a trance-like state.

Sayble closed his eyes and nodded, as if agreeing with a truth finally disclosing itself within him. Then, he opened his eyes and reached into his pants pocket, where he kept the small folded samples of the animals' hair. He rummaged through the packets until he uncovered Athanasy's fine, glowing hair. He offered some to Orinsky.

"Take this to Dr. Forbes. Have her study this in your lab. Test it. See what you can find out about this," Sayble said, smiling wryly.

Orinsky took the sample and looked at it skeptically. "What is it?"

"Ah, you tell me," Sayble replied. "It's like nothing you've ever known before." Then, the old man fell back into a gentle, swaying trance, as if being re-charged mentally from far, far beyond.

Orinsky, in beholding Sayble's state, wondered at first if he was suffering a stroke. He picked up the phone and spoke quietly into it, while keeping a steady eye on Sayble. "Get this man out of my office. Take him to Greentree. I'm done with him."

Sayble opened his eyes and said, "The insects, the mammals, the birds—all you may keep are the reptiles." His voice was deep and liquid.

Orinsky's fear was genuine now as he felt a heat emanating from Sayble's outstretched hand. "I've called the guard," he warned.

"One minute, if you please," the old man said politely. He took a small portion of Athanasy's hair from the packet and held it up between his fingers. Looking deep into Orinsky's soul, he said, quietly, "Your knowledge . . . their instinct . . ." Then, he touched the hair to his lips and vanished, leaving only a gentle, glowing light.

CHAPTER THIRTY-TWO

I'VE JUST HAD THE most disturbing dream, Neera," Athanasy said, breaking a day-long silence. "I realize no one else is truly interested in others' dreams, but might I share it with you?"

The wolf looked up from her place of rest. "It would be a great honor, Athanasy," she replied.

"Thank you." He paused and gazed about his serene domain. "There was this place . . ." he began, his voice faraway and mystical. "A void, empty space . . . a place unlike any other I've ever seen. There was not one element of nature there. Yet, there was this unseen power—a Will stronger than any I have ever encountered before. I walked into it, this Will, expecting to be replenished by its power. But instead, I was challenged by it, as though I had invaded another's soul. The challenge came from every side, yet remained invisible. I struck out with my antlers, as instinct still serves my dreaming defenses. I became savage in my desire to defend myself."

The elk paused. Neera watched him closely, aware of his sorrow. "It felt . . . like paradise," he continued, "to feel such emotion again. So I slashed the air again and again until I struck it! I carried the invisible knight in the cradle of my antlers and tossed it about, revenging my confusion and fear. Then, I heaved it down to trample it, whatever it was. And when I looked down to crush it into the dust, I saw . . . I saw Sayble."

"Did you kill him?" Neera asked.

"I do not know," the elk whispered. "My dream woke me. Perhaps I woke myself. I don't know, I don't know."

"Do you know the meaning of your dream?"

"Yes," Athanasy replied, "yes, I know. I fear his power. Sayble's power. I should have known all along this would happen. Now, I must stop him. And I'd had such hopes for the man-cousin."

"I regret this interruption, Athanasy," the Blue Heron broke in, speaking as he landed between the wolf and the elk.

"We were finished," Athanasy said, gazing down thankfully to Neera. "What news do you have, Heron?"

"Now the fish are gone, as well as the birds," the Heron reported officially, catching his breath. "And so is Et Ska. She said you have released her, that her time was over. She was magnificent in her last hours. Such speed and energy." The Heron sighed with fatigue as he recalled how many miles he'd flown.

"Where is Lordjahn?" Neera asked, looking up.

"He stayed behind at Ageon to watch over Sayble and the man-pet," the Heron continued.

"Oh, there you are, Heron!" Chanta said, landing on the bird's long bill. "My impatient blue friend looks a bit tired today. Have you been flying all night?"

The Heron was nearing exhaustion, but the bright, colorful appearance of Chanta and her concern made him smile. "Night flight always disagrees with me," he said, nodding carefully.

Chanta strutted to the tip of the Heron's bill and addressed Athanasy. "It's time for me now, Athanasy."

"What?" the elk demanded. "By whose orders?"

Chanta took flight and flew about the elk's mighty head. "Sayble's orders. I just heard him call me out. It's time for me. 'Insects, leave!' he called out. Didn't you hear him?"

"No! What you heard was the Will. Not Sayble. Only the Will has the power to beckon you, Chanta!" Athanasy admonished.

"But, it is time for me to call the insects out, isn't it?" she asked, flying toward the Heron and then back again to Athanasy.

"According to the plan, she must leave soon, Athanasy," the Heron agreed, shifting his weary weight from one leg to the other. "Yes, I know. Then go, Chanta. But, go in the name of the Will and no other," he warned. "All of us, Sayble most of all, are powerless without the Will."

"My brothers and sisters are already united!" Chanta said enthusiastically. "They've been hard at work spreading the word. Do you know how many millions of insects there are in that valley? They await my bidding. Goodbye, Neera, good wolf! Be at peace, Heron!" Then, she flew up to Athanasy and said, "Until another time." She was carried upward by a draft until she was high above the trees and heading toward Ageon.

"Where does one so small get such energy?" the Heron asked, as he watched his friend disappear.

"It's her last mission," Athanasy replied.

"What do you mean?"

"Chanta will die next. She'll join Iscariot and Et Ska. It is her season," the elk explained, turning to leave.

"But why?" the Heron persisted, flying up to Athanasy. "She's so young!"

"Compared to you, she is young. But, within her species, her cycle is completing. Don't shame me by grieving, Heron." Athanasy turned and smiled at him. "Look where you've landed, hesitant one—up to your fine neck in friendship, and thriving on it." The elk then disappeared to seek the privacy his thoughts required.

Without words, the Heron took flight. Within a few minutes, he had caught up with Chanta.

"By the Gracious Gods of Flying Etiquette, Heron! Didn't your mother tell you not to sneak up on a butterfly? I thought I was a goner for sure," the butterfly said, gasping.

"Don't be dramatic," the Heron said, flying under the butterfly. "I'm the only bird within miles of here and you know it."

"Instinct is instinct. What are you doing here anyway?"

The Heron, to avoid embarrassment, said, "Well, I thought you might need some help."

"No thank you. I'll be fine. Besides, you've come to say goodbye, anyway, not to offer your help," Chanta said while hitching a ride on the Heron. "Slow down, will you? I can't hang on at this speed."

So the Heron dropped altitude and slowly circled with the butterfly gripping his back. The two were silent for several minutes as they enjoyed the easy descent of their last flight together.

"You wanted to say something?" Chanta finally asked.

"I wanted to say goodbye, Chanta," the Heron began, awkwardly. "Before you begin your final metamorphosis. And, I wanted to say that in your honor I'll never eat another butterfly."

"Best not!" she said, taking her own wing and continuing toward Ageon. "Now, fly away and leave a butterfly to her work."

As always, the Heron marvelled at her delicate beauty and selfless courage. She was too far off to hear his exaltation, "Love, respect, and farewell, Chanta!"

CHAPTER THIRTY-THREE

THE INSECTS WERE the least noticed in their exodus, as the people of Port Hartley and Ageon unconsciously welcomed a new day without the spring flies and mosquitoes buzzing annoyingly overhead.

The people had much more on their minds. The excitement in the community was growing as the notoriety of the animals' disappearances was spreading farther out. Port Hartley was a swarm in itself with media people, reporters, scientists, sightseers, and, of course, the sayers of doom.

The protest groups seized the opportunity by capitalizing on the odd biological events and resumed their endless lines of protestation with great and zealous enthusiasm.

Cameras rolled, testimonials were recorded, and interviews were rendered from every street corner. Everyone had a lengthy opinion on the matter.

From his hillside perch, Sayble sat looking down on the increased activity below. He held his knees encased in his arms and, with a soiled blanket wrapped about him, he looked confused, childlike, and cold. At times he gently rocked back and forth as if to comfort himself and it was all Fetchit-5 could do to keep from joining in his vigil. But she prudently resisted and remained far away from her master, and kept her own vigil next to the jeep.

From far above the trees, Fetchit-5's keen ears sensed the flap of Lordjahn's giant wings and the dog was relieved to have someone to consult with at last.

The condor landed quickly and quietly. "Where is the man-cousin?" the regal bird asked immediately.

"There," Fetchit-5 motioned. "He's been like that for hours. Just sitting, watching, as though one foot in another world. I'm frightened for him."

"Has he spoken?"

"No," she sighed, laying down and placing her troubled head onto her outstretched paws. "They've done something to him," she continued. "Ageon took him away yesterday and when he reappeared in the town an hour later, he had changed."

"Perhaps he's . . . what is it the man-cousin calls it? Meditating?"

"Not Sayble. I don't know, Lordjahn. I think it's time to summon Athanasy. He'll know what's wrong."

"Talk to him. See if he answers," the condor suggested.

She rose and walked gingerly over to Sayble and sat down next to him, gracefully winding her tail about her haunches. "A biscuit for your thoughts," she said gently, watching his face for an answer. But he remained silent. "Sayble?"

Then, as if startled from behind, the old man sprang from his reverie and looked at his dog with surprise on his face. "Are you talking to me, Fetchit? What?" he asked.

"Yes, I was wondering if you're okay. You haven't eaten in a while. Perhaps . . ."

"No, I'm fine now. Look at those idiots down there." He pointed into the valley. The dog looked down on the growing populace below. "They've all rushed to see, ignoring the message. Spectators!"

"Then, we are failing?" the condor asked, coming in from behind.

"Oh, hello, Lordjahn. How long have you been here?" Sayble asked, admiring the old bird.

"Long enough to see something is wrong," Lordjahn replied.

"What do you mean by that? Everything is going just according to plan. The air creatures, the water creatures, and now the bugs . . ." Sayble said, defending his work.

"Yes, but Ageon is still a threat," Lordjahn said, indicating the action below.

"I can't help it if the idiots don't get the message," the man-cousin said.

"Look. It seems like Ageon has gathered quite a force around itself. Look at the man-cousins flock to protect it," the condor continued.

"Yes, I know," Sayble admitted, looking nervously back down to Ageon. "I know."

"But the mammals have yet to leave," Fetchit-5 offered. "Surely that will be the most impressive stunt of all!"

"Yes, the mammals. It's time for them. The buffalo, the prairie dog, the wolf . . . who's left in this conspiracy?" Sayble said, a new energy rising in his voice. "Well, nice of you to show up, Heron," he added, as the Blue Heron landed among them.

"Et Ska has died. Chanta will follow," the Heron reported, catching his breath. "A great loss."

"The fish and the butterfly dead?" Sayble asked. "Damn!"

"Why damn?" asked the condor. "They passed, completing their cycles *and* succeeding in their tasks. What more can a creature ask?"

"Yes, completion and success make fine bedding for a death-nest." The voice of Athanasy was immediately recognized by all. Only Sayble was astonished to see the great creature standing behind him, away from this Council Ground. Behind him stood Moko, Little Paw and Neera.

"Athanasy! Why are you here?" the man asked, feeling a resurfacing of that initial fear he had experienced when first he had seen the great elk.

"I am here to do what you have not," was his simple reply.

"Are you accusing me of failure?" the man asked, springing to his feet defensively.

"We will be alone," Athanasy said, looking at the two birds and the dog.

Silently and swiftly, they were gone.

The man, fighting to keep his fear in abeyance, stood his ground and asked, "Why did you come?"

"To see it through."

"You doubt my abilities?"

"No. I question your integrity," the elk said, not unkindly, but directly and flatly.

"Go to hell! I've put my life on the line for you and this mission of yours, and now you tell me you doubt my integrity?" Sayble shouted and pointed a finger toward the elk, his pride having replaced any fear inside.

"You and I have fought over power in my dreams," the elk charged.

"Dreams?" Sayble raged, pointing downhill. "Look at all that reality and you want to interpret dreams!"

"Your growing ambition troubles me," Athanasy replied, his voice quieting.

"Now, what would a man my age want with ambition?" Sayble asked, face scrunched with confusion.

"You've become very powerful, man-cousin. I have felt it consume you. Like a cancer, it grows. And looking at you now, I fear it will kill you. You have changed. You are a troubled creature. Power will haunt before it overtakes. It always happens that way." Now the elk's voice was silken and beguiling, as if the great beast sought to enchant Sayble. "I know you've felt the power. I see in your eyes the problem it has become to you."

Sayble was silent as he collected his next words. Then, he too spoke softly. "When I was confronting the man-cousin who controls this Ageon, something very strange happened to me."

"An aching warmth from deep inside?"

"Yes, that's exactly what it was like. And hell yes, it's troubled me since. I'm not used to vanishing into thin air, you know. It's a little unsettling."

"You vanished?" the elk asked.

"The damnedest thing."

The elk looked away, considering this, then said, "This is a power not meant for mankind."

"Yeah, well this mankind didn't go looking for that power!"

"And will you be able to give it back?" Athanasy asked.

Sayble looked up at the elk, wrapped the blanket tighter around his shoulders and replied, "Now, that I don't know."

"I came here with the intent of killing you, man-cousin, before your new-found power became a threat to our success."

"Now, wouldn't that be just like an elk. Killing his strongest ally before the job is done. No wonder you're extinct. Now look, all I want is to be done with this insanity so me and my dog can finish what's left of our lives which, I might add, have shortened considerably since we met you." Sayble's face lightened and there was a trace of affection in his voice. "Now," he continued, "either we consolidate our power and finish off Ageon or we all walk away. You decide."

The elk snorted a heavy, hot breath. "Consolidate," he finally said.

Sayble walked closer to Athanasy, who, in turn, lowered his magnificent head to greet the man's outstretched hand.

"So be it," said Sayble.

CHAPTER THIRTY-FOUR

W HAT'S GOING to happen now, Neera?" the buffalo asked. "They've been over there and silent for the longest time," Moko continued, nodding his great, mangy head toward the ledge where Sayble and Athanasy stood conferring.

"Yes," joined Little Paw, who, out of boredom, had begun digging a burrow. "What's going on? Are we here to fight or chit-chat?"

The restless animals had to wait only a short time longer. From their place of private counsel, Athanasy and the man-cousin appeared. The wolf was surprised to see Sayble alive at all, but said nothing. Fetchit-5 sighed a secret breath of relief, but also waited for one of them to talk first.

"I regret taking this time away from our mission," the elk said, "but Sayble and I had many plans to discuss." The wolf admired the elk's delicate wording.

"Then what's next?" Moko asked, resisting an impolite urge to paw the ground.

"You are next, Moko," Athanasy said. "From this point, you will all leave to alert the remaining animals—the mammals, wild and tame."

"It's going to take some doing," Sayble said.

The Council animals nodded in agreement.

"Such little faith," Athanasy said, with a whimsical tsk. "What do you suppose the remaining creatures in this valley are all thinking now, with the bird, insect and fish friends already gone? What are the wild ones eating these days? Don't you think by now they have noticed an imbalance? Don't you suppose their ears are already listening for our words? Look about you. Listen."

Each creature glanced about and even the keenest ear heard nothing but its own breathing.

"You see?" Athanasy continued. "As silent as the day before creation. The word of the Will precedes us. So, all we must do now is to follow the Will by encouraging the domestics, the tame, the captured, the dependents of man."

"But, how can we break the bonds?" Moko asked, looking for an answer from anyone.

"Yes, how will the latches open?" the Heron asked. "*Now* is when we need Iscariot."

"You have him! Has the Will taught you nothing?" Athanasy demanded. "Why these sudden questions? Look how far we have come already."

"Oh, I get it," Moko said, as musky enlightenment spread over his face. "We carry the Will and it does the work."

"Look, I know you guys are getting tired," Sayble said. "But, old Athanasy here and I still have a few aces up our sleeves."

"Go now," Athanasy urged gently. "Take the spirits of our departed with you. Do not be concerned with the physical. The Will gives you the speed you'll need."

"And by evening, we'll all be back in this place, dividing the spoils of war," Sayble added heartily.

The first mammals to leave Ageon were the elegant and flawlessly trained guard dogs which patrolled the inner fenced areas of the facility itself. One swift pass close to the fence by Fetchit-5 was sufficient to command the guard dogs to suddenly calm themselves and begin digging a way out under the fence, setting off a series of baffling alarm systems. But, by the time the man-cousins found the escape hole, the dogs had long since vanished, heading with a renewed instinct out of the valley.

Then, as the enchantment spread out, the locked gates opened, the barn doors secretly and freely swung open and the once-crowded fields of well-organized herds mysteriously, yet simply, emptied. And, as the confused and angered man-cousins attempted to gather their migrating beasts back together, the animals received the gifts of double speed and triple cunning. Children cried for their unfaithful pets, farmers struggled to keep their stock and mystified people started to talk of leaving Ageon and Port Hartley forever.

The sudden and altogether upsetting actions of nature were commencing to attract the attention Athanasy and Sayble had so long desired. The underground, above ground, nocturnal, and the cautious domestic had, at last, begun the final exodus. And the Council animals began to revel in the ease at which the mammals departed . . . one and all.

CHAPTER THIRTY-FIVE

W HEN HELEN FORBES returned to her lab that day, it was to the frightening news that all the lab animals, contained there for simple study, had escaped their cages and had to be destroyed, or they had died in the excitement of an Ageon chase.

By that evening, news of the domestic migration had spread to the corners of the country. Dr. Forbes listened to the reports on the radio as she put some final, hesitant remarks on a series of reports she was preparing. The hour was late and she dreaded crossing through the incessantly growing lines of protesters, reporters, and curiosity-seekers outside Ageon's gates.

She crossed the lab, which was oddly silent without the gently milling sounds of the test animals. Odd, for she had never been cognizant of the noises they once made, yet now she was suddenly aware of their absence. She organized the papers on her desk, signing several after verifying their content. Then, she picked up a vial containing the remnants of the mysterious hair samples Charles Sayble had left for examination, scooped up the papers and left the lab for Orinsky's office.

Helen calmly walked past the outer offices and, after a ritual announcement from his secretary, approached Commander Orinsky.

"I've prepared a few reports for you, Commander Orinsky. I

think you'll be interested in what they say," Helen began without any salutations.

He looked up from his desk which was uncommonly cluttered with newspapers, press releases, books, and reports. The television, neatly encased in a wall grouping of fine art, was on, but with no volume. She had never known the Commander to wear such a tired expression.

"What could your reports possibly know that all those crazy, bleeding-heart, anti-everything gossip-mongers don't?" he asked, showing her a tabloid headline. "Like Rats Deserting a Sinking Ship," he read to her, laughing. "Poor journalism on top of everything else," he added, shaking his head hopelessly. He took the reports she handed him and asked, "Now, what are these?"

"The first is my lab report on this," she said, handing him the vial.

"Don't get me wrong, Forbes, I love your lab reports, but could you just give me a quick rundown? I'm too tired to sift through your bio-jargon."

"Very well. These are the hair samples that Sayble left here. I've run them through every conceivable test and each one comes up the same—origin unknown, age unknown. I have not been able to identify even one element."

"Martian hair?" he asked, feigning intense interest in the vial. "So, what is your conclusion?"

"You cannot draw a conclusion without sufficient data. Data is derived from precedent which, obviously, is lacking in this case," she explained coldly. "In short, sir, these hairs are unclassifiable. Origin unknown," she repeated, then waited for him to say something. "Note the word: *unknown*," she added bluntly.

His only reply was, "Terrific. How positively divine." His voice was mocking. "What else do you have for me in this pile of goodies, Dr. Forbes?"

"This," Helen replied, pulling out another report.

"Oh? And what's this? Eviction notice?" he asked, with the sarcasm deeply evident in his voice.

"For me, it is," she answered. "My formal resignation, Commander Orinksy. Typed and in triplicate. Just the way the Pentagon likes it."

He looked up and his expression was far from what Helen had anticipated. Rather than appearing shocked, disappointed, or even helplessly abandoned, he began to laugh. "Oh. I see. And what am I supposed to do with this?" he asked.

Helen was infuriated with her superior for his callous treatment of her resignation. "You can sit on it until it hatches, for all I care." she said harshly, gaining anger and courage with each word. Already she could feel the relief as she stood her defiant ground. She stared at him, then noticed for the first time his crumbling condition. "Look, I'm sorry, Commander Orinsky," she began, retreating somewhat. "But my conscience will not permit me to stay here any longer. I heard your order for more guards and evacuation of all non-essential personnel. You can keep pushing back all those people out there, but sooner or later, there's going to be more of them than there is of you."

"I'm not the only villain, you know. What would you have me do? Look, like it or not, those subs and those power plants and all those nuclear warheads are with us to stay. There's nothing you or I or that Sayble or all the animals in the world can do about it!"

"Tell me, Commander Orinsky, if the decision was yours . . . totally yours, what would you do?" she asked.

"Again I ask, what would you have me do?"

Helen then realized Orinsky's helpless, empty position. Owned by the White House, leased by the Pentagon, he was left with the choice of either stoic, staunch denial of any Ageon problems, or to simply walk away, as she was about to do.

She couldn't answer his question, so she withdrew her own and merely said, "I'll come back early tomorrow morning to clear out my things, before it gets light out, before all those crowds start gathering."

"So far, 208 civilian employees have quit and over 400 military personnel have requested transfers," Orinsky continued. He found himself staring out his picture window at the long spines of the subs. His voice seemed lost as he added, "A special task force is on its way from Washington. The President's been notified. . . ."

Helen said, pulling away, "Well, Commander Orinsky, maybe one of them will slip you off the hook. You have my resignation.

I'll just say goodbye now." She awkwardly headed for the door, knowing there was nothing left to say.

"Thank you, Dr. Forbes," Orinsky replied, quite formally. He didn't smile or otherwise acknowledge her departure, but stared at his installation below, collecting his thoughts.

CHAPTER THIRTY-SIX

WITH THE CHILLY, damp darkness of the night still low in the valley of Ageon, the animals of the Great Council of Beasts slowly returned from the beckoning dreams of their faraway homes. Even though the cheerful new-day bird songs were no longer heard, each animal woke out of instinct rather than by songs of flight.

"Psssst! Little Paw, are you awake?" Moko whispered, laying next to the tiny bundle of prairie dog.

"Eh?" the creature asked, stirring. "What do you want?"

"I want to know if you're awake," the buffalo replied.

"I'm awake, I'm awake," Little Paw said, still half asleep.

"I didn't sleep much last night," Moko whispered. "But Rasslin kept me company for a while."

Little Paw rolled on his back to stretch his tiny legs in the air, then rolled back and forth to scratch himself. "Rasslin? What's new with him?"

"He asked me to tell everyone all the snakes are leaving too. They said their food was gone now and things weren't much fun around here anymore anyway, so they all packed up and left, just like all the rest. He didn't want to wake anyone, so he asked me to pass the word."

"I had a feeling that might happen," Lordjahn broke in.

"It certainly helps our cause," Neera added, stretching first her front legs, then her back. By then, they were all awake except Sayble, who was still tightly curled up in his blanket. At his side, Fetchit-5 stirred awake.

"Sayble," she said, nudging him. "Wake up. Go see what Ageon is doing. I'm afraid to look."

At first, the old man pretended not to hear his dog. Then, as the importance of the day refreshed his groggy memory, he rolled over and slowly sat up. His face was puffy and his hair stuck out at odd, sleep-pressed angles, but he was finally fully awake.

"Hold it, don't move an inch," Fetchit-5 said, looking at him. "I want to remember you always, just they way you look right now."

Sayble returned his dog's sarcastic smile. "You're no prize yourself at this hour. And why don't you brush your teeth once in a while?"

He rose and rubbed his stiff shoulders and neck. He wrapped the blanket about him, and walked across the campsite to the ledge which overlooked Ageon. Standing there already was Athanasy. The giant beast was still and statuesque, appearing as though he could hold the vigil forever.

"Ageon still breathes," the elk said, feeling Sayble's presence behind him. "See? The war-whales are still there," Athanasy added with deliberate calm.

Sayble looked down below. The lights throughout the facility still glowed their eerie, orangish light as life down below seemed to carry on as usual. Sayble looked into Athanasy's eyes and saw for the first time their infinite depth.

The elk finally took his eyes off Ageon and looked at the man-cousin. "I never dreamt it would come to this. In one's soul, a cauldron of anger constantly boils and, to keep it from spilling, one must keep careful watch. But now, I no longer care."

"What do you mean?" Sayble asked cautiously.

"You will see," the elk replied, walking toward the others.

Sayble examined Ageon through his binoculars. Fighting the rising tide of resignation, he noted the facility indeed throbbed on as usual. Then the headlights of a small car caught the corner of the lens, and he followed the vehicle's path down the winding hill and through the gates of Ageon. By her short, bulky frame, Sayble was sure it was Helen Forbes he spied getting out of the car.

"Are you coming with us?" the Heron asked, coasting in next to Sayble.

He let the binoculars swing from his neck and asked, "Where are you going?"

"We are following Athanasy down to Ageon. I'm afraid his anger is too great," Moko added from behind.

"All I ask is that you remember the power of the Will, man-cousin. You did your best," Athanasy broke in, shadowing the mighty buffalo. "Be with me," he added gently.

And so, with little more than the morning mist to protect them, the Council animals followed Athanasy down the hillside and into the arms of Ageon. The great beast towered above the rest. Flying close in on either side of Athanasy were the Blue Heron and the giant condor, like heralding banners.

Dr. Forbes, pulling empty boxes out of her car, caught the reflection of something immense in her rear-view mirror. She whirled around and stared with shocked disbelief at what she saw. She pulled herself out of the car and ran to an emergency phone across the parking lot.

"Get me Orinsky! Now!" she called into the receiver, keeping her eyes on the approaching animal battalion.

Orinsky was on the other end almost immediately, having slept close to the phone all night.

"You'd better get down to the parking lot immediately," Helen said. The tone in her voice left no room for doubt and Orinsky obeyed at once. She waited for him at the officers' entrance, knowing he would take the most direct route.

By the time he arrived, several guards had also noticed the animals descending upon them. Reinforcements were summoned to the fenced perimeters. Each brandished a rifle in front of them, awaiting assault. Like the well-seasoned troops they were, there was no talk among them.

"What the hell is that?" Orinsky demanded when Helen pointed to the creatures now half-way down the hill.

"In this fog, it's hard to say. There's that old man Sayble following behind . . . a couple of dogs, looks like," Helen said, feeling the need to whisper as the excitement of scientific discovery awakened within her. "And there are those two glorious birds!"

"Yes, but what's that thing in front? God, it's some kind of deer!"

"It's the most magnificent thing I've ever seen! If I didn't know better, I'd say that was an Irish elk."

"I've never seen anything like it!" Orinsky said, taking a pair of binoculars from a nearby soldier.

"That's because its been extinct over ten thousand years," Helen added, feeling her pulse begin to race.

Then, several hundred feet from the main entrance, the group of animals stopped. The front guards grew more and more uneasy as the giant elk drew nearer and its size became more evident. The inherent fear of the unknown was again taking root.

The Council animals stood silent for what seemed like hours. Finally, Commander Orinsky came forward and called out, "You there! Sayble! What's all this about? Take your zoo away. Not a step closer! This facility is off limits!"

It was Athanasy's game now and Sayble remained silent.

The elk walked forward, separating himself from the rest. His elegant stride cut through the fog with swift determination. His nose sniffed the air as he tossed his mighty antlers about him, as if ready to charge. He gave a deafening, frightening roar of challenge and before the echo had stopped around them, the sky began to darken. Black clouds rolled in, trapping the fog to the valley floor. So dark did it become that the automatic lights around the base obediently clicked back on.

The road was thick with cars and television vans as the cautious, courageous reporters, ready to record the story of a lifetime, descended on Ageon. Then the wind picked up and tossed the mist about bitterly. Athanasy reared up slightly, keeping his antlers perfectly balanced, and a low, growing rumble of thunder passed through the valley with such a troublesome tone that it vibrated within each being.

Athanasy stepped closer as still more guards came to defend Ageon's gates. All rifles were trained on the magnificent beast.

Next, hail the size of pebbles came crashing down upon them, causing those without helmets to seek cover. And still it grew darker. As Athanasy walked, he seemed to gather momentum. He swung his mighty head back and forth, as if marching to a secret, angry battlesong.

Finally, after a brief, hopeful lull in the valley tempest, came the lightning. First it struck the tree-covered hillsides, leaving a puff of vapor where it had met the damp ground. Its accompanying thunder shook the ground, and by now many had fled to seek protection. The lightning continued, coming down the side of the valley, spearing the ground with merciless, random strikes. Then, defying all laws of nature, a final blast struck the tail of a submarine. Again and again it struck as Ageon's attendants stood watching helplessly.

Helen had taken refuge in her car but Commander Orinsky stood his ground, confused but defiant.

When it seemed the assault was over, another low rumble started from up the valley—a different and far more terrifying sound, emanating from deep within the earth. As the ground quaked, the pavement cracked and the corners of buildings began to crumble.

"This won't work, you know!" Orinsky bellowed out, his voice screeching above the rumbling and the shouts of panicked people. "Now you listen to me, Sayble!" he cried, "Get this circus out of here! I've had it with your games!" Then he called out to the guards and ordered, "Shoot that man! He's trespassing! Shoot those animals!"

The guards hesitated and looked at Orinsky, unable to obey his commands. "Well, if you can't, I can!" He seized a rifle from a startled guard and pointed it toward Athanasy. He fired, setting off a frightening chain reaction of gunfire from the battle line. But not one bullet found its mark as the Council animals calmly stood their sanctioned ground.

The last quake was the final deathblow. It caused the tides of the bay to heave higher and higher, until the great whales of war began to roll, crushing their berths. As the waves crashed over the docks and consumed the portside buildings, emergency lights began to flash, discordant sirens sang out danger and still more soldiers scattered to emergency posts. Fires flashed from seemingly nowhere as electricity shorted and gas pipes broke.

Orinsky became lost and disoriented in the crowd, cursing whoever would listen and shouting empty commands to imaginary loyal troops. Finally, a guard escorted him away to the safety of a protective ledge.

Slumped in the corner, horrified at the destruction, Commander Orinsky looked down at his radiation detection badge and knew the impossible had happened.

Athanasy held his ground, waiting until his hooves felt the last throe of Ageon from deep within the earth. Then, feeling its death, he gave a victory cry which itself echoed joyously throughout the valley.

The paths of escape were lined with cars heading away from the facility as terrified people ran for safety and reporters ran to their editors.

After surveying his handiwork, Athanasy turned away, tremendously drained and even saddened by his labors. He began walking back up the hillside, followed by the rest of his Council, until they all gracefully disappeared into the cool, soothing sanctuary of the fog, and their dreams beyond.

The Will fulfilled . . .
It was finished.

EPILOGUE

THE NEXT DAY, Sayble started the engine of the rainbow bus, grateful that it complied. He hoped the noise muffled his shaking voice, for the farewells with the Council animals had been short, yet loving.

"Well, old girl, *now* can we go fishing?" he asked, backing the bus up and easing it out of the Council Ground.

Fetchit-5 looked up at him, panting her beautiful, chipped-tooth smile and said nothing.

"Fetchit-5?" he asked again, glancing down at her while maneuvering the bus in and out of the low hanging branches.

Again, she was silent.

"Nothing, eh?" He looked straight ahead and considered her silence. "Well, good!" he said at last with a stout laugh. "Always thought you talked too much anyhow."

The dog smiled up at him and panted contentedly, watching for adventures in the road ahead, as her dear man-cousin began humming the old but fondly monotonous tune.

Sayble took a glance in the rear-view mirror and caught the reflection of the portrait he had painted of Athanasy. The farther away he drove, the more the oils faded until, by the time they had reached the River of the North, the canvas was a mere thought.

And so, with their last songs sung, the animals left to seek their homes and families. But they took with them such tales of greatness and adventure that no bedtime story from that time on would be complete without mention of Ageon, Athanasy, the Great Council of Beasts, and of course, the man-cousin who, like the condor, seized his last chance and had done his best.